Cake Icing, Butt Budder and Tea Lids

Renee Andrews

DEDICATION

For John Rene (J.R.) Zeringue, my husband, my best friend,
the true love of my life!

CONTENTS

ACKNOWLEDGMENT

Thanks to Kaleb Zeringue at Z4Designs.com for another amazing cover!

PROLOGUE

Edna peered over the top of the clear bassinet and ogled the squirming, rolling butterball that composed the newest, and much needed, addition to the Thibodeaux family. "Why look, Delilah, she has your double chin."

Delilah Thibodeaux shot up from the hospital bed with arms flailing, curses flying and eyes glaring. At thirty-seven, Edna Thibodeaux McGill still had the power to hit her older sister below the belt at every opportunity, though this time the punch to the gut was extremely unwarranted.

"Dang it, Edna, I gave birth eighteen hours ago. Can't you at least let me recover before you start?" Delilah reached in vain for Edna's throat. "And why don't you come a little closer when you're stabbing me. Let's just see what happens."

Edna clucked her tongue against the roof of her mouth as she lifted the infant. "See, Jezze, I knew your mama was a faking. Now get up out of that bed, Delilah, and let's go. We've got the Jackson's wedding tonight, and I won't stand for your slacking." She gently placed the baby back in the transparent crib.

"Slacking? I had a child, for heaven's sake." Delilah pointed toward the door. "Now, get out of this room right now and let me rest." When Edna made no move to exit, Delilah punched the button to the nurse's station and ordered, "Nurse, get security. There's an intruder in my room." Jerking her head toward her sister, she added, "And my baby's name is Jezebel, not Jezze."

"Good Lord, Big Mama'd roll over in her grave. Naming her after a hellion, for Pete's sake." Edna grabbed Delilah's overnight bag and tossed all of the toiletries inside, the ones they'd brought from home *and* everything the hospital provided.

"I like the name," Delilah said. "It'll make her tough. Besides, it's a heck of a lot better than mine."

Edna smirked. "Your name is gorgeous. I wish I had it."

"Well, you do have it, at least part of it," Delilah said. "Deidre *Edna* Lucinda Isabelle Laila Ann Hiram Thibodeaux? It took Mr. Reynolds two complete breaths to recite the darn thing when I graduated high school."

"I happen to love the fact that Big Mama named you after members of the family, past and present. I think it's sweet."

"You know we're not related to anyone named Hiram."

Edna sniffed, shrugged her shoulders. "So she needed an 'H' to get Delilah. No biggee."

The door edged open and a nurse's head peeked timidly inside. "Everything okay?" she asked, knowing good and well it wasn't.

On cue, both sisters pleaded their individual cases, sounding bizarrely like they did when they were kids arguing over the last RC Cola in the fridge.

The nurse retreated.

"None of this matters now, anyway," Delilah said with a dism'ssive wave of her hand. "Can't you let me rest? For one small fraction of my life, would you leave me be? Let me bask in the afterglow of bringing a child into the world," she said, her voice as soft and warm as fres٦ pralines.

"Lord, what kind of trash have you been reading?" Edna asked, picking up A New Mother's Guide to Pregnancy from the nightstand and promptly dumping it in the top drawer, right next to a Gideon Bible. "Have you had a child before?"

Delilah snarled through her nose.

"Right. Well then, you can't know exactly how long you're supposed to lay around and do nothing then, can you? I mean, women do continue to live productive lives after childbirth. Even old battleaxes like yourself."

This time, Delilah stood and grabbed Edna's arm in a death grip. "I'm forty-four years old and I had a baby on my own. Now I'll be the first to admit that it wasn't the proper way to go about getting pregnant," she said through gritted teeth. "But there's not a thing you can do to change that, or the fact that she's now here."

"No, there's not," Edna agreed, "But, as I can tell by your ability to rise so easily from that bed, there's not one reason in the world that you should keep this pretty little angel in these dismal surroundings one minute longer. You're perfectly capable of leaving."

"Dismal? This is one of the nicest hospitals in the whole state of Louisiana. Why, it'd be like a vacation if you weren't here."

Edna huffed out a breath and didn't slow one lick in packing up Delilah's things.

"And you don't care whether Jezebel stays in these so-called dismal surroundings anyway," Delilah continued. "You only want to get me back at work so you don't have to do everything yourself. If you'd agree to hire someone, Thibodeaux's Cakery would survive just fine whenever one of us skipped a day every now and then. Say, for example, to deliver a baby."

"The quicker you move around, the better you'll feel. That's what Doctor Hebert said."

"He meant walk down the hall, not go baking cakes and cheese straws. And what are you planning to do with Jezebel while we're working?"

"She's a Thibodeoux. She's gonna be raised in that bakery. Might as well get an early start. And the Jackson family is counting on us."

Afraid Edna was going to pack all of her clothes before she put anything on, Delilah moved to the closet, grabbed a huge dress and flung it on the bed. She wasn't about to leave this place with her big hiney on display for the world in this embarrassing hospital gown. "You'd think there wasn't another soul in St. James Parish who knew how to bake a cake."

"There is, but none of them are Thibodeaux's. Only family in a family business," Edna said. "You remember Big Mama's rule. And in case you haven't noticed, the last remaining Thibodeaux's are all accounted for in this room."

Well, there's a bit of pressure. At least Delilah did *her* part to continue the family name. Not that Edna could help it that her Josh McGill had run off with one of those oriental fingernail sculpting gals. The newest Mrs. McGill was an unfortunate black-haired beauty who probably only married him because she couldn't understand a single thing he said. Delilah suspected they'd stay together forever. In her opinion, they had precisely the right mix for a long-lasting relationship. Looks, sex and not a darn thing else.

How could they miss?

She emitted a low, "Hmph," but Edna wouldn't know it was intended for her good-for-nothing-but-sex ex-husband. "You realize she's a newborn and she's constantly hungry. I have to nurse her every couple of hours to get my milk to come down. How do you expect me to work on a wedding while I'm attempting to feed a child?"

"Shoot, I've seen women whip it out in public all the time." Edna shrugged her bony shoulders. "No big deal." She threw a pink blanket on the bed, turned it so it was in the shape of a diamond then swaddled the wiggling infant as though she'd been taking care of babies her whole life.

Delilah's mouth gaped. "When'd you learn to do that?'

"Everyone knows how to swaddle a babe," Edna said.

"I don't," Delilah murmured, watching the child drift to sleep in the cozy cocoon that her Aunt Edna created.

"Well, sheez, I guess I'll have to teach you. Now, come on," Edna said.

Crossing her arms, Delilah flexed every muscle and held her ground. "I'm supposed to leave in a wheelchair."

"You've gotta be kidding."

Delilah dropped her still sore behind to the bed and waited. She really needed one of those cute little doughnut thingies to sit on, but she wasn't about to admit that in front of the tough one. "The least you can do is take me out in a wheelchair. It's hospital policy."

"You want me to order you an ambulance with sirens blaring to take you to the store too?"

Delilah fought the grin that pinched at the dimples in both cheeks and pushed down the double chin Edna had referred to earlier. "Heck, yeah."

She watched as Edna, with Jezebel in tow, headed toward the hall and returned pushing a shiny silver wheelchair with a black vinyl seat. Delilah stood and sat in the chair, then flipped the footrests down and moved her feet gingerly on top of the pads, as though she were eighty-three instead of forty-four.

"Are you settled in?" Edna asked, her voice mockingly sweet.

"I think so."

"Well, here. Guess you're supposed to be toting this one when we go out." She put the baby in Delilah's arms.

A sudden warmth sprang to Delilah's belly, flooding her with the euphoric sensation of motherhood. "I wonder if you'll look like your Daddy," she whispered, running a finger across the dimpled chin of her baby girl.

"You thinking about telling him about his little surprise now? Or are you going to wait until your fiftieth reunion to let him know he knocked you up at the twenty-fifth?"

"I told you not to talk about that anymore, especially not in front of Jezebel."

"I seriously doubt she's taking notes," Edna snapped. "But I'll tell you the truth, Delilah. That man deserves to know that he has a child."

"And I'll tell you the truth. From what I've heard, he and his wife got back together after the reunion. And I know we shouldn't have done what we did that night, but we did. Now I asked God to forgive me, and He did. He even blessed me with a baby," she said, then kissed Jezebel's tiny forehead. She smelled like baby lotion and sweetness, sweeter than rich butter cream icing, Delilah would say. "God obviously knew I wanted a baby bad, and He gave me one in my old age, like Sophie in the Bible."

"You're in your forties. She was in her nineties."

"Forties, nineties, tomato, to-mah-to."

"So God blessed you and gave you a baby."

"Yep, He did."

"So what do you think He's gonna do about you lying after he's given you that little blessing?"

"Lying? I haven't lied."

Edna held up the birth certificate, tapped a skinny finger on the entry for the father's name. "Unknown? Her father is unknown?"

Delilah pulled her baby close to her chest and put one palm against the side of her tiny head. Her daughter would not hear these accusations about her mother. "It isn't a lie. I meant that the father doesn't know about the baby. So his status is unknown."

Edna stopped pushing the wheelchair toward the elevator.

Delilah looked over her shoulder to see her sister, standing stone still, her head tilted and her eyes squinting as though she were bracing for a hurricane.

"What in the world are you doing?" Delilah asked.

"Waiting for lightning to strike."

— CAKE ICING —

CHAPTER ONE

According to Forrest Gump, life is like a box of chocolates. You never know what you're gonna get. Well, I agree with the "never know what you're gonna get" part. But the "box of chocolates" was where he lost the punch. Personally, I'd have compared it to a doberge cake. More specifically, a Thibodeaux's doberge cake.

With a piece of Forrest's chocolate, you bite in and are surprised by one flavor. Not so with a doberge. Uh-uh. No indeed. The famous Louisiana confection is filled with multiple layers, flavor after flavor, of delectable surprise.

Thibodeaux's holds the record for most flavors within a single cake. Thirteen thin layers compose the monstrous dessert with every one of them potent enough to send a person's palate into overdrive. I should know. I've been sampling them for the entire twenty-four years of my existence.

Lemon, caramel, raspberry, chocolate, strawberry, cherry, vanilla, divinity, blueberry, apple, peach, pineapple and coconut are interspersed throughout the treat, and honestly, since the layers are never placed in the same order, you really never know what you'll taste in a single bite.

Forrest Gump should try one.

From the time I was knee-high to a grasshopper, as Aunt Edna says, I watched my mother, Delilah, bake the renowned cake for weddings, Mardi Gras and plain ol' Cajun lagniappe. She alternated layers of icing, filling and cake, and offered to let me snitch a taste of each one (which is why I have this current situation with my butt, but we won't go there).

Anyway, this five-year-old perched on a stool beside her mother in the back kitchen of Thibodeaux's Cakery and listened intently as Mama explained the mysteries of life...in the form of a doberge cake.

"You see, Jezebel," she said, swirling a layer of butter cream icing atop the mountain of cake and cream, "Life is like a doberge cake." (See how much that sounds like Forrest?)

She formed a graceful icing curl down the side of her creation, started to apply the next line, then stopped. Grinning, she put down her icing bag and reached for the huge roll of wax paper that hung beneath a nearby cabinet.

My mouth watered. I loved it whenever she whisked off a sheet. I knew what was coming. And in spite of Aunt Edna constantly warning Mama that she shouldn't, Delilah Thibodeaux never decorated a single cake in my presence when she didn't offer me a taste. Or two. Or ten. (Again, this contributed to my current butt situation, but at the time, I thought it was sheer heaven.)

"A little sweetness for my sweetie," she said, ripping the opaque paper across a tooth-like cutter. It made a crackling sound as she placed it in front of me on the cool stainless steel counter. "There ya go," she said, plopping a glob of white icing in the center.

My skinny legs swung back and forth wildly and my unruly thick brown curls bobbed as I anticipated the creamy sugar hitting my tongue. Lord, Mama made the best icing. Aunt Edna begged to differ, saying that Mama made it too sugary, but I knew that her icing was what kept everyone in the parish coming back for more.

Mama handed me a spoon and I went to town devouring every bit while she went to town finishing up that cake and offering the same tidbits of knowledge that she offered upon each of our "kitchen talks."

"Like I was saying," she said, forming a beautiful pattern of curls and swirls along the side of the cake and gracefully hiding the stack of layers underneath. "Life is like a doberge cake. Layers upon layers of unique and different things pile on top of each other and form the story of *you*. For some folks, it starts off a bit rough and grainy, but hopefully not too bitter," she said. "Like a layer of coconut."

"That's not my favorite," I said, eyeing my mama. I always tried to skip that coconut layer, eat around it if I could. I've never cared for anything that reminds me of uncooked rice.

"I know, but one day, you may learn to like it," she said. "Besides, that sturdy layer of coconut is sometimes necessary to hold up the rest of the cake, make it stronger." Her voice softened a little as she added, "I should know."

Mama had told me plenty of times that her personal cake was composed mostly of coconut. Not the fluffy kind that comes from the Piggly Wiggly, but the hard, coarse kind that Mama makes by grating the white chunks in the kitchen. I thought a cake made of gritty, rough stuff sounded gross, but she said it wasn't so bad. She said there was a big, thick layer of butter cream near the top of her personal cake, and that I put it there. I never really understood how I managed to do that, but I was happy that her cake had at least one layer of butter cream.

She swapped the decorator tip on the end of the bag and began adding a lattice pattern to the sides of the cake. Criss-crosses of white-on-white made the dessert look like it was made of carefully stacked diamonds. "For others, their first layer starts off filled with fruit. Fun and flavorful," she continued.

"The fruit's okay, especially the pineapple, but it's not my favorite either," I said, watching her turn the cake and criss-cross her way around to the other side.

I licked my lips, looked down and frowned. I'd eaten all my icing.

Mama glopped another mound in front of me, smiled and nodded knowingly. We'd had this exact conversation enough that she knew which layer I wanted my life to start with. That's why she waited to talk about it last. You could keep the fruit and the coconut, as far as I was concerned. Chocolate was okay, and caramel would do in a crunch, but still...

"Anyway," she continued, "For other folks, it starts out nice and sweet, a layer of rich, creamy icing."

"A thick layer?" I asked.

"The thickest," she said. She finished the latticework and picked up the green icing bag. After checking the tip and discarding a hardened bit of icing at the edge, she started her wreath of leaves around the top edge of the cake. Man, my mama was good. "If you're gonna start out with icing," she said, "you need it mighty thick. Cause it'll have to hold up a heck of a lot of cake and fillings before the journey's over."

"Mighty thick," I said, nodding.

"That's right," she said with a grin. Her deep dimples pierced her cheeks, which sparkled from the blush she'd applied this morning. Mama used the glittery kind, like the teenagers wore, because she said it made her feel young. Today's color was pale pink, the exact color of the boiled shrimp that Mama and I shared for lunch.

She put down the green icing bag and took the white one again. Then she started a row of tiny white beads around the edge of the cake beneath the leaves. It looked like someone had balanced a pearl necklace on the edge of the cake. "Yes," she said, nodding as she progressed, "that icing would have to be mighty, mighty thick. Would almost be hard for a person to swallow it, I'd guess."

"I could do it," I said.

"I'm sure you could."

"And butter cream, right? It'd have to be butter cream." I licked the spoon.

"Why certainly," she said, her blue eyes shining like marbles in the middle of a sunshine of crinkles. Silver white hair piled on top of her head and flared out like a morning glory in full bloom, making her look more like a grandmother than a mama (which was what Aunt Edna always said), but I didn't care. She was my mama, and thanks to her, *my* first layer was exactly what I wanted. "Definitely thick butter cream," she said.

"My favorite." I ran my tongue across the edge of my lip to catch a wayward drop of that very substance.

"Mine too, sweetie," she said. "And I'd have to say that right now, your life is definitely butter cream."

I knew that already. She'd told me a thousand times, but I never got tired of hearing it. "Good," I said, sliding the spoon beneath another smidgen of the cream then darting it into my mouth. Three more spoonfuls and my wax paper had been licked clean again. I looked up and saw Mama unbuttoning her blouse.

Time for the flowers.

"Can I help?"

"You know the rosebuds are never as pretty unless you help," she said. Her top gaped open in the front and her industrial-strength, huge, white cross-your-heart bra peeked through, along with about four or five inches of cleavage. Aunt Edna said Mama's brassieres had to do way too much work to be called a mere "bra." So, she'd christened Mama's undergarment a new, and more interesting, name. *Over the shoulder boulder holder*. Mama didn't argue. It was the truth.

"I'll lock the door," I said. I bounced off the chair and hurried to the wooden door that separated the kitchen from the front of the store, the pastry counters, wedding displays, customers...and Aunt Edna.

Aunt Edna had a major problem with Mama's method of "freeing her creative juices," so we did our best to hide it when we were in create mode. My aunt said that the health inspector was gonna show up someday and waltz into that kitchen and see my mama in all her glory and shut Thibodeaux's down but good. But Mama swore that she couldn't decorate a cake to perfection if she felt inhibited, and I, well, I was always looking for a reason to take my shirt off (proof I was Delilah Thibodeaux's child, that's what Aunt Edna said).

I clicked the lock in place then ran to the back door, twisted the stick to make the blinds close and then locked that one too. "Got 'em," I said, running back across the kitchen and climbing on top of my stool, just in time to see Mama's massive boulders swing free.

She folded her bra and placed it on top of her blouse on the counter. A long, red flowery skirt, elastic in the waist, hung to her ankles and she swayed her hips a bit to make the fabric swirl. Her breasts moved like heavy pendulums with the action. "Feels good to create, doesn't it, honey?"

I criss-crossed my arms in front of me and ran my fingers beneath the hem of my top. Then I whipped my tiny pink T-shirt over my head and dropped it on top of Mama's clothes on the counter. Looking down at my itty-bitty mosquito bites, I compared the tiny pinpoints to Mama's magnificence and bit my lower lip. How the heck were they ever gonna manage that?

Mama noticed my observation, as she always did when we were creating. "Oh, don't you worry, Jezebel Thibodeaux," she said. "You've got plenty of time."

"I want 'em to be big," I said, honestly.

"I know you do, sweetums," Mama said. "And most men want 'em big too, which will be a point, or I should say a couple of points, in your favor one day. But we don't want a man because he loves your body. We want that special one that's been made just for you. The *right* man. And when you grow up, you'll meet him, and then you'll fall in love, and then you'll have lots and lots of beautiful babies. Yes, Jezebel, there's a fine man out there for you. I just know."

I nodded gleefully. A man. The reason for my existence, the way I saw it. Mama and Aunt Edna talked about "Jezze's man" continually. Even at merely five years old, I knew a whole bunch about the fellow.

My man would be a Cajun, good looking and strong, according to Aunt Edna, and great in the sack, whatever that meant. I remembered the words though. I figured they were important, since Mama threw a nice little tizzy fit every time Aunt Edna said it in front of me.

For Mama's part, she said he'd be a nice man who'd treat me like a queen. So basically, as young as I was, I knew everything I needed to know about this man who I'd find when I was big, big enough to date and get married and have babies. And big enough to have stars on my chest, like Mama's, instead of these tiny little dots.

Aunt Edna constantly fussed about not having any stars in her sky. She said my mama got all the goods up top. But she added that although she missed out in the stars department, her moon was pretty darn impressive. (Even at five years old, I knew what a moon was, by the way.)

Unlike Aunt Edna, Mama just called them plain ol' boobs, or breasts, or sometimes...flowers. I figured the flowers part was because she had to let 'em loose before she could make perfect flowers on a cake, like we were doing right now. When we were creating, I let mine hang loose too, though that didn't mean much. They just kind of laid there, flat on my chest. Like pennies with a speck of dirt in the middle. But one day, if dreams come true, my stars would hover near the walls of the cake, just like Mama's.

She made the big flowers; I made the buds. If you think about it, that was quite fitting, considering her flowers were real whoppers and mine weren't.

I scooted next to her and watched as the crisp wedges of pink icing accumulated from a tight center to form a picture perfect rose beneath Mama's masterful hands (and bulging boobs). My side brushed against hers as I reached across and picked up a child-sized decorator bag, already filled with pale pink frosting. Her skin was smooth and warm, like the satin case on my favorite pillow. There was nothing hard or firm about my mama. Her flesh, soft and pliable, was perfect for accepting a hug, perfect for giving one. And I always received hugs during our creating sessions.

Now was no exception.

She wrapped an arm around me and squeezed me tight. I would have enjoyed it more if I'd seen it coming. Then I could have gulped an extra mouthful of air before my face smothered into the side of Mama's left boob. But it didn't really matter. Mama was hugging me. And her hugs were the best.

"Where do you want me to put them?" I asked, after the hug ended and I started breathing normally again. I eyed the flat round canvas, already garnishing two of mama's blooming roses on one side.

"Sugar, you put them wherever you think they'd look best," she said. "It's your creation. Let the juices flow and let your beautiful little mind explore the possibilities."

I closed my eyes. Inhaled. The sweet scent of butter cream filled my nostrils, made me smile.

Opening my eyes, I saw Mama waiting, icing bag in hand. She'd watch to see where I put the buds before she determined whether the cake needed additional blossoms. I decided that a cluster belonged on the opposite side of the cake, so I set to work at putting them just so. As usual, my tongue ventured out the side of my mouth during the concentration process. And as usual, Mama chuckled at that bit of pink hanging from my mouth.

When the last bud had been placed, I grinned up at Mama.

She beamed back. "Perfect," she whispered, running her thumb along my cheek and sending a waterfall of goose bumps down my arms. "I don't think we need any more roses. We'll just connect these," she said. She grasped the green icing bag and added several stems to both buds and roses, "and then we'll be done." She swapped the decorating tip one more time to put a sprinkling of leaves along the stems then she backed up to view the final product. "Whatcha think?"

"It's beautiful," I whispered, as the locked doorknob jiggled.

"Oh Good Lord, Delilah," Aunt Edna started from the other side, "Mrs. Babin is out front waiting on the doberge cake for her party. I told her it'd be ready at two o'clock, because *that's* what you told me. Now, it's," she paused, obviously checking her watch, "two-twenty, and she wants her dang doberge cake."

"Just a second," I said, hopping off my stool and starting toward the door.

"And you had better have your shirt on, Delilah," Edna hissed through the tiny crack between the door and the facing.

I tried to slap my hand over my mouth before the giggle escaped, but I didn't make it. It bubbled out like Aunt Edna's double-chocolate fudge bubbled over the top of the boiler.

Running back to the counter, I grabbed my pink T-shirt and started pulling it over my wild brown curls. "Just another second, Aunt Edna," I called, not noticing that my T-shirt was inside-out and backwards, with the little square tag visible below my chin. I lowered my voice to a tiny whisper. "Here's your shirt, Mama."

"Now, she knows dang well I ain't gonna stifle my creative side, not for her or anyone else," Mama said, her voice raising a tad, to make good and certain Aunt Edna heard. She tossed the shirt back on the counter and thrust her bosom out a couple of notches.

Totally prepared for Aunt Edna to come in and take off across the room after my mama, I timidly walked to the door and flipped the lock.

Then I backed up. Quick.

Sure enough, Aunt Edna immediately pushed the door aside and slid through, her skinny body whisking in and slamming that door behind her in record time. "Well, at least *your* clothes are on," she said to me as she passed.

"She just put her shirt back on," Mama said. "Jezebel also enjoys expressing herself."

"Heaven help me, Delilah," Aunt Edna said, making her way across the kitchen to pull a cake box down from one of the rear shelves. "Maybe you should spend less time telling Jezze about her creative self and more time telling her how she could get arrested for displaying it in public."

"Excuse me," Mama said, "But aren't you the same woman who once told me, 'I see women whip it out in public all the time.' Isn't that what you said, merely five years ago? Heck, you're the one that started this. Can I help it if I enjoy the freedom of letting them breathe every now and then? And I do make better cakes when I'm free."

"Feeding your child is a necessity. Baring your boobs and letting them dangle not two inches from a cake that we're getting paid good money to bake is quite another. I mean, what would you do if this icing had nipple marks on it?"

"How do you know it doesn't?"

Aunt Edna let out a snarling, hissing kind of thing that reminded me of that alligator we once visited in Ponchatoula when we went to the strawberry festival. Kind of a cross between a snake and, well, an alligator. "Tell me you didn't run them things through the icing," Aunt Edna ordered.

Mama turned toward me. She put her palms high on her chest then slid them upward, so her giant breasts were looking straight at me. Like a huge brown-eyed owl. "Jezebel, do I have any icing on my flowers?"

I shook my head. "No, ma'am."

She whirled back toward Aunt Edna. "Guess I didn't venture into the cake this time," she said. "So you can get your panties out of a wad."

"At least I'm wearing panties," Aunt Edna snipped. "And what do you mean *this time*?"

Mama smoothed her hands over her rounded behind, making me wonder...*Does Mama really not wear panties?* Then she shrugged. "Take it any way you want, Edna."

"I tell you what I'm gonna take," Aunt Edna said. She inched her way around Mama as though she thought allowing those major breasts to touch her would be worse than getting bit by that great big ol' alligator. She groaned and, careful to stay clear of Mama's glory, slid the cake across the counter. Then she placed it in the Thibodeaux's Cakery box and shut the lid.

"Honestly, Delilah, what kind of example are you setting for Jezze? Do you ever think about it? And baby, tell me you didn't take your shirt off," Aunt Edna said, turning her head to peer at me imploringly. "You didn't honey, did you?"

"It feels good," I said. And then I smiled, which was, looking back, probably a mistake.

"Good heavens," Aunt Edna said. "Mama'd roll over—"

"Ah, heck, Edna," Mama said. "If she rolls over half as often as you say she does, she's probably burrowed her body half way across the world by now."

"Put. Your. Shirt. On," Aunt Edna demanded. She glared at Mama's stars, as though she'd like nothing better than to make Mama see stars of a different kind. "Put it on," she spat, her back teeth grinding as she edged out the words.

"I'll put it on when I'm good and ready to put it on and not a minute before. Jezebel and I have two more cakes to do this afternoon, and we're wanting them to be gorgeous."

"They can't be gorgeous if our shirts are on, Aunt Edna," I said, trying to be helpful.

Again, big mistake.

Her eyes rolled to the back of her head and for a moment, I thought I was going to see my favorite aunt, well, my only aunt, faint. Personally, I thought it'd be an interesting thing to see. The only faints I'd ever witnessed were in cartoons. Of course, Aunt Edna was just as animated, if not more.

She didn't faint, though. After a second or two, she seemed to come back to herself and jerked her head toward Mama. "See what you've done to the child," she seethed.

Mama looked at me as though I'd discovered the wheel. "Yes. Ain't it grand. No one's gonna stop my Jezebel. She's going places."

"Delilah, if you don't watch what you're teaching Jezze, the only places she'll be going will have bars on the windows. Or worse, poles from the floor to the ceiling."

CHAPTER TWO

Ever since that kitchen conversation when I was five, I wondered about my mama's use of undergarments. I mean, I knew she had a panty drawer, like me, but I had never seen her put any on. And it never seemed the right time to ask Mama if Aunt Edna had been telling the truth when she'd hinted that Mama didn't wear them.

With the three of us living together, I pretty much saw Aunt Edna and Mama in their underthings all the time, or at least I thought I did. But best I could remember, I'd never seen Mama in her drawers. She always had a skirt on, or a robe, or something like that. Which made me even more curious, now that I suspected she was keeping a secret.

And of course, being Delilah Thibodeaux's child, I enjoyed letting my creative juices flow by taking my top off in the kitchen. So naturally, I wanted to know if leaving my panties off would help too. Maybe that was why Mama's flowers were so big.

She was really, *really* free.

But, when it came time to get me ready to start school, I learned two important things. One, my Mama does wear panties, pretty ones. And two, Mama wears pretty panties because of one of the thick coconut layers in her personal doberge cake.

I was six years old and it was August, which, in Louisiana, means it was hot. Very hot. Hotter than your lips after you've eaten a piece of corn at a crawfish boil. (If you've never eaten it, you probably don't understand. Down here, we put corn and baby potatoes in with the mudbugs so they can soak up all the spices. And Lordy, do they ever soak them up. Your lips hurt so bad that you'd swear they're gonna fall right off your face, but the corn is so dang good that you just don't care.)

Anyway, we had two weeks before my first day of school at Riverside Academy, so Mama, Aunt Edna and I headed to Baton Rouge to do some shopping. I was real excited about getting new clothes. Granted, I liked being out of clothes more than I liked being in them, but I still enjoyed getting new ones.

I stared as we passed one swamp after another along Interstate 10. Long fingers of Spanish moss hung from the trees that stretched above both sides of the road. Some of them swayed in the wind, like they were showing us the way to my new clothes. Excited as all get-out, I started bouncing up and down on the backseat. "Where are we going first?" I asked.

"You got your seatbelt on child?" Aunt Edna asked, clutching the steering wheel as though it would fall off if she let go. (She always drove. She liked driving, and Mama liked looking at the scenery.) Using her rearview mirror, she raised an eyebrow at me and caused me to check my belt right quick.

"Yep, I'm buckled," I said, thrilled that I hadn't forgotten. Aunt Edna was in one of her "moods," as Mama said.

"Then it's sure not tight enough, is it?" Aunt Edna quipped, clucking her tongue against the roof of her mouth to let me know how disappointed she was.

"Oh, lighten up, Edna," Mama said from the passenger's seat.

"She'll go sailing right through this windshield if we crash," Aunt Edna declared. "Is that what you want, Delilah? Why, Mama'd—"

"Yeah, yeah," Mama said, "I know. She'd roll over in her grave." Mama twisted in her seat and looked at me. "Tighten your belt, sweetie. She happens to be right...this time." She turned back to Aunt Edna. "Happy now?"

"Downright ecstatic," Aunt Edna deadpanned.

Mama straightened in her seat. "What the devil is wrong with you, Edna?" she asked. "I mean, you've always got a burr up your butt, but you're even more crabby than usual. This is Jezebel's shopping trip for school clothes. Her first school clothes. We're making a memory, for Pete's sake, and you're dang trying to ruin it."

I wouldn't have thought it was possible, but Aunt Edna's grip on the steering wheel seemed to tighten even more, until her knuckles had no color at all. Then her arms started shaking a bit and her shoulders dropped. From my view in the back, it looked like my aunt was about to cry.

"You okay, Aunt Edna?" I asked, leaning forward as much as I could with the seatbelt cinched so tight.

She wasn't crying, but she didn't look too far from it, and my Aunt Edna prided herself on not being a pathetic, whimpering female.

Something was very wrong.

"I'm fine," she said sharply. "Absolutely jubilant, can't you tell?" She clenched her jaw and stared at the road in front of us.

"You realize that we could've come for her school things alone. I was trying to be nice by including you," Mama said.

Aunt Edna's head whipped around so fast that I thought the car might follow suit, but it didn't, thank goodness. "You'd better not even think of leaving me out," she snapped. "Of anything in Jezze's life. We're all she has."

"Oh no you don't," Mama started. "She's got a perfectly full life with the two of us. We're all she *needs*. That's what you should say. Isn't that right, Jezebel?"

I was used to this argument, and I knew my part. I nodded. "Yep, Aunt Edna. There ain't a happier girl in all of St. James parish." Te-dah. I grinned, waiting on Aunt Edna to cheer up, like she usually did when I made my declaration. But this time, she didn't.

Aunt Edna constantly questioned my happiness. She seemed to have a hard time dealing with the fact that I didn't have a daddy. I'm not sure why. I didn't have a problem with it at all. Matter of fact, I thought the guy was kind of cool. Mama had told me about him, plenty of times. He was a special man, tall, good-looking and kind. He wasn't the "right" man for my mama, but he was a good man, just the same. And he gave Mama a special present, a gift she couldn't get from anyone else.

Me.

"You're right, Delilah," Aunt Edna said with a sniff. "We are all she needs."

"Finally," Mama said, but I could tell she was still miffed.

"And that's not what's upsetting me now. Really," Aunt Edna said, nodding her head once for emphasis. She opened her hands on the steering wheel so that her palms and thumbs were the only things touching the leather-covered circle. Then she wiggled her fingers a bit and they started getting a tad of color back in them again. I was glad. For a minute there, I thought she was dying right in front of me, from the hands up.

"If that's not it, Edna, then what is it?" Mama asked.

"It's just that she's going to school," Aunt Edna said.

"Yeah, so..." Mama prodded.

"So, I can't help but remember our first days of school."

"Oh," Mama said.

"How do we know that won't happen to her?" Aunt Edna questioned, and her voice sounded almost scared.

"What?" I asked, curiosity getting the best of me. "What's going to happen to me?"

"Nothing," Mama answered. She turned again and gave me one of those I-love-you-more-than-anything smiles, making my insides feel warm and mushy.

"I love you, Mama," I said, and I watched her eyes water. Then I added, "I love you too, Aunt Edna."

Aunt Edna cleared her throat. "We love you, Jezze."

"So, what's *not* going to happen to me?" I asked.

Mama's smile didn't falter. "What your Aunt Edna is concerned about, sweetie, is your first day at school. She wants it to be wonderful."

"Me too," I said.

"I want it to be better than our first day at school," Aunt Edna corrected. Mama shot a warning look at her sister, but Aunt Edna didn't even glance her way. She just added, "Well, Delilah, I do."

"I do too, Edna."

"What happened on your first day?" I asked. My stomach kind of gurgled, like I needed to go to the bathroom or something, but I knew I didn't. What had happened to Mama and Aunt Edna on their first days of school? And what if it happened to me? I chewed on the inside of my cheek, looked away from Mama. Was school going to be bad? Was I about to get coconut in my cake?

"Now look, Edna," Mama said. "You've gone and made her nervous." She stretched her arm to the back and patted my leg. "Jezebel, your first day is going to be wonderful. I promise."

I blinked. "Really?"

"Yes," she said. "But Aunt Edna is right. Both of us had tough first days at school."

"Why?"

"I was fat," Aunt Edna blurted. "Huge. Like the Goodyear Blimp. And kids can be really mean at that age."

My mouth fell open. First of all, I couldn't imagine skinny Aunt Edna ever being fat. Second, I couldn't believe that any kid could say something that would hurt her feelings. Aunt Edna didn't get her feelings hurt; she got mad.

"We had the Cakery back then, of course. And Big Mama would let me eat anything I wanted, as much as I wanted, and I guess it showed." She shrugged. "By the time I started first grade, I weighed more than most of the fifth graders, but I was only half as tall. The kids kind of singled me out to pick on." She shrugged again, and I expected her to say her regular "No big deal," but she didn't.

"What happened after that?" I asked.

"I stopped eating the stuff at the Cakery. I got skinny. And I got tough. Nothing they said ever bothered me again. Nope, it didn't," she said, shaking her head with every word, as if she were trying to convince herself instead of me.

"What happened to you, Mama?"

"Nothing really happened to me, dear," she said. "I was a little uncomfortable on the playground. That's all."

"Heck, Delilah, I told her what happened to me," Aunt Edna said. She exited the interstate and started toward downtown Baton Rouge.

"Please, Mama," I begged.

"All right, sweetie. But you've got to remember, things are going to be better for you. Aunt Edna and I both started with a layer of coconut, right?"

"That's what you said."

"And you're starting with butter cream."

"Definitely," I said, grinning. "But Mama—"

"But you still want to know, don't ya?"

"Yes, ma'am."

"Well, when Big Mama and Big Daddy, your grandparents, were getting me ready to go to school, they had just opened the Cakery in Grand Point. We didn't have a lot of money, didn't have a lot of anything, and what we did have they used to get the business going. So for school, Big Mama made me a couple of dresses and we picked up a pair of hand-me-down shoes, which was fine. It was about the same as what the other girls in the parish had. Except—"

"Except what?"

"Except Big Mama tried to save money by making my underwear too. She couldn't justify spending the cash on something that wouldn't be seen. And really, I thought that was fine and dandy, until that first day of school."

"What happened?"

"The elementary school had bought some new playground equipment. Everyone wanted to play on it, particularly the monkey bars. So I quickly made some new friends and we started climbing to the top. Of course, the kids below could see my underwear."

"Oh," I said, feeling embarrassed for my mama. I sure wouldn't want a bunch of kids gawking at my undies. It was one thing to take your shirt off in the kitchen with just your mama watching. That was fun. But I sure didn't want to let someone else see my private stuff.

"Yeah, but that wasn't really the bad part," Mama said.

"The bad part wasn't when they saw your drawers?" I asked, wondering how it could've been worse.

"Nope, like I said, Big Mama tried to save money by making my panties. So when those kids below looked up and saw mine, they didn't see pretty, white cotton panties like all the other girls in the class wore."

"What did they see?"

"A flour sack cut to fit my behind, with two buttons holding it on."

Aunt Edna parked the car at the Baton Rouge Mall and shook her head even more than before. "Nobody's gonna make fun of our Jezze," she said.

I took a big breath. Swallowed. "But what if they do?" I asked.

"They won't," Aunt Edna said again, as though she would be happy to eliminate anyone who remotely acted like they'd hurt my feelings.

It made me smile. She might seem tough as alligator skin on the outside, but inside, she was as soft and gooey as Mama. Of course, I wouldn't ever make the mistake of trying to tell her that. "They might, Aunt Edna."

"You're right, sweetheart," Mama said. "And if they do, it'll make you stronger, like it made us stronger."

"Okay," I said, figuring if Mama and Aunt Edna handled it, then I could too. I am a Thibodeaux, after all. I climbed out of the car and slammed the door. "So, where are we going first?"

Mama and Aunt Edna exited the car. Aunt Edna still looked a little worried, but Mama smiled. "You'll be wearing uniforms to school at Riverside, and I've already purchased those for you, so we don't need anything like that."

"Then what the devil are we here for?" Aunt Edna asked. "I thought we were coming to buy clothes for school."

Mama chuckled, low in her throat, like she was dying to tell a secret. "We do need to get her some shoes, Edna," she said.

"All right," Aunt Edna said. "I know where the shoe stores are." She briskly circled the car, wiped the sweat that had already accumulated since we'd stepped into the Louisiana heat from her brow. "Is that all we need?" she asked, heading toward the entrance.

"Nope," Mama said.

Aunt Edna stopped. "Now you know I ain't a shopper, Delilah. I'm perfectly content buying stuff for Jezze, but I don't plan on staying in this place all day."

"After the shoes, we'll need to make one more stop."

"Where's that?" Aunt Edna asked, obviously irritated. She wiped her brow again, looked at the dampness on the back of her hand and then wiped it on her pants.

"Pretty Pony's Perfect Panties," Mama said. "I need some more thongs, and—"

"Too much information, Delilah," Aunt Edna said, holding the mall door open and sending out a blissful blast of frigid cold air. "Way too much information."

"What I was trying to say when I was so rudely interrupted," Mama said, passing through the doorway with her hand holding mine, "is that I can get what I need there *and* we can buy Jezebel some things there too."

"You are *not* sending that child to school wearing a thong," Aunt Edna declared. "Why, Mama'd—"

"Oh, get over it, Edna. I'm not buying her thongs," Mama said then she turned to me and added, "Not until you're older, anyway."

"What's a thong?" I asked.

"I'll show you when we get to the store," Mama said.

"Heaven help," Aunt Edna grumbled.

Mama chuckled and strutted through the mall like she owned it. "But we are going to buy Jezebel the prettiest little girl panties they've got, in every color and every fabric she wants. When my little angel goes to school, she'll know that she's got the best undies that money can buy."

"But you don't want me to go around showing them off, right, Mama? That'd be bragging."

Mama cleared her throat, fought a smile. "No, sweetie. That will be your own little secret. Only you, me and Aunt Edna will know that you've got the most stylish panties in all of the first grade."

"No flour sacks with buttons, huh?" I asked.

"Definitely not," Mama said, draping her arm around me and squeezing as we headed past the food court.

"So, does that sound okay with you, Aunt Edna?" I asked. "New panties, every color, but we keep them a secret."

Aunt Edna's rigid face cracked into a little smile. "No problem."

CHAPTER THREE

Grand Point. Midway between Baton Rouge and New Orleans and home to Thibodeaux's Cakery, the tiny town (well, okay, it's a few streets, but it has a name, so that constitutes a town, right?) had a shortage of residents. Blessedly, every last one of them ate cake.

And ate it aplenty.

Not that Thibodeaux's had to rely on the miniscule community as their only source for sales. Oh no, there were enough Grand Point folks to spread the word about the unique bakery owned by those crazy Thibodeaux sisters. They told every Tom, Dick and Harry (or, in Cajun country, every Rene, Pierre and Philippe) in the surrounding cities and garnered a word-of-mouth interest that big time caterers could only dream of.

Folks drove from nearby Gramercy and Garyville to partake of Thibodeaux's treats and some even came all the way from Baton Rouge and New Orleans in order to have Thibodeaux's doberge cakes at their shindigs.

Mama, Aunt Edna and I stayed busy most of the year filling orders for birthdays, weddings, festivals and parties, but when it came to holidays, well, that was something different entirely. Holidays, particularly holidays that involve a bunch of Cajuns, mean two things for caterers in the Bayou. One, lots of money, which is good. And two, lots of work. Too much work. Way too much work.

Which is bad.

It wasn't so much the work itself that hurt, although we tended to pull quite a few all-night topless bake sessions with each nearing holiday (topless for me and Mama; clothed for Aunt Edna, of course). But what stung more than the endless hours in the kitchen was Mama and Aunt Edna gearing back up in their most heated disagreement, an ongoing argument, and one that I guessed started well before I was born.

Mama wanted to hire help for the store; Aunt Edna didn't. Mama knew (and I knew too, even though I was just a kid) that there were too many orders, especially at holiday time, for two women and a little girl to fill.

However, Aunt Edna wouldn't back down. Evidently she'd promised Big Mama (my grandmother) on her deathbed that she'd never let anyone work at Thibodeaux's but a true Thibodeaux, folks that had some of Big Mama's blood in 'em. Well, even I knew that there weren't many of those left. To be exact, there were three. Aunt Edna, Mama and me.

Mama yelled and screamed and pitched hissy fits through every holiday season, but it didn't work. The deathbed bit killed her side of the argument right quick. Mama told me that she bet Aunt Edna tacked on that deathbed spiel, and then she'd fibbed so much about it she probably believed it was true. See, Mama visited Big Mama's deathbed too, and according to Mama, she didn't say a darn thing about that "only Thibodeaux" rule. Mama said it'd be just like Aunt Edna to do something like lie about Big Mama Thibodeaux's last wishes. Just to tick Mama off.

So, after several years of complaining, Mama tried to get back at Aunt Edna by changing her typical creation process during the holidays. I was ten years old when, starting in November, Mama removed her shirt for the entire cake baking, not just the flowers. I, of course, took mine off as well (like I said, I was always looking for a reason to remove my top).

I have to admit, during Thanksgiving and then on into December, I was cold. Real cold. But, like Mama said, it was a matter of principle. I still don't understand the principle of it, but I did get the gist of what was happening. Mama was mad because Aunt Edna wouldn't agree to hire help. And Mama knew that Aunt Edna didn't like her hanging out half naked in the kitchen. So Mama (and me) went half naked in the kitchen for the holidays, starting the year I turned ten.

Basically, that was it.

From that year on, I associated holidays with three things, instead of two. One, lots of money. Two, lots of work. And three, cold mosquito bites on my chest.

Of course, somewhere up north, where it actually snowed, folks wouldn't equate a Louisiana December to cold. But you've got to remember that we're pretty much frying the rest of the year, so the least little bit of a chill and we're dang near frozen. Which is how I felt in the kitchen, where I helped create rosebuds and flowers every day, before and after school. And where our own rosebuds and flowers were in full bloom.

Aunt Edna clucked at our shivers and mumbled something about stubborn, hardheaded coonazz women while she dropped spoonfuls of pralines onto wax paper. She spent more time in the kitchen during the Christmas season to help us fill orders, and she sure enough didn't care for all of the big and little boobs back there.

So the minute the bells on the front door jingled, or she could think of something else in the store that needed tending, she'd be gone. Right now, however, there was no one out front and she'd already polished the display cases, so she was stuck making the pralines.

Our schedule had us booked for a minimum of three Christmas parties each weekend right up through the actual day, and then we were equally booked for New Year's functions. Mama fussed when she saw the upcoming lineup. She said if Aunt Edna would hire some help for the holidays, then we'd all have more time to spend out at the levee, and we'd have more than a hair's breadth of a chance at winning the bonfire competition on Christmas Eve.

"Phffft," Aunt Edna said. "We'll win."

Mama shook her head, knowing the odds were better for a white Christmas in New Orleans than for a Thibodeaux Cakery bonfire to win, particularly if this year's effort was no better than last year's. "We have to spend more time on it," Mama said. "Every December, it looks half baked when they set the thing on fire."

Aunt Edna's bony back stiffened. She haphazardly dropped the remaining praline mixture on the paper in one big lumpy mess, took the mixing bowl to the sink and started cleaning up.

Mama and I watched in amazement. Aunt Edna never missed on making perfect pralines, and that hunk of stuff she'd just plopped on the counter looked like a small pile of dog poo.

"Have mercy, Edna. What're you doing?" Mama asked.

"You're right, dang it. Our bonfire is a representation of the pride we have in our business, and we should spend more time making sure it's the best it can be." She untied her apron, wadded it and tossed it on the wooden desk that held an assortment of bills and orders (and a couple of Mama's over-the-shoulder-boulder-holders that she'd forgotten to take back home). "So, how long till you two can leave here and go help me work? And for this creation, you'll have to keep your shirts on."

"That's the only bad part about it," Mama said, smiling broadly at her sister. She finished up the cake we'd started, then she hauled her breasts into her bra. "You ready, Jezebel?" she asked, her voice muffled as her head worked its way through her thick, red Christmas sweater.

Tiny, gold jinglebells were sewn across the top of the front pockets and they tinkled with Mama's every move. On a normal woman, the bells would've been suspended beneath the collarbone, well above the breast region. But on Mama, well, there wasn't much about her front that wasn't part boob, so the bells kind of balanced there as though they were on a shelf. Consequently, they drew even more attention to Mama's assets, which she didn't mind. Admittedly, Mama was still man-hunting, even though she said she didn't know what kind of man would want a fifty-four year old woman who looks like she's sixty and acts like she's twenty.

I grabbed my green turtleneck, slid it on. Picked up my red sweater and worked it over the top. Found my hat, slapped it down. Changed my tennis shoes to rubber boots, donned a puffy coat, wrapped a wool scarf around my throat and finally slid each finger into nice, warm gloves. "Ready," I said, looking more like the Michelin baby than a ten-year-old girl.

Aunt Edna chuckled through the entire procedure, but looking at me now, she laughed so hard she sounded like an excited horse.

"What?" I asked then coughed past the fuzz I'd inhaled from the wooly purple scarf that covered my mouth.

"For someone who freely goes naked in the kitchen, you sure do cover everything up for going outside, don't ya, Jezze?"

"Mama says layers keep me warm," I said, though I wasn't sure if she could understand my words through all that fuzz.

"Oh, they'll keep ya warm," she agreed. "But you're flat gonna be sweating bullets when we get to building that bonfire, child."

"She can take off her coat if she needs to," Mama quipped. "Jezebel's a smart girl. She's just trying to stay warm."

"Sure wish you two would bring that concept into the kitchen," Aunt Edna said, pulling on a black cardigan sweater with tiny red roses embroidered around the buttons. She wore her traditional charcoal gray baggy workpants, a plain white turtleneck and not an ounce of makeup. While Mama looked like an older woman trying to look young, Aunt Edna looked like a young woman trying her best to look old. Mama said Aunt Edna used to dress up a bit before "her Josh" left. I'd never met her Josh, but if he was the reason Aunt Edna stayed so ornery all the time, I really didn't want to.

"I keep waiting for both of you to come down with pneumonia and leave me to do all the holiday baking on my own," Aunt Edna sa d. "And I'll get ya good if that happens," she promised. "Good Lord, Big Mama'd—"

"Roll over in her grave," Mama and I said in unison. Then we busted out laughing.

Aunt Edna hmphed and headed out the door stomping her feet as though she were pouncing big fat Louisiana cockroaches with every step.

Within minutes, we'd driven to Gramercy, to the site Big Mama selected many years ago as the desired spot for the Thibodeaux's Cakery annual bonfire. I scanned the structures already in progress down the levee and a frisson of dread quivered through my veins. How in the world would we ever compete with those?

A Cajun tradition for generations, over one hundred bonfires are built each year like runway landing lights along the levee by the Mississippi River. They run along the edge of the cities that follow River Road, with Gramercy, Lutcher, Paulina, Reserve and Montz serving as the primary sites for the impressive arrangements.

On Christmas Eve, partying Cajuns light the bonfires to guide Papa Noel (in his pirogue; Santa doesn't use a sleigh down here) and his reindeer south, to the houses of anticipation in Bayou country.

"Wanna go take a look at the competition first?" Aunt Edna asked.

I spotted the bare patch of land where our bonfire should have at least been started and frowned. "We might not want to see 'em," I said.

Mama patted my arm. "Now, now, Jezebel, don't let those shoulders slump. Hold your chin up, sweetie. I've got an idea that'll put our name in the *L'Observateur* and the *News Examiner* for sure this year."

My eyes lit up and my heart skittered a bit. The *L'Observateur* was the big paper, covering all of the areas in St. James, St. John and St. Charles parishes. The *News Examiner* was our local paper. Delivered to the Cakery every Thursday, it was our primary source for finding out about all the upcoming festivals and general news about things in and around Grand Point. Although Thibodeaux's had purchased ads in both papers before, we'd never had an article about us—me, Mama and Aunt Edna—the last remaining Thibodeaux's. To build a bonfire that would get us noticed by the papers would be something. "Really, Mama? What is it? What kind of idea?"

Aunt Edna appeared equally surprised. "Yeah, Delilah. Whatcha thinking?"

"You'll see," Mama said. "But first, I do want to take a look at the competition. Then we'll need to buy some wood, plenty of wood. We're going to make a statement this year."

Aunt Edna circled the car around and headed down Airline Highway so we could start from the beginning of the bonfires, in Montz. Montz was about as big as Grand Point, but it had a name and folks knew where it was, so therefore, again, it qualified as a town.

We drove to River Road, where several large groups had gathered to work on their prospective bonfires. Since I'd been viewing the large compositions each year, I didn't even realize that every place in America didn't light bonfires for Christmas Eve. Evidently, Santa (Papa Noel) knew the way to every other town in the world; but for some bizarre reason, he couldn't find his way down the Mississippi unless we helped him out.

So, we did.

And it was loads of fun.

The bonfires were everywhere, all along the levee. Some were tall and towering; some were short and wide. But every one was unique. They looked like assemblages of Lincoln Logs, reaching to the sky from the top of the levee like tributes to the tower of Babel. In all shapes and forms, they were truly a sight to behold and never failed to pull a deep breath of awe from my chest.

There were towering, teepee looking ones, kind of plain, but dressed up a bit with a flag or paint. Then there were short, squatty ones, usually put together by elementary schools from the nearby towns. And then...

Then there were the "winners," the ones that made you gasp, "Coo-wah." These were themed bonfires that represented businesses, churches, or families who wanted to make their impression on the banks of the mighty Mississippi.

We drove past the Jax Beer bonfire, shaped like a tall beer bottle, complete with the Jax logo as big as a small house attached to the side. It had a wrapper around the long neck and a metal cap on the top. "Man," Aunt Edna said, gawking at the bottle. "They went all out."

"Yeah," Mama said without enthusiasm, as though a skyscraper beer bottle had nothing on her.

After the beer bottle came the gigantic coffee mug built by Community coffee. That was one of my favorites, since I loved their coffee. In the early mornings, after we'd put our first batch of cakes and pastries in the big ovens, Mama, Aunt Edna and I would sit in the cozy little breakfast area in the back of the shop and drink our coffee. Granted, mine was more cream and sugar than coffee, but I still felt big when I sipped it. Mama said that a day wouldn't start off right if it didn't begin with a cup (or two, or seven) of Community coffee. Evidently, from the amount of customers who ordered it to go along with their cake or pastry, most Cajuns agreed.

While we rode past the Community mug, a big puff of steam swirled from the center and poofed to the sky. I had my window rolled down for a better view, and I heard the cheers from the crowd who'd gathered around the tribute to caffeine. "That's pretty cool," I said.

"Yep," Aunt Edna agreed.

Mama didn't speak.

An A-framed nativity structure formed the next jaw-dropper. Aunt Edna slowed the car. On top of the stacked wood, a white angel sparkled. Her wings appeared real, with fluffy white feathers covering them completely. They moved back and forth from her sides. Inside the bonfire's frame, a hollowed area displayed a manger scene.

"Do you think they're gonna set baby Jesus on fire?" I asked.

"Well, that'll sure knock them out of the running for first place, I'd say," Aunt Edna said with a snicker. "What do you think, Delilah?"

"Probably," she said, but she barely gave it more than a passing glance. She obviously had something on her mind. Aunt Edna and I both knew it was her plan for our bonfire. Last year (truthfully, every year), our pile of logs was nothing more than that. A pile of logs. No shape or form or anything. We really didn't know what we were doing. But this year would be different.

Mama had a plan.

"Holy cow," I said, viewing the next one. A ship, complete with cannons, windows, flags and a crow's nest stretched down a long section of the levee.

"Check out the name," Aunt Edna said. "U.S.S. Coonazz." She laughed out loud. "Pretty funny, don't ya think, Delilah? Coonazz?"

"Yeah," Mama said, but she hadn't looked up. She'd stopped surveying the competition and was busy drawing on a spiral bound notepad.

"You okay, Mama?" I asked, leaning toward the front seat.

"I'm fine, sweetie," she said, still looking at her notepad.

We continued down River Road, Aunt Edna and I oohing and ahhing over each tower and Mama scribbling feverishly on her paper. When we neared Gramercy, a giant airplane bonfire with a rotating propeller stretched its mighty wings above the street.

"Now, that's the one to beat," Aunt Edna said.

There were at least forty people, drinking hot cocoa and coffee, gathered around the plane and admiring the finished product of their efforts.

"There're only three of us," I whispered, my confidence wavering. "And last year, we didn't do so good."

"We were busy baking the whole time," Mama said, snapping out of her reverie. "This year, we're going to spend several hours each day, from now until Christmas, making sure that our bonfire is special," she declared, leaving no room for Aunt Edna to argue the point. "Today's the tenth, so that gives us fourteen days till the judging. And if we have to turn down some business in order to accomplish our goal, then so be it. We're going to make sure folks know the Thibodeaux girls are a force to be reckoned with."

"We could pay someone to help us bake," I said, to which Aunt Edna briskly replied, "No." Then, perhaps realizing how sharp she'd said it, she stretched a hand to the back seat, reached my thigh and patted it through my endless layers of clothing (which were, in fact, making me sweat). "No, dear," she said softly. "We'll do fine. On our own."

CHAPTER FOUR

Those logs were heavy. Very, very heavy. I expected they'd get easier to move each year as I got older and stronger, but amazingly, as got stronger, it seemed the logs got heavier.

After Mama paid the men who delivered the truckload of cut wood to our bonfire site, I thought I'd help out by toting the pieces to the nice, flat spot that awaited my mama's biggest creation.

I thought wrong.

Toting wasn't an option. Neither was pulling, pushing, tugging or yanking. Nope, the only way to move those monstrous cylinders was to roll them. And then, they'd get to moving on that sloping levee and roll away from you before you even saw it coming. It took every determined ounce of my sixty-seven pounds to keep them from heading right into the street.

Within twenty minutes, I'd worked up enough heat in my skinny frame that I'd completely stripped off my hat, scarf, gloves and coat. I cut my eyes toward Aunt Edna, rolling logs on the other side, and ran my fingertips beneath the hem of my shirt. Mama was right. You just can't create with your top on.

Unfortunately, Aunt Edna wasn't as engrossed in her logrolling as I originally thought. She read me like a book and halted my attempt at freedom before I had a chance to proceed.

"You stop right there, young lady," she said, raising a thin brow. "We won't be getting indecent during this endeavor."

I sighed loudly. My shirt stuck to my skin like a crawfish shell. "Come on, Aunt Edna. No one's looking."

She whirled toward River Road, where a stream of cars cruised steadily along the edge of the levee. Heads poked out of windows and cameras flashed like lightning bugs as tourists and locals alike came to see the progress of the individual bonfires.

"The devil no one's looking, child," Aunt Edna said. "Everyone in St. James and St. John parishes will drive by here before the night's over. Now, you keep your shirt on. Why don't you sit down on this log and rest a minute? That'll help you cool off."

I shrugged disappointedly and plopped down on the log she'd indicated. The bark was rough against my sweat-dampened pants, but I didn't say anything about it. I was a Thibodeaux, and Thibodeaux women were tough.

Mama said so.

"And God knows you better keep yours on too," Aunt Edna said, redirecting her warning brow to my mama.

Mama shook her head. I could tell she was fighting a smile, but she held it in check as she walked toward me. "Let's take a look at this plan I've drawn up," she said. She removed her coat and stood beside me for a moment, apparently taking in everything about the December evening.

The wind from the Mississippi caught the hem of her bright green skirt and sent it whipping around her ankles. Her jingle bells jingled all over the place, sounding like the Cakery's door when a customer entered.

Her granny boots sunk a tad into the cold, soft earth of the levee and reminded me of the way my hand sunk into that plate of clay at Vacation Bible School when I was three.

Mama had hung that handprint on the wall at Thibodeaux's, right behind the cash register, so everyone could see how little my hand was back then. Of course, now my hand wouldn't even squeeze into the old impression. I'd grown, grown clean out of that handprint, and Mama was proud. She was determined to help me grow up to be the best I could be, to get everything I ever wanted. She wanted every layer of my personal cake to be butter cream.

So did I.

Mama flipped a log on its side and sat down. Aunt Edna did the same. They looked serious and intent on getting our task started right, so I tried to match my face to theirs. I had to bite the inside of my cheeks to keep from laughing, cause we looked kind of funny, all of us sitting out there on three logs in front of a pile of wood. I mean, every other bonfire on the levee was at least half finished, and we hadn't even started.

But we'd do it. We were Thibodeaux women, weren't we? We could do anything.

"Now," Mama said, her game face on, "This is what we're going to build."

Aunt Edna and I hadn't seen the diagram as of yet, and we'd been fairly anxious to know what Mama had cooked up. After looking at the plan, we saw that "cooked" was the operative word.

The picture was crude, drawn in sticks and circles with words scattered all over the page, but I knew at once what it was, since I looked at them every day.

Aunt Edna put an arm around my shoulder and leaned closer to take a better look. "Why, I'll be," she said. "Yep, Delilah, I think you've done it. This will be perfect."

"And every year, we'll move him," Mama said, circling a figure that stood to the right of the design, "closer."

"Until he's up on top?" Edna asked, more excitedly than I'd ever heard.

"Exactly," Mama said.

"Perfect," Aunt Edna said. "So, what are we waiting for?" She stood, turned around and started rolling her log seat toward the flat area where we would build.

Mama followed suit, then me.

I knew what we were building, but I didn't realize the full impact of what we were doing. Little did I know that Mama's brainstorm would cause a ripple effect that would last through the next fourteen years, bringing folks from far and wide to Gramercy.

If we built the bonfire the way she'd designed it, all of St. John, St. James and any other parish that came for the Christmas Eve lighting would know exactly what Mama and Aunt Edna wanted for me.

A man.

CHAPTER FIVE

Mama, Aunt Edna and I rolled and stacked logs until the pitch black of the Bayou sky became so thick we couldn't see the product of our effort. Our palms stung from the roughness of the bark. Cheeks blazed, wind-blistered and chapped. Eyes burned from a combination of the Mississippi's wind and the tiny bits of debris cast off by the levee. Backs ached from bending, standing, bending, standing.

When we couldn't work any longer, we trudged back toward the car with Aunt Edna's knees cracking like Snap 'n Pops with every slow step.

"I can't drive," she announced. "I really can't." She braced a palm against her lower back and moaned louder than the gusty wind whipping across the river's surface. "Good Lord, I don't think my foot could even push the pedal. See?"

We looked down at Aunt Edna's leg. It shook like a drenched dog after a dip in the Bonnet Carré spillway.

"How're you doing that?" I asked, impressed.

"I ain't," she said. "Trust me child, I ain't."

"If you weren't so bony, you could take the heat," Mama said, grabbing the keys from her sister and heading to the driver's side. "All that food we cook every day and you're so dang skinny a good breeze would blow you out to the Gulf."

"Ah, shuddup," Aunt Edna hissed, inching her way to the other side. She held the passenger's door open long enough for me to crawl through to the back, then she cautiously edged her way in and slumped her body in the seat.

We sat in the car for a moment and stared at the beginning of our masterpiece. A sliver of a moon, God's thumbnail, pushed its way through a cloudy veil and displayed the silhouette of today's work. The circular structure wasn't very tall yet, but it would be. When we were done, it'd be huge, like the other bonfires scattered along the levee's edge.

I figured our wooden interpretation of a Thibodeaux's doberge cake was at its second layer, with eleven more to go. That wouldn't take us long if we worked real hard, I hoped.

"I reckon tomorrow we'll have to bring a ladder," Mama said, peering at the collection of wood that stood atop our section of the levee.

"Yep," Aunt Edna said, as though her mouth was too tired to form any additional syllables.

"I hurt all over," Mama said. She rolled her neck from side to side. Speckles of mud and tree bark dotted her white hair, and her cute little pom-pom on the top didn't remotely resemble a morning glory anymore. It looked more like a used Kleenex. "What about you, sweetie?" she asked. "You hurting, Jezebel?"

"Yes, ma'am," I answered, rubbing the two noodles that masqueraded as arms hanging from my shoulders.

Evidently, an entire day working at the Cakery followed by an entire night pushing logs was too much for Aunt Edna. Her body curled over in the passenger's seat and shook, almost identically to the way her leg had been shaking outside.

I jerked my head toward Mama. "She's crying," I whispered, knowing I had never in my life seen my aunt shed a single tear. The closest she'd come was that day we went to buy my school panties, but even then, she'd held the salty drops in.

Mama tilted her head, glanced toward Aunt Edna. "Nope," she said. "Look again."

Leaning over the console in our Buick Century, I ducked down low so I could peer up at Aunt Edna. Thankfully, the dome light in the car still glowed, allowing me to get a better view. Aunt Edna's bobbed salt-and-pepper hair hid the majority of her face, so I lifted my hand (which hurt, since my arms were so sore) and gently pushed it out of the way.

Her eyes, a shade bluer than my mama's, were absolutely sparkling. But not with tears. They kind of glistened, like a bright turquoise twinkle light on a Christmas tree. And her lips curved into a cheek-stretching smile.

I edged closer, studying her new appearance. My face was merely three inches from hers when she nearly scared me clean out of my skin with a high-pitched cackle that sounded almost girlish. Then she grabbed her sides and hooted with laughter.

After I caught my breath, I laughed too. I couldn't help it. Something about seeing Aunt Edna's usually stern face scrunched up in an honest-to-goodness-holding-nothing-back smile made me forget that my body had worked harder than it ever had in my entire ten years. It made me forget most everything except the urge to laugh.

Mama must've felt the urge to giggle too, because she joined in wholeheartedly, and before we knew it, all three of us were sitting in the car and fogging up the windows with our wild cackles.

"Wh-what's so funny?" I finally managed, holding my stomach to keep it from hurting. Tears trickled down my cheeks. Man, we must've needed a good laugh.

At my question, Mama and Aunt Edna increased their hilarity even more. If the *L'Observateur* or the *News Examiner* would've shown up right then, they'd probably have put us on the front page of both papers for sure. And the headline would've been a doozy.

The REAL Fruitcakes from Thibodeaux's Cakery.

In the end, I figured none of us knew exactly what was so funny. Maybe we'd worked our minds and bodies so much that they flat gave out, got tired of putting up with our foolishness and called it quits for the day. At any rate, Mama, Aunt Edna and I ended up staying on that levee's edge until nearly midnight cause we were too tickled to drive the car home.

When we finally did get our bearings enough for Mama to steer us back to the house, we took long hot showers and then went straight to bed. But I didn't sleep. And I bet Mama and Aunt Edna didn't either, though I'm not for sure. I imagine, though, that they were probably in their rooms doing exactly the same thing as me, staring out the window at God's thumbnail and wondering if He might find it in His heart to help two women and a little girl do the impossible, build a wooden doberge cake.

In time for Christmas.

The next morning was Saturday, so I planned to help Mama with the baking all day. We woke bright and early to get started. Our tiny, shotgun-style house sat on the lot behind the Cakery, so we didn't have far to go to begin.

As usual, Aunt Edna manned the shop out front while Mama and I cooked in the back. We started the day like every other day, drinking our coffee and making dozens of beignets, which sold as quick as we pulled them out of the fryer.

Mama handled the frying part. Then she dumped the puffed squares into a wire basket in front of me. I'd put three on each plate and sprinkle powdered sugar on the top. Sprinkling that sugar, I dreamed that snow had miraculously appeared in Grand Point, if only in the Thiboceaux's kitchen.

During the Christmas season, we increased our inventory to include chocolate-dipped cherries and fruitcakes. We also made specialty breads for holiday dinners, with our artichoke bread leading the pack in popularity.

Normally, we'd cook well into the night, but to get our bonfire finished on time, Aunt Edna flipped the sign on the door from *Open* to *Closed* at precisely five o'clock, and we headed toward Gramercy.

The first few nights that we worked, it didn't seem we were going to fare any better than the years before. No matter how hard we tried, the wood didn't take shape. It looked like we'd simply converted the lumpy pile that the guys had delivered to a taller, but still lumpy, pile for our bonfire.

"What are we doing wrong?" Aunt Edna huffed, glaring at the wooden mess as though it were a mound of snakes instead of trees.

"I don't know," Mama said with a sigh. She flipped a log on its end and sat down. It wasn't quite large enough for her behind, so she wobbled a bit, but then she caught her balance, dropped her palms to her knees and let her head tilt forward in defeat.

"We're Thibodeaux's," I said, puffing out my chest (best I cculd). "We can do it." I hoped I sounded more optimistic than I actually felt, because the pile really did look pitiful, particularly when you looked downriver and saw the wings of that enormous plane.

And now the Piggly Wiggly had started theirs on the other side of the airplane, and even though they'd only built the bottom half, I already recognized the big, stubby snout that extended toward River Road.

Our whole pile looked like a snout, standing on its end, with snot running from the center. (Well, okay, it wasn't that bad, but it didn't look like anything else either. Certainly not a doberge cake.) However, I wasn't going to let a little thing like that bring me down. No way. Thibodeaux's don't give up. Mama said so. Even if she didn't look like she believed it right now.

"We *can* do it," I repeated.

"Sure you can," a very deep, very male voice said from behind us.

We all turned. For the past three nights, we'd watched cars drive slowly by, surveying the progress of the bonfires, or in our case, the lack of progress. A few folks waved, some even shouted hello, but none stopped. No one offered to help or even to give a bit of advice about where our project had gone south. But now...

Zip DuBois, one of the most notable men in St. James Parish, and consequently, one of my favorite Cakery customers, stalked assuredly toward us. He wore a purple and gold LSU jacket, a pair of worn faded jeans and hiking boots. He looked like an angel.

In purple.

Aunt Edna had brought a couple of gas lanterns to help us see what we were doing. They were perched on two logs on either side of our pitiful pile and they cast a creamy gleam of yellow toward Mr. DuBois, making it appear as though he was the lion or maybe the tin man walking to Dorothy on the yellow brick road.

Except Zip DuBois didn't look like a lion. Or a tin man. He looked like my Ken doll, but with wavy white hair and a darker tan. His teeth were whiter too. Oh, and he was older than Ken, way older, but, well, he still looked a lot like Ken. I had actually mentioned the resemblance to Aunt Edna one day after he'd purchased a coffee and beignets at Thibodeaux's. She told me to go ask my Mama if she still felt the urge to play Barbie every now and then.

I didn't get it, but I asked her. Her face turned a tad red and she said something about Aunt Edna minding her bee's wax, then she went back to icing her cake.

"Hi, Mr. DuBois," I said, waving from my log seat. I twisted around to see Mama, her head still staring at her hands on her knees. "Mr. Zip's here," I said, and goodness if her face wasn't red again. "You okay, Mama?"

She nodded, straightened on the log. Then she smoothed back the hair on top of her head and fingered her morning glory bun. "Yes, of course, sweetie. I'm fine," she said. "Hello, Zip."

He reached forward, his eyes studying my mama. He took her hand, didn't shake it or anything like that, just held it for a second. "Delilah," he whispered. "Always a pleasure."

She gave him a small smile, and her face turned a deeper shade of rose. I could see it, even in the lantern light. It made her look younger and very, very pretty. Though to me, Mama always looked pretty.

Everyone was quiet for a couple of seconds before Aunt Edna jumped up from her seat. "Well, Zip, we'd love to sit and chat with you about whatever it is you came to say, but I guess we need to get back to our bonfire." She kicked a log from the original heap and started rolling it toward our confused stack. "It's a cake," she said.

It was probably a good thing that she let him know, since there was no way in the world he'd have figured it out on his own. She hustled the log on top of the others, then turned and looked pointedly at Mr. DuBois. "What do you think of what we've done so far?" she asked, sounding like she was challenging him to a fistfight.

Zip cleared his throat. The corners of his lip twitched up for a slight second, but he caught it quick and straightened his mouth into a serious line. "Edna, I think it's a fine effort," he said, releasing my mama's hand

and walking toward the flat, crooked cake. He balled his fist, brought it beneath his chin and stared at our mess.

"Really," Aunt Edna said, not hiding her disappointment. "You think it's fine?" Even I heard the sarcasm in that question.

"Yes, it's a fine *effort*," he repeated. "And I don't believe any women in Louisiana could've done any better."

"That's because we're Thibodeaux's and we're tough," I said.

A low chuckle rose from his throat, but he turned it into a cough. "That's right, Jezebel," he said. "But you know what's wrong about this?"

"What?" I asked.

"You're the only group on the levee composed of all women," he said matter-of-factly.

"So?" Mama spouted. Her shoulders straightened. She'd added the air of coolness to her tone that I knew well. Zip DuBois had said something wrong.

"So," he continued, undeterred by Mama's single word reprimand. "Aren't you afraid that all of the men out here will feel discriminated against if you don't at least ask one if he wants to help? I mean, you don't want every male in the local parishes boycotting Thibodeaux's because you didn't think they were good enough to assist you in this spectacular bonfire display, do you?"

Aunt Edna's face lit up brighter than both of the lanterns put together. Mine did too. But they weren't anything compared to my mama's. She looked at him as though he'd promised that crawfish season would start a month early next year.

"No, we wouldn't want to upset the men," she whispered, her dimples dipping into her cheeks like the first drops of rainwater on a puddle.

Zip walked toward her, extended a hand and helped her from her seat. "Well then, would you like to invite a man to help? To keep the peace around here, of course."

"Of course," she said. "Do you know of anyone who'd be interested in the job? It's strictly volunteering, you know. We won't pay him for his services."

"As a matter of fact, I have just the man for the job." He grinned broadly. "Do you happen to know the meaning of the name DuBois, Delilah?"

"No, I don't," Mama admitted.

"It was given to a man who," he removed one of the clumsily placed logs from our pile, repositioned the ones beneath it, then set the top one back in place, "worked with wood."

Mama laughed out loud. "Is that so?"

"Have I ever lied to you, Delilah?" he asked.

"Only once," she said.

At that, Zip moved a hand to his heart as though she'd sucker-punched him. "Now, don't say that yet, Miss Thibodeaux. The way I see it, that remains to be seen." He slid out of his shiny purple jacket and tossed it toward me. It smelled brisk and tangy, a scent that wasn't at all familiar. I brought it to my nose and inhaled.

"Smells good, doesn't it?" Aunt Edna whispered. She crouched beside me while Zip looked over Mama's drawing and helped her define a new strategy for building that cake.

"Yes," I said. I whispered too, though I didn't know why. "What is it? This smell. It's different."

"Why, that's simple, sweetie. It's called...the right man, and it's different for every woman." She nodded toward Mama and Mr. DuBois, who had started gathering cane reed from back the levee and stuffing it inside of our cake. "That particular scent is for one particular woman alone."

"Mama?" I asked, my eyes widening.

Aunt Edna nodded.

One of my wayward brown curls spiraled in front of my left eye. She gently pushed it back and tucked it behind my ear.

"But it has to stay our secret. She hasn't figured it out yet." Aunt Edna paused, looked at Mama and Zip. "Wait. I take that back. She's figured it out, but she's fighting it."

"So why can't we just tell her to stop?" I asked, thinking that I should head on over and let Mr. Zip know he was Mama's right man. She'd been waiting for the right one for as long as I could remember. She'd said so, in several of our kitchen talks. I couldn't fathom a reason she should have to delay having him one minute longer.

"That's the funny thing about finding him," Aunt Edna said. "Some women hunt their whole lives to get the right fellow. Others find him early on, but they don't realize he's the right one, and they let him get away."

"Then what happens?" I asked, knowing that each year I got older, I was getting closer to beginning the search for mine. Even though the two of them had been telling me about him for years, I still wanted to be totally prepared for what I should do when he came along. "What happens if you let him get away?" I asked again.

"Sometimes, he's gone for good," she said.

"Like your Josh?" I asked, before I thought better. "Josh" was one of those four-letter words. You know, not the typical four-letter words that grants you a telephone call from the principal to your mama, but the kind of dirty word that's specific. In this case, specific to my Aunt Edna. I guess the jolt of learning that Mama's right man had been living in our town and she hadn't even made an effort to truly pursue him put my knowledge of our own private four-letter word on the back burner.

"I made a mistake," Aunt Edna said. "Josh McGill wasn't the right one for me. Heck, I haven't found mine yet. Not sure I ever will."

"Of course you will, Aunt Edna," I said. I scooted toward her and kissed her cheek.

She grabbed me in a tight hug and pulled me close, causing Zip's jacket to bunch up between us. "We'll see, Jezze."

"Is that what happened to Mama? Did she fight it and then she lost him?"

"No child," Aunt Edna said, still gazing across the patch of earth that separated us from the bonfire and the two people talking on the other side. "Your Mama was blessed to have two right ones."

"Two?" Now why hadn't anyone ever mentioned that to me?

"Yep."

"Where's the other one?" Heck, if one was living in St. James parish, the other might be there too. And why hadn't Mama ever told me?

"God needed him to come on up and visit with Him, I suppose," she said.

The corners of my mouth dipped down and I bit the inside of my cheek. I knew exactly what that meant. It was the same thing she'd told me when my pet guinea pig, Andouille, died when I was seven. Well, shoot. Poor Mama. I was real torn up over Andouille dying, can't imagine how hard it was for her to lose a right man. My lip quivered.

Poor, poor Mama.

"Now, now," Aunt Edna said, putting her skinny arm around me and patting my back. "It's okay. Like I said, your Mama had two right ones given to her. She's just being a bit stubborn about the second one."

"But she told me that she's still looking for her right man, that she wants to find him someday," I informed, recalling all of our kitchen talks about that very subject.

"Well, truth of it is that your Mama's a bit gun-shy. See, it hurts pretty bad when you lose someone that suits you so well, and she's afraid of getting hurt like that again. At least I think that's the problem."

"And would she get hurt again?" I asked, looking at my mama and praying that she'd never be sad again. Ever.

Aunt Edna shrugged. "Heck, sweetie. You can get hurt doing about near anything. But isn't finding the right man worth the chance?"

"I guess so," I said, seeing Zip help Mama move a log and noticing the way his hand laid on top of hers.

"You'll understand one day, Jezze, when you find yours. Zip's been waiting a mighty long time to show your Mama he's the right one."

"How long?" I asked.

"So far, thirty years," Aunt Edna said. She moved toward a stack of logs and pushed one down from the top. "But I think she's starting to see the light."

CHAPTER SIX

Finding out information about my mama and Zip DuBois was about as easy as peeling a shrimp that had been boiled too long.

Nearly impossible.

But then again, nothing's totally out of reach for Thibodeaux women (that's what Mama says) and I set about to prove that as a fact. So I started asking her questions about the right man, how someone knew when she found him, what she should do about it, and what to do if she lost him. We'd talked about that kind of thing before, since it was such an important part of growing up (according to Mama), so she didn't seem to think it was odd that I asked so many questions about him now.

The problem was, she didn't talk about *her* right man like she usually did. She seemed much more interested in talking about mine. Or the one I'd find, rather, when I grew up.

For the next few days, Mama and I baked in the kitchen and I dilly-dallied around with learning more about Zip DuBois. And with why Mama didn't want him. Then at night, Mama, Aunt Edna and I drove to Gramercy and watched Mama's right man in action.

I'd always liked Mr. DuBois. He was one of the few customers who insisted on a trip back to the kitchen to say hello every time he came in Thibodeaux's. And he came to the Cakery a lot.

Of course, there had been plenty of times when he'd about near caught us with our shirts off. One day in particular, he'd come in while Aunt Edna was righting a sample wedding cake that had gone to leaning a bit. She'd heard the bells on the door when he came in; she'd even said hello. But she'd assumed that he would want to browse a tad before he made his purchase, surely before he went to the back of the store to say hi to Mama and me.

Typically, Aunt Edna would start talking real loud when she rang up Mr. DuBois' sweets, then she'd stomp down the hall doing that kill-the-cockroach move she'd perfected and then jiggle the doorknob a bit like it was stuck (in case we didn't hear her yelling and stomping).

I'd hop off my stool, whip my shirt on and head toward the door to unlock it, while Mama got dressed and Aunt Edna bellowed her conversation with Zip.

"SO, HOW ARE THINGS DOWN AT THE CAMP?" Aunt Edna would scream, her hand working that doorknob like a booger she was trying to shake loose.

When Aunt Edna asked about the camp (Mr. Zip owns a fish camp on the Tickfaw River), we knew that they were at the door. So, while she screamed about Mr. DuBois' private getaway, the message Mama and I heard was "GET YOUR SHIRTS ON. WE'RE COMING IN."

We got a real kick out of Aunt Edna's tactics, so it never failed that when Zip entered the kitchen, we were nearly crying with a case of having our funny boxes turned over. I bet he thought we laughed all day.

Then again, some days we did.

Anyway, on this one particular day, he took advantage of Aunt Edna's preoccupation with that leaning cake and headed down the hall. And wouldn't you know it, I'd forgotten to lock the door.

I had just finished a patch of yellow rosebuds on a birthday cake when I heard the door creak open. "Mama," I whispered, kind of panicky, and grabbed for my shirt. I caught a glimpse of his forearm, the big hand wrapped around the knob, and I knew this wasn't Aunt Edna heading into our kitchen. "Mama," I repeated, still at a whisper, but a loud we're-about-to-get-caught whisper.

"Lord Almighty," she said, dropping a chocolate icing bag and hurrying to drape her shirt around her big bosoms.

I yanked my T-shirt over my head and shot toward the door knowing if I didn't get there soon, the *L'Observateur* and *News Examiner* could have eye-catching headlines about those crazy Thibodeaux women...

Grand Point's Naked Chefs.

I even imagined what the local television station would report if they got wind of it...

Topless at Thibodeaux's. Film at eleven.

By the time I reached my side of the door, Aunt Edna had realized what was happening and had started down the hall at an all-out run. Problem was, before she could slow her pace, she barreled into the back of Zip and knocked them both inside the kitchen.

Straight into me.

The three of us hit the tile floor like mating love-bugs splatting against a windshield (and yes, I've heard the joke—at least they died happy).

"Mercy, Edna," Zip said, "You need to slow down, woman."

Aunt Edna had that Darth Vader breathing thing going. She couldn't say a thing, and if she had, I'd have expected it to be, "Luke, I'm your father." In any case, she remained wordless, with that hiiiii-huuuuu hiiiii-huuuuu rasping along while she gawked at Mama, buttoning up her shirt.

Zip cleared his throat. I don't know if it was because he caught a glimpse of Mama's pride and joy (she actually calls them that; her left one pride, her right joy), or if he just needed to loosen the crud in his windpipe at that moment. But when he did it, everything got real quiet.

"Hello, Zip," Mama finally said, breaking the awkward silence.

He stood, walked over to my mama and took her hand. "Delilah."

And that was it. They mixed a little social talk. You know, "How's the cooking going?" and "How's the camp?" but neither of them mentioned her shirt. So I figured we'd pulled it off (or pulled it on, you could say, if you're referring to our tops).

Looking back on that day, I didn't think too awful much of the episode at the time. I mean, I made certain to lock the door after that, but I didn't consider that Mama's right man had just fallen into our kitchen. Of course, I was only five or six when it happened. I wasn't old enough to spot the right one yet. But now, at ten, I was practically grown. Mama said so. And smart enough to realize that I needed to know more about Mama and Mr. Zip.

It took several days of hinting to Mama during our kitchen talks before I finally got tired of pretending. And wouldn't you know it, all I had to do to find out everything I wanted to know...was ask.

"Mama, why do they call him Zip?" I blurted, sliding my hands into disposable gloves, then filling several stocking shaped boxes with chocolate-covered cherries. I kept my eyes on the red and white striped stockings in front of me, in case Mama decided to give me one of her you-know-better-than-to-ask-that looks.

But I stole a peek, and to my amazement, she grinned, an opening-the-first-present-on-Christmas-morning type of grin. She looked tickled with the question, almost like she'd been waiting for me to ask.

"It's a nickname he got in high school," she said, "when he ran track for Lutcher. He was the fastest thing St. James parish had ever seen. He ran the four-forty, the two-twenty *and* the mile relay. The last leg of course." Her eyes closed a little, as though she were about to go to sleep, then she shook her head, and her face reddened a bit.

"Sorry, sweetie," she said, staring at my confused look. "That means he ran one time around the track in a race, then halfway around in another one, and finally, he'd be the last runner in a race where they each ran one lap around, for a total of four times."

"Wow," I marveled. "So, he must have been really, really fast."

"Yeah," she said. "After he got the track scholarship to LSU, the name followed him there. Then he graduated and started coaching the college's team. Stayed until he retired. He's been 'Zip' as long as I've known him."

"So, what's his real name?" I asked. I stopped distributing the chocolates and turned to face her.

She was topless, of course, but she reached for her shirt and put it on. "His name is John-Paul," she said, her voice soft and low. "John-Paul DuBois."

"You finished decorating the cakes?" I asked, staring at the line of doberges stretched across the counter.

"No," she said, still grinning.

"You put your shirt on," I informed, as though she hadn't noticed.

"I guess I got a chill."

Okay, that was a new one on me. Mama didn't care about how cold she got when she was in create mode, but evidently, this was a different kind of chill.

"Oh," I said, grabbing my shirt and wrestling it on. (No need in being cold all by myself.) "Did you know him back then? Mr. Zip?" I asked, starting back up with the chocolate distribution.

Mama sat down on the stool beside me and seemed to forget all about those doberge cakes that needed decorating. She stretched her hands out and caught my wrists, eased them down and waited for me to drop the two pieces of chocolate that dangled from my fingertips into a stocking box. "Jezze?"

I bit my lip. Guess I hadn't been as subtle as I thought. "Yes, ma'am?"

"Why don't you take a break from those candies and ask me what you really want to know."

I blinked. Well, I should've thought of that to start with. "All right," I said. "Aunt Edna said that you have two right men. Or," I amended, "You *had* two right men."

Her full lip pulled down for a second, but then slid into an easy smile. "Well, I don't know about that, but I did fall in love when I was young. Very young, actually."

"How young?"

"Fifteen."

Fifteen. Just five years older than me.

"With your first right man?" I asked.

"I guess you'd say that," she answered. She blinked, and I watched an extra layer of shine spread across her eyes. Man, I didn't want to make Mama cry.

"That's okay, Mama. We don't have to talk about it," I said. I did my best impersonation of an adult, patted her forearm (the way she did mine whenever I was upset), and flashed her my brightest smile, hoping that it'd help her forget my questions.

"Oh yes we do," she said, "But I had expected us to talk about it when you were a bit older. Guess I forgot what a big girl you are now." She took a breath. "His name was Rene. Rene Couvillion. We were boyfriend and girlfriend, I guess you'd say."

"We call it going out," I enlightened, to which she gave me a deep-dimpled grin.

"Oh, I see," she said, nodding. "All right, then you'd say we were going out."

"Okay," I said. A couple of girls in my grade were going out with guys already, but I'd decided to stay single for now. At least until I finished fifth grade.

"I met him at the Lagniappe Festival the year I turned fifteen," Mama said. "Actually, we met on the same night that I met Zip."

"Mr. DuBois?" I asked, wondering what the odds were for Mama to meet two right men on the same night.

Mama nodded. "A lot of the teens from the local high schools went to the festivals back then. At that time, that was the best way to meet other kids your own age. Probably still is," she added.

"So what happened?"

"Nothing out of the ordinary," Mama said. "I met lots of people that night, but two boys kind of stood out from everyone else."

"Rene and Zip?"

"Rene and Zip," she repeated. "As a matter of fact, they both took an interest in me. Truthfully, it was quite flattering."

"But you liked Rene best."

"Oh, I suppose I liked them both the same at first. But Rene was my age, fifteen. He wasn't quite as confident as Zip, not as determined, and I think I was more comfortable with that back then. Zip DuBois could be a little intimidating, even when he had his eye on you."

"How old was he?" I asked.

"Seventeen, and he'd just accepted the scholarship to LSU, so I knew he'd be moving to Baton Rouge for college. I suppose that had a lot to do with me choosing Rene."

"Did Mr. DuBois get mad?" I asked, infatuated with the whole idea of two boys fighting over my mama.

"No," Mama said. "When I told him I had agreed to take Rene's class ring—that's the way we let people know we were going together back then—Zip backed down, like a real gentleman."

"Then what happened?"

"Zip went on to become a star at LSU. In truth, he was the hometown hero, the boy who made it really big. And Rene, well, I fell head over heels in love with him. We dated for three years until we were eighteen, and then he asked me to marry him."

"You were married?" I asked, my brows shooting up a span and my eyes bugging out real big. Shoot, I'd never even considered that.

Mama shook her head, her lip thinned. "He was in an accident, a car accident, two weeks after he asked me," she said. She lifted her shoulders and sighed. "Wasn't meant to be." Cupping my chin, Mama leaned forward and kissed my forehead.

"You okay?" I asked.

She nodded. "Yes, sweetie, I'm fine. Some things are a little tough to talk about though."

"More coconut in your cake," I said.

"Yep." She drew me toward her chest and held me tight. "That's exactly it. More coconut in my cake."

"So then you and Mr. Zip never were boyfriend and girlfriend? You never went out on dates?"

"No," she said softly. "After I lost Rene, I wasn't much interested in getting that close to a man again. I decided I'd rather keep my mind on working for Big Daddy and Big Mama at the Cakery."

"So you didn't talk to Mr. Zip again?"

"Oh, he came around to check on me every now and again. After a couple of years, he even asked me out for a date, but I said no."

"Why?"

"I suppose I was afraid."

"Of getting hurt?"

Mama nodded. "Eventually, after a good deal of time passed, he met a girl in Baton Rouge and they married."

"Is he still married?" I asked, shocked. I hadn't even thought of that either.

"No, sweetie."

"What happened?"

"Well, I know they've had a rocky patch at love over the years, and I think the road eventually just got too tough for them to handle," Mama said. "From what I hear. I haven't asked Zip specifics. Some things are best not talked about."

I thought about that for a minute then I remembered one of Mr. Zip's comments from that first night he'd shown up at the levee. "Mama?"

"What, honey?"

"You told Mr. Zip that he'd lied to you once. What did he say?"

Her eyes deepened from blue to sapphire and she had a subtle, secret smile when she spoke. "He made me a promise back then," she said, and a hint of a giggle crept from her throat. "On the night I met him. Lord, he was so sure of himself."

"What kind of promise?" I asked.

Mama touched a finger to the cleft in my chin and looked directly into my eyes. "Well, sweetie, that man promised me that he'd marry me some day. Can you believe that?"

I smiled back at my mama. Then I wrapped my arms around her neck and hugged her tight, knowing that her cake was due another round of butter cream and believing that Zip DuBois could make it happen. "Yes, Mama," I whispered, my words smothered since my head was buried in her chest. "I can."

CHAPTER SEVEN

Twelve inches. The precise amount of space that Mama, Aunt Edna and Mr. DuBois determined my "right man" should progress each year toward his goal. Oh, and that goal would be...

Me.

Yep, Mama's prediction held true. On Christmas Eve, the *L'Observateur*, the *News Examiner* and practically everyone else in the Gramercy vicinity came out in record numbers to see the Thibodeaux's bonfire display. More folks gaped and gawked at our cake than the ship, the beer bottle, the pig and the airplane put together.

And my life would never be the same.

See, Mama's vision for our bonfire wasn't meant to be a one year exhibition. Oh no, she planned on telling a story, a story that would reveal itself in the form of that bonfire each Christmas for the next fourteen years.

The Cajuns in the parish loved it. The *L'Observateur* loved it. The *News Examiner* loved it. Mama, Aunt Edna and Zip loved it.

But me? Well, I wasn't so sure.

By the time I finally realized exactly what we were building, there was only one day left before the judging, and it was way too late to change Mama's mind. Plus, I didn't want to hurt her feelings, particularly not when she was so excited (and when her right man was so excited too). But geez, I never realized...

"Mama, are we going to paint the layers different colors?" I asked, standing back to admire the huge, perfect doberge cake that towered on our spot of the levee.

"Now, why would we do that, sugar?" she asked. "We'd only paint them different colors if it were a doberge." She held the ladder in place while Zip scuttled to the top to straighten a dislodged log.

"It's not a doberge?" I asked.

"No, sweetie," Mama said. Her brows knitted together as Zip's big male body wobbled on top of the ladder. She seemed to hold her breath until he steadied himself, then she whispered, "I thought you knew what we were building, Jezebel. It's not a doberge, but you're gonna like it just as much. As a matter of fact, it's even better than a doberge."

"Then what," I started, but stopped when Aunt Edna came rambling up the levee in Zip's truck. In the past ten days, since Zip had shown up at our bonfire spot, he'd become a regular fixture around the Cakery and the levee. He'd hauled wood, stacked it, brought dinner for all of us to share picnic-style by the bonfire site, loaned us his truck...

And stolen our hearts.

I sure hoped that Mama was half as happy having him around as I was, because truly, I didn't want him to go. And I certainly didn't want to see her lose the smile that had christened her face ever since the first night he'd surprised us on the levee.

Mama was pretty anyway, but when she looked at him, she was downright beautiful.

Aunt Edna wheeled up the levee like she was trying out for a monster truck exhibition. I gasped. She always drove our Buick as though she were expecting someone to plow into us at any moment, never even achieved the speed limit and certainly didn't punch the accelerator.

Like she was doing right now.

The back tires spit dirt and gravel everwhichaway as she cut the wheels toward our bonfire. I put my hands over my face to protect my eyes from the cloud of dust she kicked up when she finally, blessedly, slammed on the brakes.

"You think she'll climb out the window like Bo Duke?" Zip called from the ladder.

I'd seen a few Dukes of Hazard reruns, so I watched the driver's door in anticipation, holding my breath and refusing to blink. If Aunt Edna's skinny body came sailing out that window, I sure didn't want to miss it.

To my disappointment though, the door opened normally. Then Aunt Edna hopped out.

And squealed.

"IIIII-EEEE," echoed down the levee as she let loose a Cajun shout that made the other bonfire builders stop and laugh.

Paying no attention to the onlookers, she darted to the back of Zip's truck and opened the tailgate. "I've got my part," she said. She waved her hand like a Price is Right girl to display the small pieces of wood in the bed of the truck.

"Looks good," Zip said. Three rungs from the bottom, he jumped from the ladder, took Mama's hand, kissed it then led her over to look at the new supplies.

"What do you think?" Aunt Edna asked.

"Perfect," Mama said. "It shouldn't be too hard to create the rest from this."

I looked at the cake, which looked as finished as it could get, in my opinion. So exactly what were they planning to do? I mean, we could paint it to make it look a bit better, but we didn't need more wood for that. In my opinion, it already looked pretty dang good, particularly if we made each layer a different color.

But Mama said it wasn't a doberge.

So if it wasn't, what was it?

"What are you going to do with all that?" I asked, thinking that whatever it was, it better be something we could build fast, since the thing would be judged tomorrow.

"She doesn't know?" Aunt Edna asked, shock apparent on her face. "Come on, Jezze, didn't we tell you?"

"I thought we were building a doberge cake," I said. "Since that's our specialty and all, and everyone knows about us holding the record for the most layers, I thought we'd be painting the cake all different colors. One for each of our thirteen layers. It'll look cool," I added, trying to let them know they were missing a golden opportunity to make our bonfire really spectacular.

"Oh, sweetie," Mama said. "We're doing something that will be even more," she paused, looked at Zip, and winked *(Mama winked!)*, "Cool."

Zip wrapped an arm around Mama and pulled her close. I swear they looked like some of the teenage couples at the high school. Only happier. I was glad about that, but still a bit confused about the pieces of wood in the back of his truck.

"What're we going to do with all that?" I asked.

Aunt Edna dashed back to the cab of the truck and withdrew a long, white gauzy scarf. She held it up and smiled. It took me a second to look at the fabric; I was too shocked by her face. She'd smiled more in the past two weeks than in my entire life. I was sure of it. And right now, it seemed that the additions that she, Mama and Zip had planned for the cake were the cause for her uncommon mood. "See?" she said, nodding her head victoriously at Mama and Zip.

"Oh yes," Mama said, clapping her hands together. She walked to Aunt Edna and took the fabric, ran it through her palms, then pressed it to her cheek. "A shame we'll be burning it tomorrow."

"What?" I asked, totally confused. Were we going to drape the stuff around the top of the cake? Like icing? Because I'd have gone for something thicker. That thin stuff would never pass for butter cream.

"Did you get a dress?" Zip asked.

"Sure did," Aunt Edna said, ignoring my question and moving straight on into his. She dove in the truck again. Her bony bottom wiggled in the air a bit while she searched around. Then she withdrew...

A wedding gown.

My eyes shot from the gown to the cake. "Oh," I said. "I get it." Relief flooded over me. It wasn't as though I'd been totally in the dark. We had built a cake, after all. Not a doberge cake (though that's the kind I'd have preferred), but a wedding cake. And Thibodeaux's was known for outstanding wedding cakes as well, so I supposed it would do (if they had their minds set against a doberge). "We're going to put a bride and groom on top, right?" I asked.

"Just the bride," Mama said. She fingered the beaded bodice on the gown. "Goodness, Edna, did someone actually throw this thing out?"

"There's a wine stain on the back," Aunt Edna explained. She turned the garment so we could see the big red splotch that started in the center, then dribbled down the entire length of the gown. "Mrs. Jeansonne said we could have it. She thought our idea was brilliant, by the way."

"Remind me to send her a thank you note tomorrow," Mama said. "Right after we win." She laughed. "And it is a brilliant idea, even if it was mine."

"What idea?" I asked.

Mama walked away from Zip and headed toward me. She crouched over so we were eye-level, then she took my hands in hers. "This cake is yours," she whispered.

"It's all of ours," I said. I wasn't about to let them give me all the credit when we'd all worked our behinds off to get the thing done. "Yours, Aunt Edna's, Mr. Zip's and mine."

Mama leaned forward, ran her palm across my temple and down my cheek. "No, sweetie, that's not what I meant."

"What did you mean?"

"I meant that we're building a cake that's going to tell a story."

"What kind of story?"

"Your story," she said.

"My story?"

Mama nodded.

Realization dawned and my face burst into a smile. "Then we need to make it a doberge cake, with a thick layer of butter cream at the bottom."

Mama laughed. "Well now, that's true," she said. "That would tell the story of your life, but we're going to tell a different story with this cake. And you're going to love it."

"What story?" I asked, my repetitive question reminding me of that Minah bird at the Grand Point gas station. I could almost see its shiny black wings and hear the squawking, cracked voice. "What story? What story? What story?"

"I got it," Zip called. A long, brown garment bag draped across his arms and bent down heavily on both sides. It reminded me of the backbends Mrs. Benoit made me do in gym class.

Mama and I stopped talking long enough to watch him reposition the bag, unzip it and withdraw a black tuxedo.

"For the groom," he said, his white teeth nearly blinding against his tan face.

Mama returned the gesture.

For a moment, I just sat there, staring at Aunt Edna, holding the wedding gown, Zip DuBois, holding the tuxedo, and Mama, holding her right man's heart with her smile.

"What do you think?" Zip asked, breaking the Kodak moment.

"It's perfect," she said. "You sure you want to donate your tux?"

"It's an old one," he said, shrugging. "I've got a few more, believe it or not. Besides, I want Jezebel's cake to look terrific." He and Aunt Edna returned the wedding clothes to the truck's cab then moved to the back and started pulling the pieces they needed for the bride and groom.

"Mama?" I asked.

"What, sweetie?"

"What story?"

"Honey, it's going to be perfect. Our bonfire is going to be a wedding cake. Your wedding cake. And the bride, *you*, will be right on the top."

Okay, I didn't miss the fact that something, or someone, was missing from that sentence. "What about the groom?"

"That's where the 'story' part comes in," Mama said. "See, the first year, he's going to be standing on the ground, a little ways out from the cake."

I nodded, having no idea where she was heading and afraid to ask.

"Then each Christmas Eve, he'll move closer to the top. Until your right man is directly beside you. Each year, everyone who sees our bonfire will know how much closer you are to finding him," she explained.

She sounded practically joyful, so I didn't have the heart to tell her that I wasn't so sure I wanted the bulk of Cajuns from the surrounding towns watching my progress. I swallowed, looked at the size of the cake. Suddenly, the top didn't seem all that far from the ground. How fast did they plan on my wooden groom making the journey? And what would happen if he got there, and I still hadn't found the guy I'm looking for?

What if I never found him?

A drop of sweat trickled down my back as though it were July instead of December. "How long will it take him to reach the top?" I asked, working hard to keep my voice steady.

"He'll move twelve inches each year, and we're starting him fourteen feet from the top, so—"

"Fourteen years," I whispered, thankful my ability to do simple math hadn't disintegrated as a result of my shock. Okay, so I have to find the fellow by the time I'm twenty-four, which should be possible, right? Mama found hers at fifteen, found two actually. Surely I'd find mine by twenty-four.

Then again, Aunt Edna was still looking.

"Yes," she said. "But if you find your right man early, we can move him quicker."

"What if I find him later?"

"Oh, sugar, I doubt that," she said. She pulled me close. "But if it is a little later, we'll slow his journey down a bit."

I nodded, swallowed. "Okay." Taking a deep breath, I worked on convincing myself that this wouldn't be so bad. I was a Thibodeaux, wasn't I? I could handle having my wedding cake on display for the general public for the next fourteen years. No problem. Or, as Aunt Edna says, no biggee. They'd root me on as I tried to find my groom. It'd be fun.

Right?

"Okay," I repeated. I leaned back from Mama, grinned. "Piece of cake," I said then laughed at the pun. "Guess we should go help build my groom."

"But of course," Mama said.

Within a few hours, a bride stood atop our cake. Her long, white gauzy veil billowed behind her as though calling to the mighty Mississippi to send her a man.

A few hours later, the groom arrived. Only he was stuck on the ground with his head peering longingly toward the woman he loved.

"Hmmm," Aunt Edna said. She stood away from the completed structure with her skinny legs braced apart and her back arched so she could see the top. "I'm not so sure."

"About what?" Mama asked. "I think it's perfect."

Aunt Edna looked from the bride to the groom. "He looks sad."

Zip stepped between the two sisters, draped his arms across their shoulders. "It's tough waiting on her to realize she needs you up there."

He gave them both a squeeze, then left them standing there while he headed toward the bonfire. Then he scooped up the long ladder, carried it across the levee and deposited it in the back of his truck. "Poor fellow," he said, moving back to stand by Mama and Aunt Edna.

They stared at him accusingly.

Zip smirked. "Gotta feel sorry for the guy, huh?"

Mama crossed her arms in front of her stomach. (I know, most people cross them in front of their chest, but for Mama, that isn't an option.) "Maybe he's debating whether he's at the right cake, and she doesn't want to let him up there until she's sure he won't go back to the old cake...again," she said.

He smirked. "Or maybe that old cake has burned to the ground for good, and he's sad because all he really wants it the new cake. And he's pretty sure the girl at the top of the new cake wants him too."

"Well, maybe he's so dang cocky she doesn't know if he's worth the trouble."

Zip laughed out loud. "Reckon how long it'll take her to decide?"

"I guess he'll have to wait and see," she said crisply, though I heard the humor in her tone.

"Well, if you ask me, he's been waiting long e—" Zip started, but halted mid-sentence when a shiny pickup with a *L'Observateur* stamp on the door started up the levee.

A reporter who looked like he was barely old enough to be driving jumped out with pen and paper in hand. "Can I ask you a few questions about your display?" he asked, walking toward us. He wore glasses and a tie, but it didn't help him look any older (or any less nerdy, in my opinion). "Won't take but a minute," he said.

"Why, take all the time you need," Mama said, smiling as though she'd won the lottery. Not the regular one, but the PowerBall.

Within minutes, the guy had his interview underway.

"Is it a wedding cake?" he asked.

"Of course," Mama replied.

"I can't help but notice that something looks amiss," he said, raising an eyebrow as though he'd found a flaw in our plan.

"Really?" Mama asked, feigning surprise. "And what would that be?"

"The groom. He's at the bottom. Is that because the bride has already decided she doesn't want him? Is this the story of love gone bad?" he asked, his voice intense and his pen moving rapidly across the page. "A divorce? Separation? An affair? Or maybe a couple who wanted to marry, but couldn't? Is it a depiction of something that actually happened? Tell me, what's the story?"

Again, I heard the Minah bird. "What's the story? What's the story? What's the story?"

Mama enlightened the fellow about our story (guess you could say *my* story) and we could actually see the exhilaration bristle on his skin, the anticipation in his hungry eyes. We'd given him a winner. A legend that would last fourteen years (or longer, if I didn't get a move on).

He called his office and had a photographer there within thirty minutes. They took pictures of the bonfire, the bride, the groom, Mama, Aunt Edna, Zip.

And me.

Lots of pictures of me.

I didn't mind it at the time (I've always been a camera hog), but later I wasn't so sure.

That night, Aunt Edna picked up twenty copies of the newspaper's special edition (they always put out a paper to let folks know about all the bonfires they can see on Christmas Eve). I knew something was up when she waltzed into Thibodeaux's singing.

Aunt Edna—singing?

"Delilah," she called, bouncing in with her arms full of newspapers. She bumped the door closed with her bony hip. Humming, she started down the hall.

I heard her coming, turned to Mama, who was finishing up the last of the doberges that had been ordered for Christmas Eve. "Is that Aunt Edna?" I asked.

"Sounds like it," Mama said. "Go on, open the door."

Jumping off my stool, I jerked on my sweater and moved to the door.

Mama didn't make any effort to don her shirt; there was no need, since we'd been closed for two hours. (We had our bonfire finished, so we took advantage of having another night to wrap up our cooking.)

I opened the door.

Aunt Edna sashayed inside and plopped the stack of papers on the stainless steel counter. "Guess what," she said, grinning at Mama.

Mama looked down at her chest. I guess she was checking to make sure she was actually half naked, since Aunt Edna didn't holler at her or anything. Then Mama shrugged, making her boobs lift a bit before they fell back into place. "I give. What?"

"Take a gander," Aunt Edna said. She lifted the top paper, turned it toward us.

Mama slapped her hands to her cheeks, which sent a tiny puff of flour drifting around her face. She blinked a few times then focused on the images. "Oh," she whispered.

With an awed smile, Mama walked across the room and carefully accepted the *L'Observateur* from Aunt Edna, as though it were made of glass instead of paper. "My goodness."

"The judging won't happen until tomorrow, of course," Aunt Edna said, "But the paper already has us pegged to win."

"Look, Jezebel," Mama said, as though I hadn't been gawking at the headline from the minute Aunt Edna lifted the page.

I nodded, shut my jaw and smiled. What else could I do? There, on the front page of the local paper, the one that all of my friends and everyone who lived anywhere near Grand Point would see, were four pictures. The wooden bride, her long veil flapping in the breeze, standing on top of our cake. Her tuxedoed groom on the ground. Mama, Aunt Edna and Zip standing beside the bonfire. And me. A picture of me, all by myself, blown up twice the size as all the others.

But the photograph wasn't what made me speechless; it was the headline that made my throat go dry and created another round of sweat droplets that pooled down my back.

Jezze's Man.

One day I was Jezebel Thibodeaux, plain ol' fifth grader at Riverside Academy and only child to Delilah Thibodeaux, one of the kooky Thibodeaux sisters who owned the Cakery in Grand Point. And the next day...

I was a ten year old on a manhunt.

Or a groom hunt, I guess you'd say.

By Christmas Eve night, the *Times-Picayune* in New Orleans had picked up the story, along with the *Advocate* in Baton Rouge, the *Daily Star* in Hammond and the *Courier* in Houma. And those were just the papers that were relatively close. Evidently, the news made it as far south as Morgan City and as far north as Natchitoches, because reporters showed up from those places too. Heck, the story of the fifth grader already on the prowl for her groom was front-page stuff.

And we won't even discuss local TV.

I half expected to hear that David Letterman had a top ten list in my honor. Let's see, what would he call it...

Top Ten Ways for a Ten Year Old to Snag a Groom

10) Get some wood.

9) Start a fire...

Seriously, Cajuns and tourists alike drove hours to see the bonfire that had subsequently been entitled "Jezze's Man" by the judging committee.

"I think we're going to win, Jezebel," Mama said, holding an arm around me on Christmas Eve while we waited for the announcement.

Blinking past all of the cameras that flashed in my face, I tried to smile at Mama. "I hope so." For all this trouble, we'd sure enough better.

Reporters kept firing questions at me from all directions, almost as rapidly as the photographers snapped pictures.

"How does it feel to have a bonfire in your honor?"

"Did you know what you were building when you started?"

"What if you find your groom early, Miss Thibodeaux?"

"What if you find him late?"

"How much did y'all spend on the bridal trousseau?"

"Will you burn a bridal gown and tuxedo every year?"

"Won't that be expensive?"

"Do you know the name of your groom, Miss Thibodeaux?"

"Do you have any prospects? Boys at your local school, or perhaps someone here tonight at the festivities?"

"Where do you think you and your groom will go on your honeymoon?"

That last question brought on a coughing fit that I flat couldn't control. It was worse than breathing in when you eat a beignet, when all that powdered sugar hits the back of your throat and gets you to hacking. Worse than when you're eating a pickle and the pickle juice trickles down your windpipe.

I about near died coughing out there, and the photographers loved it. They took pictures of me with my tongue hanging out, my eyes all watery and then with both of my arms yanked above my head as Mama and Aunt Edna tried to help me out.

When I finally stopped, I glanced around at the reporters, every one of the scribbling across their papers. Unfortunately, I saw tomorrow's headlines in big letters on one of the pads.

It took all I had not to groan out loud.

All Choked Up About Finding Her Groom.

Super, I'd given them more ammo.

At last, the judges announced the winner. No surprise, Jezze's Man won by a landslide.

Then, the judges torched it, starting with the groom. Obviously, Zip's old tuxedo was ultra-flammable, because the fire consumed my right man in nothing flat.

Then they lit the base of the cake.

Orange, red and yellow flames licked their way toward the top, heading toward the bride. I stared in awe, as more and more cameras flashed, attempting to capture my expression when "Jezze" burned.

I looked down the levee. One by one, each structure went up in flames, until the Mississippi's typically brown, murky waters were golden from the reflected inferno. Christmas Eve was officially here.

I smiled. Quite a feat, I'd say, particularly when I stared up at that bride on the top of my cake and realized that I didn't agree with Aunt Edna's interpretation. She'd said the groom looked sad. But she got it wrong.

He couldn't have looked sadder than the bride.

CHAPTER EIGHT

Thirteen days. The number of days between the lighting of the bonfires, December 24th, and my first day back to school, January 6th.

Each morning during that span of time, I slept a little later. And later. And later.

On those cold, dreary winter mornings, I'd crawl out of bed, put on my endless layers of clothing then head down the rock pathway that connected our house to the Cakery. A plate of warm beignets with mini-mountains of powdered sugar would inevitably be waiting on the wrought iron table in the breakfast nook.

Mama and Aunt Edna had told me I should stay home, watch television or play with some of my new Christmas things instead of working during the entire winter break. They wanted me to experience the vacation, but they should've known I couldn't stay away from the Cakery. I loved working in the Thibodeaux's kitchen with Mama.

Besides, I didn't see staying home as an option. I had to stay busy to keep my mind off going back to school.

I had no doubt that every kid in fifth grade, probably in the whole school, had seen my picture on the television or in the newspaper. Heck, most of them had been standing out there on the levee when the judges announced the winner.

And not a single one of them talked to me when it was over. Then again, I was drowning in reporters and photographers at the time; they may not have had a chance. In any case, I had no earthly idea what they thought of the fiasco. And I wasn't so sure I wanted to find out.

Sitting in the breakfast nook, I sipped on my cup of coffee and begged the sweet taste of chicory to lift my spirits.

It didn't.

The kitchen was empty and fairly quiet, save the low humming of the refrigerator and the clicking of the big round clock on the wall. It smelled of coffee, butter cream icing and yeast. In other words, it smelled like complete heaven to a ten-year-old in the dumps.

I figured Aunt Edna and Mama were out front straightening the displays, so I didn't go hunting them, just drank my coffee and inhaled the aroma of the kitchen in silence…while wondering what my life would be like in three days.

I glared at the red marker that hung from a looping strand of blue yarn beside the dry erase calendar on the back wall. Three empty squares were all I had left. Three. After today, there'd be two.

Gulping down too much coffee, I coughed past my scalding throat and stood. No need to put it off until the end of the day. I walked to the calendar, grabbed the marker and made the biggest, fattest red X of all.

"Hmph," Aunt Edna said, entering the kitchen and passing behind me as she took her coffee mug to the sink. She rinsed it then poured another cup. "The day's not over yet, Jezze. What's your hurry?" She leaned her back against the counter, winced at her first sip of coffee then eyed me suspiciously.

"No hurry," I said. And I meant it. Lord knew I wasn't in any rush whatsoever to get back to school. I could almost taste the grainy coconut creeping into my cake.

Sitting back down at the table, I turned my attention to the remainder of coffee in my cup.

"Is that so?" she asked, in her I-know-better-than-that tone.

I nodded, praying she believed me. "Where's Mama?"

Aunt Edna went along with my attempt to change the subject.

For now.

"Zip asked her to help him take some things over to the camp. I told her we'd be fine on our own. Don't reckon we'll have a lot of customers today, since the winter holidays have passed."

She was right. Thibodeaux's had a few days of down time each year after Christmas and New Years. Right now, we were smack dab in the middle of those days.

"I figure they'll be back late this afternoon," Aunt Edna continued. "Zip planned to take her for a ride through the swamp too, so it could be a while."

"Did she layer up?" I asked. A swamp ride in January didn't sound all that great to me. I was almost always up for a tour of the marsh, but not in the winter. Those boats moved pretty darn quick, and I could only imagine that frigid January wind slapping my face, stinging my cheeks, making my eyes burn with unwanted tears, causing my lips to chap and bust open and bleed. Thanks, but no thanks. Shoot, I never get warm enough in the wintertime to begin with; there's no way you could convince me to go cruising in a swamp boat now.

"She had on more layers than I could count," Aunt Edna said. "If she was a tree and they were trying to determine her age from her rings, they'd have to say she'd been here since the beginning of time."

I laughed. "Good."

"Delilah started to wake you before she left, you know," Aunt Edna said. "She asked me if I thought you'd want to go, and I figured you'd say no. I guess she decided that was probably true, so she let ya sleep."

"You figured right," I said. "She's gonna freeze her behind off, and I'd just as soon not."

Aunt Edna snorted, sipped her coffee again and swallowed. "Yeah, I imagine she will."

"Besides, I went on a swamp ride with Sophie in October," I said, speaking of my friend from school, Sophie Fontenot, whose uncle owned one of the swamp tour companies near Baton Rouge. "And I was cold then."

"I remember," Aunt Edna said. "So you think your Mama won't enjoy it, huh?"

"No," I said quickly, then amended, "Well, maybe."

"How's that?"

"If Mr. Zip is with her, she might."

"My thoughts exactly," Aunt Edna said. She grinned over the top of her coffee mug.

Aunt Edna and I'd been talking about Mama and her right man ever since she told me about Mr. Zip back before Christmas. We didn't say too much to Mama about it; Aunt Edna said it was important for her to decide on her own that Mr. Zip was the right one.

Consequently, Zip and Mama started spending more time going places, though Mama didn't say anything about them "going out." They'd usually invite me to tag along, and I'd usually decline. Not because I didn't want to go, but because I wanted to give my mama more one-on-one time with her right man. The way I saw it, if I was going to hand-pick a Daddy, I'd pick Mr. Zip.

Then again, I never hurt for not having a father in the house. Mama and Aunt Edna always made certain that I had everything I needed. And, truth be told, I didn't think there was a girl in St. James parish any happier than me. But that didn't mean I wouldn't be tickled to have Mama's right man hanging around permanently. It did me good to see her so happy. And heck, Mr. Zip made me happy too.

So I didn't mind Mama spending time with him while they "figured things out," like Aunt Edna said. Besides, it'd been a long time since I'd spent a spell with Aunt Edna. (She could be loads of fun, by the way, if she wasn't in one of her "moods.")

"So, what are we going to do today?" I asked. (Ten year olds get bored without an agenda.)

"Well, for one thing," she said, "We're going to talk about that big red X on the calendar."

I frowned, took another too-big sip of my coffee and started coughing. I hadn't put but one spoon of sugar in my cup. Usually I put three, but I figured if my cake was about to get bitter with coconut, my coffee might as well match the theme.

"Don't worry. We don't have to talk about it now. We'll get to that later." She downed the rest of her cup then placed it in the sink.

"All right," I said, happy to buy my time. "So, what're we going to do now?"

"Well, I figure we best make some King Cake dough, don't you think? Carnival season starts in three days."

Man, I'd forgotten all about that. I looked back at the calendar on the wall. I'd been so caught up in my first day back to school that I hadn't even noticed the tiny "Twelfth Night" printed at the bottom of the same square. Twelfth Night, or January 6th, officially marked the beginning of Mardi Gras season.

And consequently, the beginning of rampant King Cake baking for Thibodeaux's.

"We should've already made some," I said, biting my lower lip. Folks in St. James and St. John parishes typically started celebrating early, and we hadn't made a single King Cake yet.

"Nah, we're doing fine," Aunt Edna said with a shrug. "I took our first orders this morning from some of the businesses in Gramercy. As long as we have them ready for pickup on Monday morning, we'll be running right on schedule. We'll make extras to be sold out front, a couple for display, and I thought we'd make one for you to take to school on your first day back."

"To school?"

"Sure," she said. "It's still cool for a kid to bring something sweet to class, isn't it? You haven't outgrown that already, have ya?"

"No," I said, kind of letting the word draw out a bit while I thought about it. "Actually, Mrs. Landry likes it when we bring something for the class to share. Especially if she likes it too."

"And who doesn't like King Cake?" Aunt Edna asked.

"Nobody I know."

"Then it's settled. We'll fix one up for you to take to school on Monday. You'll make everybody smile with a King Cake in your hands that first day back."

I thought about that. Would a Thibodeaux's King Cake help them forget that I'd been burned at the top of a bonfire Christmas Eve?

I doubted it.

"That'd be cool, wouldn't it?" Aunt Edna prodded.

"Probably."

"All right." She shot another glance at the calendar. "Ready to talk about that X?"

"Not yet."

"Fine then. But we will. Eventually. For now though, let's check our supplies for those King Cakes."

She gave me a list of the items we needed, then she rummaged through the shelves and cabinets to see what we already had. By the end of our inventory check, we'd learned we had everything necessary for the dough, but were missing some of the key ingredients for the icing. And a King Cake without icing was nothing more than sweet bread.

"Looks like we'll have to run and pick up a few things today," she said, eyeing the list.

I nodded. "We don't have the icing stuff."

"We've got the confectioner's sugar and the lemon juice," she said, "but we're missing the coloring paste for the green, purple and gold. And we're slap out of babies."

Everything about the famous cake was significant. Unlike some of the desserts where we could "improvise" (as Mama says), the King Cake had to be precise. The shape, the colors of icing and even the plastic baby that was hidden inside all had a meaning. So we couldn't very well sell a King Cake without everything picture-perfect.

Generally, several tourists stopped by Thibodeaux's during carnival season and purchased them for Mardi Gras parties. They never failed to ask if we knew the history of the cake, so Mama and Aunt Edna made certain I knew every detail. That way, no matter which Thibodeaux woman they asked (including me), our customers learned exactly what they needed to know about the Louisiana specialty.

Flat and round with a hole in the center, a King Cake reminded me of the track that circled the high school's football field. Except the cake's circle wasn't smooth; it was twisted. And of course, there was a reason for the shape. It represented the route that the wise men took to see baby Jesus. They went in a wide circle, making several twists and turns to confuse King Herod, so he wouldn't find and kill the baby.

Back when people first started making the King Cakes (and Mama says that folks aren't absolutely certain when that was), they hid a bean or a pea or a coin inside the cake. The person who got the hidden item was declared King for the day, or was supposed to have good luck for the next year. Since then, the bean, pea and coin were replaced by a plastic baby. Baby Jesus. He's hidden in the cake and you have to try to find him, like the wise men tried to find the babe.

The person who gets the baby in their piece is supposed to carry on the carnival fun by buying the next King Cake (which helped us to sell even more of them, by the way, but it truly is part of the history, so we told our customers about it...and then we sold them another cake).

Even the colors of icing on the King Cake have a special meaning. Traditional Mardi Gras colors, the tinted sugar is gold for power, green for faith and purple for justice.

I looked at the list in my hand. Plastic babies hadn't been included, but Aunt Edna was right. We couldn't very well sell a King Cake without a baby in it. That was the neat thing about the cake, seeing if your piece contained the tiny, naked doll (I never figured out why they didn't clothe baby Jesus. Seems like that'd qualify for a sin, but no one else ever mentioned it, so I kept that opinion to myself).

One of the boys in my class at school, Cale Bouvier, said that he broke his tooth on a baby that was in his piece last year (I still think he was fibbing about that one. Cale'd do anything to get attention).

"Tell ya what," Aunt Edna said. "We'll go ahead and mix the dough, then we'll head out to get everything else we need while it's rising."

"What about the store?" I asked. "We could have some customers while we're gone."

Aunt Edna grabbed an apron and tied it around her waist, then started pulling everything we needed from the cabinets and fridge. "Phfft," she said, slamming a big tub of flour on the counter. "It'll keep. No biggee."

I grinned. It was rare that Aunt Edna would take off in the middle of a workday, and it made me feel special that she was willing to do it with me.

"Want me to separate them?" I asked, pointing to the tray of eggs she'd placed on the counter (you only use the yolks in King Cake dough).

"Sure," Aunt Edna said. She watched as my fingertips grazed the bottom of my sweater and began to tug it up over my belly. "But keep your shirt on, child," she instructed. "Lord, Mama'd roll over in her grave."

"Sorry," I said, choosing not to jump on her "roll over" quip. Heck, I was so used to cooking topless, it felt kind of funny to leave my shirt on, but I didn't want to ruin her good mood, so I suffered through it (Mama was right though; you can't create near as well with your glory confined).

We mixed the dough, covered it then left, with the store smelling deliciously of rising yeast dough.

"You sure this is okay?" I asked, hopping in the passenger's seat of the car and buckling up.

"Hey, we're entitled to a little time off every now and again, don't you think?"

I nodded, thinking that Aunt Edna was the second coolest woman in the world, next to Mama.

It took us a little over an hour to drive to LaPlace, complete our shopping and pick up some lunch at the Frostop. I munched on a shrimp po-boy as we started back toward Grand Point. Aunt Edna picked at her grilled chicken tenders. I knew those tenders were good. I'd had them plenty of times. But nothing could beat a Frostop shrimp po-boy, and it irked me to no end that Aunt Edna never got one.

"Aunt Edna?" I asked, mid-chew.

"Yes, child?"

"Why won't you ever eat anything that's good?" I bit off another hunk of delicious shrimp, fresh bread, tomatoes, lettuce, mayonnaise, mustard and ketchup (yeah, the bite was way too big for my mouth, but I worked with it).

Her lip quirked to the side, jaw tensed. "My chicken *is* good," she said, tearing off another tiny piece and popping it in her mouth, then taking a sip of her water.

I grabbed my root beer from the cup holder and took a big slurp. "You never eat anything sweet," I said, remembering all my conversations with Mama on this very subject. "Never eat anything fried either. Matter of fact," I said, on a roll now, "You don't ever eat much of anything. Mama says when you stick out your tongue, you look like a zipper."

She frowned, put her chicken back in the little pirogue-looking box it came in, then pulled the car over to the side of the road.

I looked out the window at where we'd stopped. We had just passed Reserve and were about halfway home, which meant we were in sugarcane country. Freshly planted cane fields stretched out from both sides of the road as far as my eyes could see. The plants were tiny right now, but by the summer, those stalks would be firm and tall. And by next fall, they'd be ready for harvest.

"Look at all that sugarcane," I said, deciding I should've kept my mouth shut about her eating quirks. Maybe if I talked about the scenery...

"Tell me something, Jezze," Aunt Edna said. "You think I'm an ornery ol' cuss, don't ya?"

Evidently, her question made my grip loosen on my sandwich, cause three shrimp fell out the back end. I placed the sandwich back on the white sheet of paper in my lap then I picked up those three pieces of shrimp and chomped on them while I wondered...*should I lie*? I swallowed, took a deep breath to gain my courage and decided that the truth never killed anyone.

Yet.

"Yep, Aunt Edna," I said, "Sometimes you're an ol' cuss." Then I figured if I was going for it, I might as well go for broke. "Mama says you're an old fart, but I don't say that word. Not usually, anyway."

"Hmph." She straightened in her seat. "And why do you and your Mama think that is?"

"Mama's never told me," I said honestly, "But I think I know part of it."

"What part is that?"

"Well, I don't know why you always seem so fussy, but I think I know why you don't eat anything good."

"And why do you think that is?" She twisted in the seat and draped her skinny arm across the back, so that her fingertips rested against the back of my head. I'd been letting my wild brown curls grow to see if they might tame up a bit with some length, and she wrapped one of them around her finger while she waited for me to speak.

"Well," I said, staring at the sandwich in my lap. "I think it's because those kids made fun of you for being fa-" I stopped the word, knowing that it wasn't the best one to use, "er, healthy, on the first day of school. I think you stopped eating cause you were worried they'd make fun of you again if you stayed—so healthy." I lifted my eyes to look at my aunt, and to my horror, her lower lip trembled.

Well shoot.

She sniffed, quirked her lip to the side again. "You know what, Jezze?"

"What?"

"You're absolutely right."

"I am?" I asked, completely flabbergasted.

"You sure are," she said. "All of these years, I have been so afraid that someone would make fun of me again that I didn't let myself enjoy one of the simplest pleasures of life."

"Good food?"

Her brittle face cracked into a smile. "That, and other things."

"Well then," I said, picking up the edges of the white paper in my lap and wrapping it around the remaining half of my sandwich. "Here." I held it toward Aunt Edna. "No time like the present."

She gawked at the paper-wrapped sandwich like I'd offered her a live crawfish.

"Go ahead, Aunt Edna. Try it." I extended it another nudge. It hung in mid-air, about four inches from her nose. I knew she could smell those shrimp (Frostop spiced them up right).

She slowly accepted the gift, placed it in her lap. "My stomach won't know what to do with it," she whispered.

"I bet it'll surprise ya," I said, eagerly watching as she picked up the sandwich and took her first bite of really good food in years. "Well?" I asked.

Tears slipped from Aunt Edna's eyes as she chewed the treat, then swallowed. "Have mercy," she whispered.

I laughed. I couldn't help it. Aunt Edna looked like a kid who'd tasted her first praline.

We sat there by that cane field for a while, Aunt Edna finishing off my sandwich while I finished off her chicken tenders (which were pretty good as well, just not as good as a shrimp po-boy).

She polished off the last bite, wiped the corner of her mouth with a napkin and leaned her head back in bliss. "Thank you, child."

"You're welcome," I said, and goodness knows I meant it. I couldn't wait to tell Mama about what I'd seen today. Aunt Edna, eating a shrimp po-boy by the side of a cane field. Who'd have dreamed it?

"Now while we're here, I want to tell you something that these cane fields reminded me of," she whispered.

"What's that?"

Aunt Edna lifted her head, turned toward me. "On those first days of school, your Mama's first day, and then again on mine, Big Mama took us to the cane fields after our school day ended."

"What for?"

"To talk about our day," Aunt Edna said. "I'd nearly forgotten, but today, something about our talk reminded me. She brought an old pink checked blanket and sat it out at the edge of the field then she traipsed to the stalks and cut one for us to share. We sat there, chewing on that sweet sugarcane all afternoon while Big Mama kept cutting more for us and while she kept listening to us talk. She said that the first day of school was special, and she wanted to do something that'd help us always remember."

"But you nearly forgot it," I reminded.

"I know," Aunt Edna said, another tear trickling down her cheek. "I'm afraid I tried so hard to forget how cruel the kids were on that first day, that I made myself forget how wonderful the remainder of the day was, when I got home from school and spent the entire afternoon with Big Mama and Delilah."

"So that afternoon was wonderful, wasn't it?" I asked, happy to hear that Mama and Aunt Edna's first days at school weren't total disasters.

"Oh, it was the best," Aunt Edna said dreamily. "The best."

"Did you tell her?" I asked. "Did you tell Big Mama about what the kids said?"

She nodded. "I told her. And your Mama told her too, when it was her first day, about her troubles on the playground."

"What did Big Mama say about those kids? What did she do about it?" I almost expected her to say that Big Mama went down there and whupped up on 'em. Or at least gave them a come-to-Jesus talking to. But, as Aunt Edna continued, I learned that wasn't at all what she did. And what she did was, well, right.

"She told us that we were Thibodeaux women, and that Thibodeaux's are strong, that we can do anything, and that we would. And," Aunt Edna added, "she said that worrying about things won't change nothing, and it's a waste of valuable Thibodeaux time. Oh, and she also called those kids a few names that I'm not going to repeat." The corners of Aunt Edna's lips curled up a bit. "But every one of them was true."

"Mama never told me about your trips to the cane fields."

"Maybe I'll have a talk with her," Aunt Edna said, peering out over the tiny green plants that currently composed the fields, "Make sure that she remembers."

"About that worrying part? That's what you're gonna ask her, isn't it? You think Mama worries about getting hurt again. That maybe she's afraid to love Mr. Zip cause she's afraid she'll lose him like Rene?"

Her eyes deepened a shade. "I think that'd be fair to say. I think she needs to let her heart go and realize that he's the one...without me, or anyone else, telling her."

"And what do you worry about?" I asked.

"I did worry about food," Aunt Edna admitted. "Though after that po-boy, I think I'll only worry about how long it'll take me to taste everything I've been missing." She chuckled deep in her throat. "And I suppose I worry every now and then that I'll never," she paused, tensed her jaw and a single tear slipped down her cheek, "never find *my* right man."

"You'll find him one day." I knew, particularly after the bonfire, that finding your right man could put quite a bit of pressure on a girl. At least Aunt Edna didn't have a fourteen year deadline to meet.

I leaned across the seat, wrapped my arms around her and squeezed. She was so skinny that I felt the bones shift beneath my arms. "Maybe you're not looking in the right spot."

Her throat pulsed against my forehead as she laughed out loud. "Lord, you make me smile, child. Truth is, after what happened with that crazy Josh McGill, I haven't been looking at all."

"Then it's high time you start," I said, leaning back and smiling up at her while she stroked my curls.

"I suppose it is." She cleared her throat, brought a finger up to my chin. "And I also believe it's high time you tell me about that red X on the calendar."

My back stiffened for just a second, but then I realized that there was nothing in the world that I could do to keep my determined aunt from finding out. "I'm wondering what the kids at school will say about the bonfire," I blurted.

"Wondering? Or worrying?" she asked.

"Worrying," I admitted, then bit my lower lip. "Definitely worrying."

"If there was some sugarcane in those fields, I'd wade through the muck and grab a stalk, then we'd chew on cane for an hour or two while we talked about all the reasons you shouldn't be worrying."

"There's not any cane now," I said.

"Right. So this coming fall, we'll have to come back out here and make up for the time we missed."

I grinned. "Okay."

"But for now, we'll have to improvise." She reached beneath her seat and pulled out her purse. Opening it, she dug around inside and finally withdrew a pack of sugarless gum. "Here," she said, handing me a piece then taking one herself. "I know, there's no sugar in it, but it'll have to do for now."

"All right," I said, chomping down on the gum.

Aunt Edna leaned her head back and rested it on the seat while she chewed. "What's the worst thing that can happen when you go to school on Monday?"

"They could laugh at me," I said. "Make fun of me. Not talk to me. Not sit with me. Think I'm a freak. Make jokes. Show me the pictures from the paper."

"And?" she prodded.

"And that about covers it."

"And?" she asked again, tilting her head and raising her brows.

"And," I repeated, then I took a breath and smiled. "And, I'm a Thibodeaux, and I'll be fine."

Grinning, she nodded. "Exactly, child. You know, I was so worried about you when you were first going to school. Not this year, but the very first year. I don't know if you remember."

"I remember," I said. "It was when we went to Baton Rouge to buy panties."

"Yeah. Lord, I wish I would've remembered what Big Mama had said back then. That worrying don't do ya one iota of good."

We stayed there, chewing our gum and chatting about life in general, for another thirty minutes. Then we headed back to the Cakery, both of us feeling better. And less worried. About food. And right men. And bonfires.

And even school.

Mama and Zip had made it back from the swamp. She was busy working on the King Cakes and he was manning the front of the store. Amazingly, Aunt Edna didn't even comment about the fact that he didn't have Thibodeaux blood in him. I suppose being a Thibodeaux woman's right man qualified a fellow to be okay for the job.

By Monday morning, I had my worries under control (mostly) and Aunt Edna drove me to school. Normally I took the bus, but since I was toting a King Cake, we opted for the Buick.

"You're going to be fine, my little Thibodeaux," she whispered. "Just fine."

That prickly part in the back of my throat started tingling like it does right before you blowchunk. And I sure didn't want to lose my breakfast in front of the entire fifth grade. With my hand on the door handle, I stalled. "You sure, Aunt Edna?"

"Positive, child. And when you get home after school, we'll share some beignets to celebrate."

My head jerked toward her. I'd never in my life seen her eat a beignet. "You'll let me put sugar on yours?" I asked.

"As much as it'll hold," she said. "Hey, we're celebrating."

"What are we gonna celebrate?" I asked, stalling, and noticing that several cars were in line behind us and ready to drop off their kids.

"We're going to celebrate you, Jezze. The youngest Thibodeaux," she said. "And the strongest, I suspect."

I nodded, stepped from the car, started inside...

And became a star.

With my hands filled with the King Cake box, I couldn't enter the school. Staring at the metal double doors in front of me, I debated whether to try to knock with my foot. I had just shifted my weight and lifted my right one from the ground when the doors burst open.

"Jezze!" Sophie squealed, grabbing the cake and smiling broadly. "We've been waiting for you."

Every kid from my class gathered behind her like an oversized football huddle (where I, of course, was the quarterback and they all waited for the play).

"You have?"

"Sure," she said. "Tell me all about it."

She turned, cake in her arms, and started clearing a path through the crowd for me to follow. "Out of my way," she hissed to some third graders. "Let her through, bucko," she blurted to Cale Bouvier. They all backed away, giving us room to pass, and making me feel like Moses.

"So, tell me," she said, cutting off the crowd like a herd dog would cut off a calf, until the two of us stood alone at the end of a row of lockers.

"Tell you what?"

"How does it feel?" she asked, her words bursting with excitement.

"How does what feel?" I asked, at the same moment the bell rang.

"Oh, dang," she said. "We've got to get to class."

I followed her, still carrying my cake, down the hall to Mrs. Landry's room. "How does what feel?" I repeated as we neared the doorway to our class.

"Jezze!" the entire class screamed as we entered. They were all smiling, all asking questions, all wanting to sit next to me, talk to me, be friends with me. Then I realized what Sophie had been asking.

How does it feel to be famous?

And I'd have to say...it feels darn good.

From that day forward, I would forever remember January 6th, Twelfth Night, as the best day of my life (at least until I got married, had babies, and all that other grownup stuff). But for a kid, it didn't get much better.

It started with my class, totally captivated by the events of Christmas Eve. As I suspected, practically all of them had been on the levee that night and had seen my bonfire burn. They'd seen my picture in the paper and on the television. And they thought it was way cool.

By the time I finished answering all of their questions, and all of Mrs. Landry's questions (she was pretty excited to have a television star in her class), we'd flat talked through first period and it was time for break.

I was afraid she would make us work through our break, since we hadn't done a lick of schoolwork yet, but she didn't. She said she was dying for a piece of the King Cake I'd brought. So, we cut the cake, and wouldn't you know it—Aunt Edna had added a bit of assurance to make sure my day went well.

Every piece of that cake had a baby in it.

By lunchtime, I'd become quite accustomed to my newfound fame, but I still hadn't adjusted to the boys. Lots and lots of boys. Boys my age. Older boys. All of them asking me out.

Me. Jezebel Thibodeaux.

I think they figured that asking me out would get their name in the paper, but I didn't knock it. I said no to them all (like I said before, I planned on staying single through the fifth grade). And instead, I made a ton of new friends. I have to admit that I was tempted to say yes to Johnny Langlinais. He was a sophomore (*a sophomore!*) and a star baseball player. But I can only imagine what Mama and Aunt Edna would do if I announced I was going out with a sixteen-year-old hunk. I figured I'd wait at least a year or two.

Anyway, by the end of the day when Aunt Edna and Mama picked me up (I was supposed to take the bus home, but they couldn't wait to see what happened), I had received sixteen requests to "go out." I'd also answered so many questions about the "right man" that I felt like a fifth grade therapist.

And I loved every minute of it.

"Here," Aunt Edna said, handing me a stick of gum (this time with sugar) as I hopped in the car.

"Everything went okay?" Mama asked, turning in her seat to gaze at me in the back.

"Better than okay," I admitted, blowing a big bubble, then peeling it off my face when it burst.

"So, no reason for all that worrying, huh?" Aunt Edna said, and I could see her smiling in the rear view mirror.

"Why should I worry?" I asked. "I'm a Thibodeaux."

Mama laughed in the front seat. "That's right, sweet Jezebel, you are."

We drove to the Cakery (they'd left Mr. Zip running things while they were gone) and ate beignets until our stomachs hurt.

The next day, I rode the bus to school, but I was the only fifth grader who did. All the rest of them had fulfilled their duty, and that required a ride in a car. See, since every one of them had gotten a piece of King Cake with a baby in it, they all had to bring one to share.

A King Cake topped each desk in our room. All twenty-two. Mrs. Landry didn't complain. She sent an announcement to the office that the entire school could pass by her classroom throughout the day if they wanted a piece of cake.

And once again, I was a star.

CHAPTER NINE

For two and a half years, Mama and Mr. DuBois continued "courting" as they called it, and I continued spending more time with Aunt Edna (Not that Mama and I stopped having our kitchen talks, but I tried to vacate as much as possible so she could be with her right man).

Aunt Edna got in on the act too, inviting me along on all of her ventures away from Thibodeaux's.

"It's clear out front now," she said, walking down the short hallway that connected the front of the store to the kitchen. Her cheeks were full and rosy, her hair streaked with pale highlights. She wore tailored black pants that molded around her curvy hips and a crisp white blouse, tucked in at the waist. Ever since that day by the cane field and that first bite of shrimp po-boy, my aunt had transformed from a fairly old biddy into a not-so-old mass of sass.

She looked healthy and happy, and Mama and I couldn't have been more pleased.

"No customers, for the time being," she said. "By the way, Zip called and said he's on his way over, so he can help you out, Delilah. I need to go to the pig." She crossed the kitchen and snitched a petifore from the tray in front of me.

I grinned, still enjoying the look on Aunt Edna's face when she tasted something good. She'd barely swallowed the tiny cake, white with blue baby-booties on top, when she reached for another.

"We need five dozen of those for Amelie Oubre's shower," Mama said. "I made twelve extras for you, Edna. If you need more than that, you need to tell me now," she said, grinning as she stirred the batter.

"Oh, don't get your panties in a wad," Aunt Edna said, her mouth dropping a few cake crumbs as she simultaneously spoke and chewed.

"I'm not wearing…" Mama stopped when Aunt Edna slapped a hand over her mouth.

"Trust me, Delilah," she said. "It's bad enough you don't wear anything up top. If you're free down south, I sure as heck don't want to know about it."

Mama laughed. She had a sneaky smile on her face that made me think perhaps she'd left today's thong in the drawer.

"Good Heavens," Aunt Edna started, studying Mama's guilty smile, but before she could finish her thought, Mama said, "Please, Edna, don't make her roll over again. I think she passed China last year."

"Phfft," Aunt Edna hissed, reaching for a third petifore. "You're gonna come to the pig with me, aren't ya, Jezze?"

"Yes, ma'am."

"Fine," she said, glaring at Mama, whose pride and joy had created a nice little wake in the side of a doberge cake.

"Delilah Thibodeaux, there are valleys in that cake," she snapped.

Mama glanced down. "Mmm-hmm."

I stifled my giggle.

Mama looked at Aunt Edna as though she dared her to speak.

Of course, Aunt Edna was always up to a challenge. (If she'd have been that kid on Christmas Story, you know, the one who was double-dog-dared to stick his tongue on the telephone pole, she'd have done it in a heartbeat. Or less.)

"We will not sell a cake that you have contaminated," Aunt Edna declared.

"I'm not selling this cake," Mama said. She moved to the sink and began washing her hands. "It's a gift for Zip, and for your information, he doesn't have any problem whatsoever with my valleys. Or my peaks, for that matter."

"TMI, Delilah," Aunt Edna said sharply.

Mama looked at me and winked.

I beamed back. Man, it was good to see her happy all the time, even if she and Mr. Zip hadn't got hitched yet.

Aunt Edna turned to me. She dropped her eyes to my chest. The mosquito bites from two years ago had plumped a bit and looked more like swollen bee stings. Mama said they were "on their way." Personally, I was ready for them to arrive already.

"If you're going with me, Jezebel, you've gotta wear a shirt."

"Yes, ma'am." I reached for the bright green T-shirt I'd hung on the back of the chair.

"And the bra," Aunt Edna added.

I looked back to the strap of my pathetic little bra, dangling from the same chair that held my shirt. Mama's over-the-shoulder-boulder-holder hung impressively from the opposite site. "You sure?" I asked. I didn't like shirts, much less bras.

"Definitely," Aunt Edna said.

Frowning, I slid my arms through the straps and fastened the back. Then I maneuvered the shirt over my head, but I'd forgotten about the mass of curls that I'd yanked into a high ponytail. My hair hung halfway down my back in long chaotic waves, and right now they had no interest whatsoever in cooperating by passing through the neck opening of my shirt.

"Oh, good grief," Aunt Edna said, stomping across the room to help. "If you'd keep the thing on, you wouldn't have this problem."

"But those baby booties wouldn't look as good," I said, wedging my mouth above the crew neck.

She shook her head and spat out a sentence that included "Delilah" and "head examined," but I didn't catch the rest.

"You ready to go, Aunt Edna?" I asked, slipping my feet into flip-flops (being barefooted also helps one to create, I've learned).

She nodded then held a finger of warning toward Mama. "Delilah, you're gonna have to man the front if anyone comes in while I'm gone. At least until Zip arrives."

"That's fine," Mama said, working on a lattice series on the top of a chocolate iced cake. Her pride and joy weren't touching the chocolate, but they were mighty darn close.

"So put your shirt on," Aunt Edna demanded.

Mama took her time finishing the cake, pouted for a second, then slid into her shirt. "Happy now?"

"And the bra," Aunt Edna declared, eyeing the thick white fabric still hanging by a wide strap on the back of the desk chair.

"Listen here, sis," Mama said, retrieving a box from the shelf and gently placing the cake inside. "I'm putting on the shirt. Don't get greedy."

"Good Lord," Aunt Edna said, twisting me around and leading me out the door, "Big Mama would—"

"Roll over!" Mama yelled. I couldn't tell if she was completing Aunt Edna's sentence, or issuing a direct order. In any case, my aunt pushed me on out of the shop.

And I laughed all the way to the car.

Most of the items we needed for baking were delivered directly to Thibodeaux's, but occasionally we'd run out of one thing or another and end up having to make a trip down to the Piggly Wiggly, or as Aunt Edna called it, "the pig." Even if she didn't invite me along, I'd always ask to go.

Mainly because I didn't want to miss the show.

For as long as I could remember, Aunt Edna had declared her own silent war against William LeBlanc, the man who owned the tiny grocery. I liked to watch them do battle, especially since both of them tried to act like they didn't know what was going on.

Mr. LeBlanc had dark gray hair, a thick mustache and a big smile for his customers. Always. He looked like he was about the same age as Aunt Edna and Mama. Old, but not too old. I'd never seen him when he wasn't in his work clothes, a white pullover shirt with a grinning red pig on the pocket, short-sleeved (even in the winter) and black pants. In a way he reminded me of us, the Thibodeaux women, because he was always busy. Every time we went in, he was stocking shelves or helping customers or running a cash register. He owned the store, but he worked harder than any of his employees. That was the big difference between Mr. LeBlanc's Piggly Wiggly and our Cakery. He had employees. We had...us. (Of course, we were in the process of changing that, by adding Mr. DuBois to the mix.)

Aunt Edna yanked a buggy from the corral and steered it toward the produce section. She picked her way through the fresh artichokes and finally decided on a few. It wouldn't have taken her so long if she'd concentrated on what she was doing, but she never concentrated all that well at the pig. She was too busy scouting out the terrain for Mr. LeBlanc.

"Have you seen him yet, Jezze?" she whispered, picking up an artichoke that was way too little and plopping it in her plastic vegetable bag without looking.

"Not yet."

"Well, he's here somewhere," she said. "I can smell him."

I started to ask her if he smelled anything like Mr. Zip, because I liked the way he smelled, but I decided that she might take offense to the question.

She wheeled us down a few aisles and attempted to be discreet in her search for the enemy. After the fifth row, and still no sign of Mr. LeBlanc, she sighed. "Looks like fast hands Willie is out to lunch, huh?"

Giggling, I nodded. She'd dubbed him the funny nickname when this whole feud thing started. After seeing him in action a few times, I had to agree. The name fit.

We quickly found baking flour, eggs, spices, powdered sugar, mandarin oranges and cherries, the remaining items on the list of things we needed. Then we rounded the corner of the last aisle in time to see Mr. LeBlanc walking in. He did a quick scan, as though he were looking for someone. Then his eyes halted on us.

I waved.

Aunt Edna slapped my hand down like it was a mosquito.

Mr. LeBlanc laughed out loud.

"Sorry," I whispered. "I forgot."

"Nonsense, child," Aunt Edna said. She whipped the buggy back around and started down the last aisle, even though I knew we'd found everything we came for. "He's conniving, that one," she said. "Smiling at you and making your insides quiver and all, he should be ashamed."

"My insides didn't quiver," I said.

"Hmph," Aunt Edna said. She darted down that aisle like she was on that television show Supermarket Sweep, except she didn't pay any attention to the prices or the items she threw in her cart.

She hit the snack aisle by storm, flinging Zap's chips and ginger snap cookies toward the buggy like they were Mardi Gras beads and she was on the top tier of the float. I for sure knew she wasn't paying attention now. We *never* bought snacks and sweets at the pig. We had plenty already at the Cakery. But I got into the excitement of it all too and pretended it *was* Mardi Gras.

"Throw me something, mister!" I yelled in my best parade voice. Thinking she'd like the joke, I jogged down the aisle, turned and waved my arms in the air. Then I did that little shimmy move that always gets me extra beads.

I seriously thought she'd laugh.

She didn't.

Oh no, she clucked at me and shook her head in disapproval.

"Sorry," I whispered, though I had to fight the urge to let loose a big belly-busting snort.

Aunt Edna tightened her grip on the buggy handle until her knuckles were white, then she took off running—*running*—down the aisle. The wheels clattered and clunked as she progressed. I knew where we were headed, so I ran alongside and wished my legs were longer, since it took three steps for me to match every one of Aunt Edna's impressive leaps. For a woman who could barely move without creaking two years ago, she sure had added some whip to her step.

The wheels on the buggy screeched when we skidded to a stop in the produce section.

"Things to weigh," she said, eyeing the fruits and veggies with extreme scrutiny. "What do you think, Jezze?"

Knowing the type of thing she was looking for, I studied the bins. "Sometimes the grapes roll out of the bag when he weighs em," I offered.

"Good girl," she said. She loaded up a thin plastic produce bag with seedless white grapes until the thing was about near splitting. At first she twisted the bag around to seal it up, but then she thought better and loosened it. "That should do him in," she said. "Now we just need to get everything in order."

We moved to the back of the store, right between the dog food and the cleaning products, where no one else was shopping at the moment.

"Help me spread these fruits and vegetables out, child," Aunt Edna said, rearranging the items in our cart. "That'll slow him down.''

I nodded and wondered if she finally had her game plan down pat. It sure would do Aunt Edna a world of good if she could beat him.

Just once.

Then again, I really enjoyed the challenge of our shopping trips to the pig. It was like being on a live game show every week! And truthfully, I thought Mr. LeBlanc was pretty darn super.

"Now," she said, lodging the grapes in the back of the cart, high enough that they wouldn't get smashed, but far enough back that they would be one of the last items to hit the conveyor belt at the checkout.

"That should buy us more time," she said, pulling a stem of grapes out of the bag so it dangled off the side. "Now we're ready."

She took a deep breath, exhaled and slowly made her way toward the front of the store, as if we hadn't just run a marathon up and around and down every aisle in the place.

The back of my shirt was damp with sweat and a small puddle had accumulated in the center of my wimpy bra.

"There he is," she hissed. Her lips didn't move a bit when she spoke and her smile didn't falter in the least. Aunt Edna had gotten really good at this game. She should try ventriloquism. Maybe I could get her one of those dolls for Christmas. They'd probably be selling them at the Gumbo festival. Then she could practice that little part of the scheme at home in the mirror.

Pushing the cart up to the sole register in the store, Aunt Edna beamed at Mr. LeBlanc (it would have looked more convincing if she hadn't had a mustache of baby sweat beads above her upper lip, but I wasn't about to point that out). "I thought I saw Bess at the register," she said, casually moving in front of the cart to unload our items.

"I gave her a break," he said, grinning knowingly at Aunt Edna. "How are you doing today, Edna?" he asked.

"Oh, I'm fine," she said sweetly. Way too sweetly, like thick Tupelo honey.

She placed the first items, a large bag of flour and a jar of mandarin oranges on the conveyor.

He whisked them through the beeping scanner and waited for more.

Aunt Edna fought her frown.

"That's good," he said. "And you, Jezze?" He grabbed Aunt Edna's next items, some of the chips and cookies that were nearly crushed from their hurl into the depths of our buggy, and whizzed them across just as quick.

Aunt Edna's face paled, but her eyes still looked determined.

"I'm fine," I said, handing the eggs to Aunt Edna.

She grinned. Eggs always slowed him down. He had to bag them separately.

I watched as Aunt Edna strategically put one item after another on the conveyor, with her pace increasing as she went. Faster and faster she flung the food toward the man, and faster and faster he swiped the items through and bagged them up.

By the time she got to the grapes, Aunt Edna was nearly in tears. She put them on the counter then reached for the last item in our cart, a box of powdered sugar. I knew she was hoping it would take him a second to weigh those grapes, but it didn't. He slid them through, bagged them and had his hand extended for the box of sugar when Aunt Edna turned around.

Her shoulders slumped in defeat.

His grin curled into his cheeks.

"You sure are fast," I said, marveling at the man.

Aunt Edna shot me a look that told me I'd be hauling in all the groceries when we got back home.

"In a business like this," he said, then paused, "Well, in most things, I reckon, it pays to have talented hands." His brow twitched a hair when he said the last two words. I noticed, and I bet Aunt Edna did too. "Wouldn't you agree, Edna?" he asked.

"Hmph," she mumbled. Then she read the total on the cash register out loud. "Eighty-three fifty," she said, her face the exact color as the embroidered pig on his shirt. "Is that right?"

"That's it," he said, double-checking the figure.

She fished the exact amount of cash and change from her purse while he placed her bags in the buggy.

"You want help with these?" he asked, indicating the surplus of sacks in our cart.

"We'll manage just fine on our own," she said. She smiled, but it didn't look like a very happy one.

After we passed through the sliding door that led to the parking lot, I tapped her arm. "Aunt Edna?"

"Yes, child."

"He won again, huh?"

"Yes, Jezze, he did."

I waited a beat then and, too foolish to know better, started back up. "Aunt Edna?" I asked again, while helping her fill the big trunk of that Buick with the items we'd bought, the ones we needed and the ones we didn't.

"What is it, Jezze?"

"I was just wondering—"

"What were you wondering, child?"

"Are his hands really *talented*?"

She stopped moving, kind of stood there for a second with a bag full of artichokes suspended mid-air between the buggy and the trunk.

I blinked. Heck if Aunt Edna didn't look like she was in a trance or something. I debated on whether to run inside and ask Mr. LeBlanc to call 911. Then she snapped back to life and began rummaging through the bags.

"Aunt Edna, you looking for something?" Want me to help?"

She didn't answer, but withdrew the jar of mandarin oranges and whipped the top off in nothing flat.

I gaped as I watched her poke three in her mouth, chew and swallow. She glanced at me, smiled (kind of) and then tossed two more inside.

"You okay?" I asked.

She nodded, still chewing.

"So, *are* his hands really talented?"

She put the jar to her lips and tilted it back like it was a cup of water, ate as many of the sweet oranges as she could, then shrugged. "Jezze, I wouldn't know."

CHAPTER TEN

Little did we know at the time, but that one particular visit to the pig when I was twelve changed both of our lives, Aunt Edna's and mine, forever.

First of all, Aunt Edna's thoughts were plagued by Mr. LeBlanc. Specifically his talented hands. And like I said, I was twelve, so I wasn't totally in the dark about such things. (Besides, I overheard my aunt asking Mama if she thought Mr. LeBlanc had any other hidden talents. Of course, I decided not to admit that I'd been eavesdropping on that, um, interesting conversation.)

So, for our subsequent trips to the pig, Aunt Edna dabbed a bit of perfume behind her ears and on her wrists. She even took to borrowing Mama's glittery blush every now and then and putting a finger of petroleum jelly on her lips to make them shine.

In other words, Aunt Edna started her own odd version of courting, which involved sparring with Mr. LeBlanc over the items at the checkout line (he always won, by the way). But now, instead of glaring at him and snarling through her nose, she smiled and made these funny giggling sounds in the back of her throat. Sounded an awful lot like those turkeys I'd seen during my school's field trip to the New Orleans Zoo last year, but

I wasn't about to tell her that. At twelve, I finally had a better handle on when to keep my thoughts to myself around Aunt Edna.

It took everything I had not to laugh out loud at her flirting. But from the admiring look on Mr. LeBlanc's face, she had it down pat.

Now, as far as how my life changed...

Basically, Aunt Edna's haphazard flinging of items into our cart resulted in us buying a unique product that we'd never purchased before, but a product that would factor prominently into my life from that point on.

Babineaux's Butt Budder.

"What's this?" Mama said. She pulled the yellow tube from the brown paper bag with the red pig on the side (Aunt Edna requested paper instead of plastic because she thought it took longer for Mr. LeBlanc to bag the groceries that way).

"I don't know," Aunt Edna said, putting the half-empty jar of mandarin oranges in the fridge, then turning to look at the bright yellow item in Mama's hand. "Toothpaste?"

"You bought it, didn't you?" Mama questioned.

"Yeah, but I guess I didn't pay attention," she admitted. "I thought it was toothpaste. No biggee," she said, shrugging. And refusing to look Mama in the eyes. "So, what is it?"

"Butt budder," Mama deadpanned.

"*Butt* budder?" Aunt Edna repeated.

I busted out laughing, but had the wherewithal to snap my mouth shut when Aunt Edna cut her eyes in my direction.

"That's what it says, Edna." Mama turned the yellow tube toward us so we could read it. Sure enough, a cute little naked baby smiled back from the front of the tube. A bright blue blanket draped across his lap, covering whether or not he was actually a *he*, and a red rattle rested beside his chubby leg. He looked very...happy. Above his head, written in big, bright red letters, was the product's name.

Babineaux's Butt Budder.

"What the devil is butt budder?" Aunt Edna asked, her face about the same color as the letters on the side of that tube.

"You should know, Edna," Mama said. "You bought it."

"Oh, shuddup." Aunt Edna stormed across the room and reached for the yellow tube, but Mama whisked it behind her back.

"Seems like you've been buying a lot of stuff we don't really need, Edna," Mama accused. "You're not still trying to beat Will LeBlancin that shopping cart war, are you?"

Lord, I wished I'd known Mama was gonna bring that up before I got a beignet to my mouth. I sucked in my breath and ended up hauling a mound of powdered sugar right down my windpipe. I started coughing and gagging and hacking until both of them were shoving glasses of water at me and telling me to calm down.

"I'm—fine," I managed. "I am." But the tears running down my cheeks didn't do anything to emphasize that point.

Finally, the coughing subsided and I started chugging the water.

"Just tell me what butt budder is for," Aunt Edna said, at the same moment that Zip entered the kitchen.

"You got some butt budder?" he asked. He carried an empty cookie tray to the sink, washed and dried his hands, then hugged Mama. "Stuff's awesome, isn't it?"

"You've seen it?" Mama asked, her eyes wide with surprise.

"I carry a tube everywhere I go," he said. And to our amazement, he pulled a tiny, travel-sized yellow tube of the stuff from his pants pocket.

"What do you use it for?" Aunt Edna asked.

"Shoot, dang near everything," he said. "Mosquito bites, chapped lips, cuts, poison oak, poison ivy."

Mama flipped the tube around and read, "Diaper rash, jock itch, hemorrhoids..."

Aunt Edna lifted a warning finger at Mama. "Don't even go there, Delilah."

"I was merely going to ask which ailment you made the purchase for, dear."

Not wanting to get choked again, I chewed fiercely on the b te of beignet.

Aunt Edna swirled on one heel and took off down the hall toward the front of the store doing her kill-the-cockroach stomp. Mama and Zip laughed loudly, but not loud enough to drown out Aunt Edna's yelled reply.

"Jock itch!"

— BUTT BUDDER —

CHAPTER ELEVEN

After four years of dating, Mama was bound to expect a ring from Zip for Christmas. I sure expected her to get one; Aunt Edna did too. And it probably would've happened on that December 25th when I was fourteen…if I hadn't learned the truth about my father.

Now, I know how it sounds, like the fellow found out he had a daughter, searched my mama down, then tried to hone in on our happy little family. But that isn't at all how this reunion with my "Daddy" occurred. Oh no, in typical Thibodeaux fashion, I learned that the details of my conception were as bizarre as every other aspect of my life. Then again, it wouldn't have been true to Thibodeaux form if they hadn't been.

We'd stayed up late on Christmas Eve waiting for my future groom, the wooden version, to burn to a crisp. The fellow had now advanced forty-eight inches toward his eventual goal. Consequently, we had to anchor him to the side of the cake. He looked like a mountain climber tackling Everest. Needless to say, it took a little bit longer for the sucker to burn with a wooden man hanging off the side, but the *L'Observateur* and the *News-Examiner* loved the drama. I mean, it was quite the show, that fiery fellow suspended above the ground glowing all orange and red with forked flames licking the cold December air merely feet away from the spectators. While most of the bonfires merely had a fire extinguisher on hand in case things got out of control, Jezze's Man was equipped with the entire Gramercy Volunteer Fire Department.

We took first place in the contest, no surprise there since we'd now held the coveted title for four years running. However, the next morning, Christmas Day, was *full* of surprises for the Thibodeaux women.

I woke up early, layered up real good and headed over to the Cakery. This had been the first year that I'd bought Mama and Aunt Edna real Christmas presents, not the kind you could buy in the Santa Secret Shoppe at school, but gifts I'd purchased at the Baton Rouge Mall on a shopping trip with Sophie and her mom.

It'd been tough to figure out what the two would like, but I thought I'd done a super job. Sophie and I found a store specializing in unique kitchen supplies. At first I thought there wouldn't be anything in there that the Cakery didn't already have, but I was wrong. There were plenty of neat little gizmos and gadgets that I honestly had never seen before. So, with Sophie's help, I picked out a bunch and had the store fix them up real pretty in a big bulky basket for Aunt Edna and Mama.

I couldn't wait to see them when they found their surprise. And I truly wanted it to be a surprise, so I placed it on the stainless steel counter in the middle of our kitchen, turned off the lights, locked the door and hid in the back of the breakfast nook.

Crouching down on the floor behind the table, I had a good view of the basket and knew I'd be able to see them when they found it. I figured it wouldn't be nearly as good of a surprise if they saw me; besides, this was much more fun.

Mama usually arrived at the Cakery first, around six a.m., and today was no exception. I heard the key wiggle in the door and held my breath, hoping she wouldn't turn on all of the lights.

Thankfully, she didn't.

The kitchen illuminated, but the breakfast nook remained in the shadows. I grinned and tried to keep from giggling out loud. My stomach flittered, my heart raced, and I decided that surprising Mama and Aunt Edna was much better than getting presents.

"Well, what's that on the table? Jezze?" Mama called.

I swallowed, but stayed quiet.

She crossed the kitchen and stood beside the basket. The lady at the store had wrapped it in thick red cellophane and put a huge green bow on the outside. I'd bought a Hallmark card (cause they deserve the best) and had tucked it in the bow.

Mama fingered the card, then removed it and began to read. Even from my spot on the floor, I could see her chin quivering.

"Brrr," Aunt Edna said, entering the kitchen and slamming the door behind her. "Have mercy, it should be outlawed to be this cold in Louisiana. Why haven't you got the coffee on, Delilah?"

"Look," Mama said, pointing to the basket as she turned toward her sister. "It's from Jezebel."

"Where is she?" Aunt Edna asked, quickly moving to stand by Mama. She peered at the card.

"I guess she's still sleeping. I didn't check her room, just headed on over. I thought she'd be here already, being its Christmas and all." She held the card out so Aunt Edna could finish reading it. "Guess she snuck over last night and left this for us."

"Little angel, isn't she?" Aunt Edna beamed, and sniffed.

Well shoot, I didn't mean to make them cry. I pressed my palms to my thighs and got ready to stand up, but I stopped when Mama started removing the bow. "Look at all of this," she said.

Cellophane rattled as they pushed it out of the way. I waited, anxious to hear their exclamations of pure joy at all the neat little kitchen toys I'd purchased. And that's exactly what I heard. They were bragging on me like I was the first person to ever fry dough (that's all beignets are, by the way, fried dough...with a heaping mound of sugar on top).

Once again, I prepared to come out of hiding, but then I saw Mama point to another basket perched over in the corner. Now how did I miss that? I guess I'd been so anxious about putting my present out that I totally missed the other basket, easily twice the size of the one I'd bought.

Was that for me?

I should've let them in on my presence—I know I should've—but I couldn't help it; I wanted to hear what they said.

"Can you believe she fixed this big ol' basket for us, and I fixed a big ol' basket for Zip? Look, they even look the same."

So that one wasn't for me; it was from Mama...to her right man. I smiled. I was good with that. This was going to be a special Christmas for my mama and Mr. Zip. I just knew.

And Mama was right. The other basket was decorated almost identical to mine, with red cellophane and a green bow and everything, but bigger.

"Like mother, like daughter, I'd say," Aunt Edna said.

"She is like me, isn't she? And she's like her Daddy too," Mama said. "All thoughtful and sweet."

My breath caught in my throat, heart kicked it up to triple time. All these years, I'd heard tidbits here and there about my father, but I still didn't know the exact details. Mama said she'd tell me more when I was old enough. I figured in Mama's opinion I still wasn't there yet, so I should stand up right now and let them know I was hiding out in the kitchen.

I should.

But I didn't make a move. And in my whole life, I was certain my ears had never strained so hard to hear every word.

"She *is* like her Daddy," Aunt Edna agreed. "So...are you finally going to tell her who he is?"

To my gleeful surprise, Mama's morning glory pompom bobbed as she nodded.

She was going to tell me? When???

"But first, I should probably tell him he has a daughter," Mama said with a secret smile.

Tell *him*? My daddy didn't know about...*me*?

My heart's triple time screeched to a near halt, and I was certain I could feel the thing thudding in my chest. *Ba-bum. Ba—bum. Ba. Bum.* I guess the whole fact that Mama had always told me Daddy that gave her the gift of *me* made me think that he'd at least been aware of the fact. And I admit that for the past few years, probably since I was ten, I'd been wondering why he never even wanted to see his gift.

Now I find out that he didn't know the gift existed!

"You're telling him? When? Today?" Aunt Edna's eyes were so wide that I could see the whites all the way around the blue. They locked like they were trying to pop right off her face, like Garfield's dog Odie. Other days, I'd have laughed. But not right now.

Oh no, I stayed stone still and hoped they'd say more.

"Yes, I'm telling him today. I think this may be the day he plans to tell me—or ask me—something rather special, so I thought I'd tell him something special too." She continued running her fingers along the big green bow on Zip's basket as she spoke.

The back of my neck started to tingle, like I had all of the answers, if I'd just put them together. And I could literally feel the pieces of the puzzle sliding slowly into place.

If my daddy was going to be asking Mama something today, then he was nearby. Probably in Grand Point. Could my daddy actually live in our tiny little town? For some reason, I'd always pictured him living somewhere similar to the beginning of Star Wars.

In a galaxy far, far away.

Where was my Daddy? Who was my Daddy?

And then, as if God heard my silent pleas and decided to answer all of my questions and then some, the door to the kitchen opened and the most shocking Christmas Day of my life...got even more shocking.

"Brought you a little lagniappe present to get your Christmas started off right," Zip said as he entered the kitchen.

Mr. Zip, my mind whispered.

Could it be?

Dear God, please.

"Zip," Aunt Edna said, her hand patting her chest as though she'd just run a marathon. "We—we didn't hear you come in."

"The bell sounded loud and clear." He lifted a stark white brow. "What were you two talking about that had you concentrating so much you wouldn't hear the bell?"

"The store's not open," Aunt Edna said, still looking a little flabbergasted. "It's Christmas. We weren't listening for the bell." She peered down the hall toward the front of the store. "How'd you get in?"

Aunt Edna looked weird, like she'd stolen a King Cake or something. And when I peeked at Mama, she also looked like a kid who'd been caught stealing an extra praline.

Mr. Zip held up his LSU key ring with his key to the Cakery dangling from the end. He'd had a key for as long as I could remember, ever since he started helping out pretty much all the time at the store. How did Mama and Aunt Edna forget that?

"I used my key, of course," he said, still holding that one brow up high like he couldn't figure out what in the world was wrong with the two Thibodeaux women in the kitchen (yes, there were actually three Thibodeaux women in the kitchen, but he didn't know about me in my hiding spot, and for the time being, I wanted to keep it that way.)

"Last night, at the bonfire, you two promised me Christmas morning beignets, remember?" Mr. Zip said. "We were going to celebrate the holiday with Jezze, eating beignets and opening presents, the way we've done for the past three Christmases. Now what's going on that made you forget our tradition? And where's Jezze?"

"Still sleeping," Mama said. She turned to Aunt Edna. "Edna, can you go check on Jezebel? I can't remember the last time she slept in. She might be sick."

"I sure hope she isn't. It'd be a shame for the child to be sick for Christmas." Aunt Edna said, still looking at little odd...and like she was perfectly happy with getting to leave the uncomfortable conversation. She slid her arms back into her thickest coat and heading toward the door. "Especially this Christmas. Cause from the look of things, it's gonna be a doozie."

"A doozie?" Mr. Zip questioned, but Aunt Edna merely nodded her head in one sharp jerk then bolted out the door as if the Cakery was on fire.

I knew I should fess up to my hidden status, but again, I didn't. Instead, I prayed it'd take Aunt Edna a few minutes to figure out I wasn't sleeping...and that it wouldn't take Mama more than a few minutes to say something that would let me know more about my daddy. Maybe even let me know whether he was the guy I already loved who always wore purple and gold, was standing in our kitchen and was consequently Mama's right man.

Let it be Mr. Zip. Let it be Mr. Zip.

"Did you say you brought me a lagniappe present?" Mama asked, obviously trying to throw him onto a different subject.

Mr. Zip wasn't fooled, and neither was I. She was stalling, and he wanted to know the truth.

So did I.

"Delilah, what are you keeping from me?"

"I don't get my lagniappe present?" she asked.

"Not until I figure out why you and Edna looked so incredibly guilty when I entered this kitchen. Something is up, and I'm not budging until I find out what."

"Not even for some beignets? Because I've got to heat up the oil if you're wanting to have them anytime in the near future, you know."

"I've been helping you out here too long to fall for that," he said. "Doesn't take no time to heat that oil, roll the dough and cut the squares. And I'll help you do it...as soon as you tell me what's you're up to."

She edged toward the huge honker basket and nudged it along the counter until it was directly in front of Mr. Zip. "Okay, but a lot of it has to do with your lagniappe present from me, so you'll have to open it first."

"This giant thing is a lagniappe gift?" he asked. "Delilah, I'm fairly certain you know, but lagniappe means a 'little' something extra. Nothing about this basket is little."

She laughed, but it sounded awkward. Mama seemed worried, or nervous, or something. And it had to do with whatever was in that basket. I scooted up a little to get a better view and my knees popped. I had no idea whether they made noise or not, because my heart was pounding so loud I couldn't hear the things, but I squinted and prayed that Mama and Mr. Zip didn't hear it.

They didn't. He tugged on the green bow with no regard whatsoever to the fourteen-year-old hiding out in the kitchen. The cellophane seemed louder on his basket and made that same kind of echo sound that a peppermint wrapper makes when you try to open it in church. Nothing quiet about it.

Finally, the crinkling and crackling died down, and I listened to Mr. Zip describe the odd assembly of things in the basket.

"A menu?" he asked, withdrawing a long peach-colored laminated sheet of paper.

Mama's smile pulled into her cheeks. "From Copeland's. You remember going to Copeland's?"

His mouth quirked to the side, and he looked a little confused, but nodded. "Sure, I've been to Copeland's several times. One of my favorite restaurants. Is this a gift card to Copeland's?" he asked, looking at the menu as though it was the oddest gift card he'd ever seen.

She laughed, but it wasn't a real laugh. Mama seemed kind of embarrassed...or something. "No, it isn't a gift card. It really is just a menu, the take-out menu. So it probably doesn't click yet. We didn't get take-out."

Mr. Zip looked even more confused. "Who didn't get take-out?"

She laughed, the same odd chuckle again, then said, "Look at the rest of the things in the basket. Then you'll put it together."

"O-kay," he said. He withdrew a long bottle. "Champagne?" he asked. "We celebrating something, Delilah?"

"No, I mean, well, yes, maybe. I think we will," she said, and this time had a strange giggle, but her cheeks had started turning even more red than when she wore her reddest glitter blush. "I mean, we didn't have champagne, but I couldn't remember exactly what it was."

"Delilah," he said, shaking his head. "I think I'm missing something here."

"Look at the rest," she said, pointing to the basket.

I began to wish I was near a window, so I could see when Aunt Edna was heading back. This was going way too slow, and I was beginning to think they wouldn't get to the real meat of the matter until after Aunt Edna came back and announced I wasn't in my bed.

Come on, tell me something about my daddy, I silently pleaded.

Mr. Zip withdrew a framed photo. I couldn't see the picture, so I hoped he'd say what was in that frame, and he did.

"Well, I'll be. It's us, at the twenty-fifth reunion," he said, smiling. "You looked gorgeous in that red dress, Delilah."

"That's what you told me that night," she said.

"Well, it's true." His smile slid into a frown, and he shook his head.

"What is it?" she asked, while he stared at the picture.

"I'm sorry, Delilah. It's just that I was in such a rough place at that time. You may not have known, but Sela had just left me for the other coach at LSU, and I was in a rough spot. I went to that reunion to get my mind off of it."

"I do remember. We talked about it that night."

"Yeah, I guess I probably talked about it with everyone, huh? Hope I wasn't too pathetic."

"You were precious," she said, "talking about how you wish you'd found your true love the first go-around…and then you talked about how you wished I'd have picked you instead of Rene back when we were in high school. That you'd have been married to me instead, and that you had no doubt our marriage would have lasted," she said, rattling it all off as though she'd remembered his words over and over again through the years. And I suspected she had.

"I said all of that?" he asked, his white brows inching up. He grinned. "Well, heck, I sure didn't leave much to the imagination there, did I?"

"You don't remember?"

"I'll tell you the truth. I don't remember anything much about that night, except that I went to the reunion. You know I don't drink, never have. But that night I did. Can't even remember what all I had, but I do know that I went to the reunion, woke up the next morning with a horrible hangover and no recollection at all of the night before." He lifted the photo. "And now I know that I spent time with you. I'm so sorry. I'd give anything if I could remember, Delilah. But I can guarantee I'll never do anything like that again, not with us, not with me…and you."

Her mouth fell open, and she didn't speak. I saw the shocked look on her face, but Zip didn't. He'd returned his attention to the items in the basket.

"A baby rattle?" he said, lifting the small pink item. "Was this supposed to be in the basket?"

Tears trickled down my mama's cheeks.

"Delilah?" he asked. "What's wrong? I'm sorry that I'm having a difficult time figuring out the basket theme. Do you want to go to

Copeland's to dinner? Recreate the fun we had on the reunion night? Because I can tell we had a good time from this picture. I just wish I remembered it."

"I do too," she whispered. "And the baby rattle is part of the story." She visibly swallowed. "A story you don't even remember. The best story of my life!"

The back door open, and Aunt Edna bustled in. "Have mercy, now the wind's blowing in off the Mississippi, and it's even colder. I don't think I'll leave this kitchen the rest of the day. And Jezze isn't..." She stopped talking when she took a good look at Mama. "Delilah? What on earth is wrong?"

"He doesn't remember. The whole night of the reunion. He was drinking, and he doesn't usually drink. And I didn't even realize it. And we had all of that champagne, or whatever it was, and then—and now—he doesn't remember."

"Oh, Lord have mercy," Aunt Edna said.

"Listen, I have no idea what you two are talking about. What's this about the reunion? And why are you so upset, honey?" he asked Mama.

"I would have told you back then, but you'd already gotten back with Sela and given her another chance by the time I knew. And then I thought when you started spending time with me and with Jezze that you'd figure it out, but you didn't. And then I thought that was because she came a month early. But I really wondered why you didn't consider the fact," Mama said, her words coming in spurts because of her sucking cry in between sentences.

"Lord have mercy," Aunt Edna repeated.

"Delilah? What are you saying?" Mr. Zip asked, but his face said that he'd started putting it together...just like I already had.

My Daddy.

And my mama had let me be around him nearly every day for the past four years and hadn't told me. Or him!

"We were together that night, Zip," Mama said. "And we made Jezze that night."

Mr. Zip's face turned nearly as white as his hair, and I fell backward to land on my bottom. True, the whole time I'd been sitting here eavesdropping I'd been hoping that I was about to learn who my daddy was, and then that my daddy was the man I'd grown to love. But to hear Mama say it, and to realize that he hadn't known about me from the whole time since I was born...made me a little shocked. And a lot mad.

Why didn't Mama tell me?

Or Aunt Edna?

Why didn't *somebody* tell me?

But apparently, I wasn't the only person ticked by this earth-shattering news. Mr. Zip's face had gone from that albino white...to redder than my bonfire groom.

"Delilah," he said, his voice stern and his body seeming to grow another three inches in height and width as I watched, kind of like a banty rooster when he's ready to crow. "Are you telling me that you and I slept together that night? We've...slept together?"

Mama sniffed, shakily brushed tears from her cheeks. "And you don't even remember it!"

"Don't," he said, his tone full of warning, "Don't you even attempt to get onto me right now, young lady," he said. "I have a daughter? Jezze is mine?"

She nodded, while Aunt Edna muttered another stream of Lord have mercies.

"And you let me go fourteen years without knowing the fact? What would you have done if I hadn't come back around four years ago? Would I never have learned I had a daughter?"

Mama's eyes widened. "I—don't know. You went back to Sela."

Mr. Zip said something I can't repeat, then inhaled through his nose and growled when he blew it out his mouth. It was pretty impressive, and I'd have probably applauded him, if I wasn't rooted to the spot and waiting to see what was going to happen next.

"You knew how badly I've wanted kids," he said. "I've told you over and over about how it killed me that Sela didn't want any. And I've told you over and over again how lucky you were to have Jezze!" He drug a hand through his white waves, making them stand on end and making him look even more infuriated. "I asked you who her father was, and you said you weren't ready to tell me yet."

"I wasn't," she said.

"That wasn't your secret to keep, Delilah!" He shook his head again. "She's mine too!"

"Well, I kept wondering why you never put it together," she sputtered. "Why you never at least considered the possibility. And why you never mentioned us being intimate before."

He said a few more things I'm certain I shouldn't have heard and definitely shouldn't repeat, then when Mama reached for him, he pushed her hand away. "No, Delilah. Don't even try. I need to think this through." Then he left the kitchen and headed toward the front of the store, the bell sounding loudly as he apparently slammed the door on his way out. Out of the Cakery.

And out of my life?

"Lord have mercy," Aunt Edna repeated for the umpteenth time.

"Oh hush up," Mama said, wiping away more tears. "What are we going to do now?"

"I told you to tell him years ago, Delilah," Aunt Edna said. "How do you think he's going to forgive you for keeping his daughter from him for ten years—fourteen if you count the years he was around her and still didn't know. That's bound to tick a guy off."

Mama picked up the reunion photo. "He doesn't even remember."

"Well, didn't you ever consider the fact? I mean, how many times has he told us that he doesn't drink, that he doesn't like the way it messes with his memory?"

Mama's brows shot up beneath her platinum bangs. "What are you saying, Edna? Did you think he might not have remembered sleeping with me?"

"No," Aunt Edna said. "Heavens, no. But I'm just saying…" she held up her hands in defeat, "oh I don't know what I'm saying. It's a mess. A big fat mess. And I don't know what we're gonna do about it now."

"I need to see Jezze."

"You're gonna tell her now?"

"No, of course not. Not until I figure out what's going on with Zip. But I just need to see her. Where is she?"

"Goodness, I almost forgot. She wasn't at the house, wasn't in her bed, anyway, and I didn't see her anywhere else. I was coming back here to see if she might be in the front of the store picking up some pastries or something."

"Zip would've seen her on his way in," Mama said.

Up until this point, I'd pretty much held my emotions in check and merely sat there hunkered down, albeit uncomfortably, in the darkened recesses of the breakfast nook. But this new bit of information regarding my conception—and the fact that they'd finally figured out I was MIA— gave me the courage I needed to stand up...and give the two crazy Thibodeaux sisters a piece of my fourteen-year-old mind.

"How could you have kept it from me?" I asked, standing from my hiding spot and gawking at the two of them. "All of those years, you told me my daddy gave me to you as a gift, like he was at least aware of the fact. I thought there was some reason I hadn't met him. Maybe he was in the army. Or maybe he was the governor. Or something! But never did I think that he could've been around all the time, that he would have been around all the time, if he'd known I existed. And then, after Mr. Zip started coming around, you could've told us. I could have known he was my daddy. I could have had someone to celebrate Father's Day with this year."

"We did celebrate Father's Day," Mama said. "All of us...with Zip. Remember?"

"But I didn't know! And neither did he!" I darted through the kitchen so fast I ran into a chair on the way out. The edge hit the top of my leg, and I knew I'd have a nice black bruise as a reminder of this Christmas morning. Maybe even a scar. And wouldn't that be fitting? A scar to remind me of how much being a daughter to one of the crazy Thibodeaux women...hurts.

CHAPTER TWELVE

An hour had passed since I left them in that kitchen and I hadn't seen hide nor hair of my mama or my aunt since. I scratched out the last word on my notepad. I'd always been somewhat talented at poetry before, but today my muse was on leave. Or maybe it just up and vacated the premises this morning when it learned that my father was probably semi-conscious at best during my conception. And my mother and aunt were in cahoots on keeping the truth from me—and him—for fourteen years.

"Cowards," I grumbled, running my pencil eraser violently through another botched attempt.

"I'd say I have to agree," Zip said, peering into my room, where I was sprawled across the bed in full pout mode.

I pulled my legs underneath me and scrambled upright to get a better look at him. Cocking my head to the side, I surveyed his eyes, nose, mouth. The shape of his face. Then I turned and looked in the mirror.

"Well?" he asked, almost humorously. "What's your take?"

I didn't want to answer. I'd felt a connection with Mr. DuBois my entire life. In truth, finding out that I shared his genes only seemed fitting.

But should I admit that now?

"If you ask me, I'm surprised we didn't realize it sooner. Of course, I'd have needed a bit of information to at least realize it was a possibility," he said, moving across the room to sit on a white wicker chair.

He looked odd, a big, bulky man on that feminine chair, but he didn't appear uncomfortable sitting in my bedroom. Nope, he looked right at home. And, I had to admit, I liked that.

"So you think it's true?" I don't know why in the world I was asking. I already knew the answer. Guess I just wanted to hear him say it.

"Would it be so bad if it were?" He gave me a slight grin while he waited for my response.

"No," I said quickly. I'd been thinking about that possibility nonstop since I'd retreated to my room. Shoot, having Zip DuBois for a father was—perfect. "That's not it," I said, and took a deep breath as I attempted to explain the hurricane of emotions spiraling through my body. "She said that I was a—well, a gift—from my daddy to her." I blew a rogue curl out of my eye. "Oh, I don't know how to explain what I'm thinking."

"Tell you what," he said, crossing his leg so his right ankle rested on his left knee, "Why don't you let *me* try to guess what you're feeling now?"

Grateful, I nodded. "All right."

"With your mama, you're wondering how she could've lied to you all these years, telling you about the man who'd freely given a part of himself so she could be blessed with you. The story had seemed honest enough, yet now, you know that each time she told it, she was lying."

I blinked, nodded again.

"And with your Aunt Edna, you're wondering how she could've kept the secret for so long, particularly for the past four years, while she watched you, Delilah and I interacting and she knew that we belonged together. The three of us, as a family."

Another nod, and a thick swallow to hold back tears.

"Is that the gist of it?" Zip asked.

"Pretty much."

"Now, if you add to that the distinct irritation with knowing that someone you've trusted and grown to love kept you away from the child that you would have loved more than life," he said, bracing his palms on his thighs, "Then, you'll understand how I'm feeling too."

I hadn't even thought about what *he* was feeling. I mean, I was ticked off at Mama and Aunt Edna, but he's the one who they'd really duped. "I'm sorry," I said.

I expected him to tell me how awful they were, how he never wanted to see Mama or Aunt Edna again. And I hoped he wouldn't feel the same way about me, but I didn't anticipate what happened next.

Mr. Zip smiled.

Oh, I know, he'd smiled at me before, plenty of times. But this smile was different. This was the kind of smile that Mama gave me when her heart was near to bursting with love. I knew because she'd told me, nearly every time.

Zip smiled at me with a unique Daddy-loves-his-little-girl smile. A smile that I'd seen before in movies and on television and even with the fathers of some of my friends.

But I'd never been on the receiving end myself.

Tears moved up and over the ridges of my eyes, trickled down my cheeks. My throat got even thicker than before and my chest swelled. "You're not mad at them, are you?"

"Oh, I'm disappointed in their deceptiveness, in their willingness to keep a secret," he said. "That's for sure. But I have to admit that the thought of one day being your daddy has been a dream of mine for quite a while. I had assumed the possibility of having a biological child with Delilah had long since passed. But now, I've learned that both dreams are one and the same. And, honestly, it isn't all that bad of an outcome. In a sense, I think I've always felt something special toward you, Jezze."

"I've felt it too," I admitted.

"So, they're not perfect," he said with a chuckle and a shrug. "But who is?"

"Did you tell them you're not mad?"

"Nah," he said and winked. "I figure it'll do them both some good to stew on it a bit. Lord knows they've earned a bit of worrying keeping this big a secret, don't you think?"

I laughed. "So, are you the reason they haven't come to check on me yet?"

"Certainly," he said. "As a matter of fact, I told them to keep to the kitchen and give you some time to sort things out. Then I headed over here as well and hung out in the family room a while so you could have a little time on your own."

"And so they could suffer," I said.

"That too."

My smile bubbled out toward this wonderful man that was my daddy.

"So," he said, uncrossing his legs. "How about a hug for your old man?" He stretched out his arms then waited for me to crawl across the bed and latch onto his neck. "We're all going to be okay," he said, his words feathering against my curls.

I leaned back. "Are you sure?"

"Jezze, I'll never lie to you."

My smile instantly slipped into a frown. "She did. Both of them did."

"I'm assuming they thought it was for your own good. And mine," he said. He loosened his hold around my back and I returned to the bed.

"So, when are you going to tell them everything's okay?" I asked, picking up my notebook and looking at the hysterical rhyme I'd produced, then smirking.

"I'll give them another hour or so, then I figure both of us can go tell them we'll work it out," Zip said. He scooted the chair closer to the bed. "Whatcha got there?"

"I, uh, came up with my own version of The Night Before Christmas."

"Based on today?" he asked, an amused expression on his face.

"Yeah."

"Care to let me take a look?"

"It's not finished," I said. "And I don't think you'd like it."

"You know, I tend to scribble jibberish type poems when I'm frustrated," he said.

"Really?"

He nodded. "Perhaps you inherited that trait."

Had I? The thought of having traits like him amazed me. How many things that I did were similar to Zip DuBois—to my father?

"Can I see?"

"I guess so," I said, handing him the pad.

He read aloud, "Twas the night of the reunion and all through the house, my mama was waiting for Zip to get soused."

I dropped my head into a pillow, but raised it again when I heard his deep, rolling laugh.

"Not bad." He covered his mouth with his palm, but I could tell by the way his cheeks lifted that Zip DuBois was grinning big time.

"You like it?" I asked.

"I'd say it's a perfect start to an interesting poem," he said. "Now then, you ready to go put them out of their misery?" He stood and waited for me to climb off the bed once more.

"I reckon we should."

"You know, odd as it sounds, I don't think they meant any harm. And truthfully, it isn't all that bad of an outcome, in my opinion. I've always wanted a daughter."

"I've got Thibodeaux blood," I reminded, poking out my chin. "That means I'm gonna be a bit on the crazy side too, you know."

He laughed out loud. "Jezze, dear, I wouldn't have it any other way."

CHAPTER THIRTEEN

Picture perfect, the spot on the levee that had boasted Thibodeaux's famous bonfire for the past five years was the ideal location for a wedding. In merely three months, Jezze's man would make his annual steep journey toward his bride. But today, another bride would claim her right man on the very same spot.

And on this gorgeous September Saturday, rose petals blanketed the bare circle of earth where the wooden wedding cake stood each Christmas Eve.

Gusts from the Mississippi shifted the tear-shaped petals to and fro like an ever-changing red, white and pink patchwork quilt.

Red for lovers.

White for friends.

And pink for everything in between.

Guests gathered along the levee's incline. Men's shirts rippled wildly against their chests as if tiny fingers skillfully massaged tight (or in some cases, flabby) abdomens. Skirts whipped around women's legs as though attempting to catch hold of the wind and set themselves free, free to join those shifting rose petals and actively participate in the ceremony that would join two soul mates.

Some folks dressed in their Sunday best. Others wore casual attire, jeans or shorts, as if attending a crawfish boil rather than a wedding. One older gentleman donned a worn, ripped pair of overalls with no shirt underneath. His overlapping, gigantic belly poked out from both sides and jiggled when he laughed at the uncharacteristic scene.

The place certainly didn't have a normal wedding appearance. But then again, Delilah Thibodeaux would cringe to be classified as anything remotely similar to normal.

"Come as you are," the invitation had read. Evidently, many Cajuns took that directive to heart.

Multicolored, whimsical kites darted across a cyan sky like kaleidoscope crystals. Mama had asked specifically for the kites to hover above the Mississippi to remind her of when she'd met her right man. Not the time that she'd met him again five years ago, when he'd approached us on this levee or when she met him to make me at their twenty-fifth reunion, but when she'd met him that very first time...at the Lagniappe Festival when she was fifteen.

Aunt Edna decided to take that wish one step further by hiring clowns to man the kite strings and stroll along the levee during the ceremony. She remembered that night at the festival too, since she'd been there with her big sister. And she wanted everything to be as close to that memory as possible. So Aunt Edna, a stickler for details, also rented cotton candy, caramel apple and other festival stands to serve the guests after the knot had been officially tied. She even borrowed a dunking booth from one of the local schools.

Sunbeams bounced off the Mississippi River, reflecting images of passing barges and boats, as well as colorful diamonds from the kites that flew overhead.

Zip's request that the event be "like a big, Cajun, make-you-want-to-slap-your-mama shindig," had been answered with gusto. Grilled sausage and burgers produced a tantalizing sensation of sizzling grease and mouth-watering meat. Monstrous black cast iron pots bubbled with combinations of smoked andouille, shallots, seasoned chicken and rice...traditional Cajun Jambalaya.

Children waiting for the couple's appearance tossed red Frisbees to Black Labradors and Golden Retrievers (yes, dogs were welcomed too).

A jazz band decked out in crisp red and white striped shirts with black vests and pants belted out New Orleans jazz (and occasionally, on the groom's request, "Hold that Tiger").

The scene was flawless, only to be made better by the situation. Delilah Thibodeaux, at long last, marrying her right man, who, consequently, was my father.

When Zip appeared, driving his truck no less, the crowd cheered and shook purple and gold pom-poms like they were at a Death Valley victory line. (I still thought of him as "Zip", by the way, though at times Daddy did slip into the vocabulary.) He hopped from the cab, removed his top hat and bowed with grandeur. Then he joined in the fun while we all awaited Mama's arrival.

At her request, he wore a snappy black tux with tails. He had to buy a new one, since we'd offered every last one of his previous tuxedos to the bonfire gods. Even a man who owns a few tuxedos for his fancy-shmancy LSU alumni dinners runs out of those type duds eventually. Especially when your fiancée and daughter torch one every Christmas.

Mesmerized by every detail, I took the scene all in. The kites, the wind, the food, the party, the fun. And I wondered if I'd have a wedding like this, which naturally made me also wonder...

Would I ever find *my* right man?

At fifteen, I'd finally conceded to going out with a guy. (I was trying to wait until I found the right one, but at this rate, I figured I'd never find him. I hadn't experienced any of those famous feelings Mama had told me of. Maybe I was doomed to marry him at fifty-nine, like Mama. Or to be like Aunt Edna, fifty-two and still looking.)

Specifically, I said yes to Cale Bouvier in May. So for the past four months, I'd been obligated to talk to him each afternoon when he called, go to the movies on Saturdays (we met up with a bunch of friends; I couldn't single date until I turned fifteen, and I just made fifteen last week), and basically told the other kids at school that we're going out. He walked me to class. We ate lunch together. Yada yada yada. As Aunt Edna says, no biggee.

But Cale Bouvier wasn't my right man, and I knew that. He's okay in a crunch, came in handy for tough situations. You know, a yeah-I've-got-a-boyfriend-so-buzz-off kind of thing. But there weren't any fireworks going off. No ringing of bells when I saw him. He's good to look at and a fairly good.

(Yeah, I kissed him, and it was okay. I mean, he didn't like, inhale, or anything like that. Derrick Walker did that to Sophie during a game of spin-the-bottle at Macie Roussell's birthday party when we were all thirteen. She came up gasping for oxygen, you know, like she was in an airplane and it was going down, but the little mask thingy didn't drop. That kind of thing.)

Anyway, kissing Cale was all right, except his lips always seemed a little too wet. And a lot too cold. Kind of slobbery, you know? But I could handle it. I figured he'd get better eventually (not that I really knew what "better" was). In any case, kissing was as far as it'd go. Like I said, he's not my right man.

"Jezze, come see!" Sophie stood beside a funnel cake setup that I'd missed during my first scan. On the plate in front of her, she had one of the lace-looking pastries with a glob of strawberry topping and a tower of whipped cream sliding around on the glaze.

My long, blue skirt tangled around my legs and dang nearly tripped me as I made my way up the hill toward Sophie. I stopped, straightened the material then started back up again. The wind flapped my brown curls everwhichaway as I made my ascent. They slapped me in the face like long brown whips and occasionally landed in my mouth. I blew one out of the way to speak.

"You know you should wait and eat that for dessert," I said. "We've got awesome jambalaya. Mr. Duhon made it."

She shrugged her shoulders, ran a finger through the cream and fruit, then stuck it in her mouth and licked it off. "Who says I can't have another one for dessert?" she asked. "You want some?" She broke off a piece and ate it. "It's still hot."

I glanced down River Road. Mama told me her entrance would be unique and that she planned to be "fashionably late." Since the wedding wasn't set to start for another ten minutes, I figured I had at least twenty to share the dessert with Sophie. "Sure," I said. "Why not?"

She grinned and led the way to the tiptop of the levee, where we found a big log and plopped down to watch the long, gray barges stalk powerfully through the murky water.

"Excuse me, ladies," a clown with a gigantic, fat smile said as he stepped around us.

"No problem." I squinted up to see the kite he manned soaring high above with its colorful tail streaming wildly in the breeze.

"So, are you excited?" Sophie asked.

"About what?"

"The wedding, silly. Your Mama finally marrying Mr. DuBois. He'll be your Daddy now," she said. "Officially."

"I know," I said. "I can't wait." I finished chewing a man-sized piece of funnel cake then licked the surplus of strawberry glaze from the outside corner of my lip. Have mercy, it was good. Aunt Edna and I had been so busy helping Mama get ready for the wedding this morning that I'd forgotten to eat.

Eventually, I swallowed the bite, reached for another and added, "It isn't as though I haven't been expecting it. She's been going out with him for nearly five years now. I'd say it took them long enough. They started dating when I was ten, for Pete's sake."

"Yeah, that's a long time," she agreed. "Heck, back then you were still flat." She indicated my chest. Sophie was always pointing them out, mainly cause she was still waiting for hers to kick in. She wasn't really jealous or anything like that (at least she said she wasn't). As a matter of fact, she said that seeing mine gave her hope.

Over the past couple of years, my stars had come out in full form, and I sure didn't mind. In my opinion, my sky had been in total eclipse for way too long, which was particularly noticeable when I worked alongside Mama in the kitchen. Now though, I figured I was well on my way to having my own pride and joy. I even had to start watching the cakes I decorated to make sure I didn't leave nipple marks.

"Don't you think it's romantic?" Sophie asked, taking my attention off of the assets I'd inherited from Mama. "They met so long ago and they've waited all this time to get it right. Isn't that incredible?"

Shoot, now why did that question make me think about the bonfire? If my groom had to wait that long, he'd be hanging by his toes from the top of that cake. He only had ten feet to go now. And after Christmas, it'd be nine.

Nine years left. Nine years to find someone that, as far as I could tell, I hadn't even met yet. "Real romantic," I said.

"So, you think you and Cale will have a wedding this big?" she asked. "Wouldn't that be something? If you got married here too? In the very spot where everyone sees your bonfire each Christmas?"

"I've told you," I said, "He isn't the right one. That is *not* Cale Bouvier on my cake."

"You like kissing him, don't you?" she asked. "He told Rooster that you really get into it."

My eyes bugged. Rooster (his name was Terrance, but his redhead gained him a nickname that'd stuck since Ms. Duhon's class in first grade), Sophie's twin brother, had to be the biggest, cockiest, bragging blabbermouth in all of Riverside. And he was on the football team. Which meant that every dang player knew what was happening between Cale and me. "He told Rooster?"

Sophie nodded as though this was no big deal, which of course, it wasn't. Maybe. Or maybe it was. Shoot, I didn't mind people knowing I'd kissed him. Folks would think something was wrong if I hadn't, since our boyfriend-girlfriend status was official and all. But what if Cale didn't tell the truth? What if he said that I...

"Yep, but don't worry. He didn't mess with your rep or nothing. He told Rooster and the guys that you weren't ready for, you know, yet. But he did say that he thought you were getting there," she informed, smacking another hunk of fruit-coated funnel cake.

"He—what?"

"So, *are* you thinking about it? Cause I haven't done it yet, you know, and I was hoping, since we're friends and all, that you'd be willing to tell me how it is."

"No," I said, my back teeth clenched. I looked around the levee. Cale had been buying a candied apple the last time I saw him. I mentally pictured him lying on a table, like one of those pigs at Thanksgiving, with that apple rammed in his mouth. The stick, of course, piercing his throat.

And all of it courtesy of me.

"You won't tell me?" Sophie asked, disheartened.

"I'm not going to do that with him," I said. "Or with anyone else who isn't the right one. As a matter of fact, Cale Bouvier will be lucky if I even speak to him again, much less anything else."

"You're breaking up with him? Goodness, Jezze, I didn't mean to cause trouble between you and your right man."

"I've told you, Sophie," I said, trying to keep my composure, (I didn't want to lose a best friend just because I'd picked a jerk as my first "going out" boyfriend. I'd liked guys before this year, but never officially said yes to going out. Until Cale. The pig.) "Cale isn't the right one."

"What makes you so sure? Dang, Jezze, he's the best looking guy in our grade, and he's head over heels for you. Shoot, most girls would..."

I dropped the piece of cake that'd been heading toward my mouth back on Sophie's white paper plate. How did I know he wasn't the right one? Maybe because I suspected the only reason he asked me out was because my boobs had started to grow. He sure stared at them enough. I couldn't remember the last time we'd talked that his eyes had even remotely neared my face. "When I meet the right one, I'll know it," I said.

"How?"

"Mama told me how it felt for her. I figure I'll feel the same."

"How's that?"

I couldn't fight the smile that tugged at the corners of my mouth, in spite of my irritation with Cale Bouvier. Mama had described it over and over, that feeling of finding the right one, and each time, I'd wanted it even more. That feeling she'd experienced when she'd met my father.

Problem was, I knew for certain I hadn't felt anything like it.

Yet.

"She said your chest gets real tight and your head feels kind of swimmy, like when you've eaten ice cream too fast."

"Brain freeze," Sophie said. "Don't you hate it when that happens?"

I nodded. "And your stomach kind of knots up, like you're gonna hurl, but you don't."

"Great," Sophie said, frowning. "With my luck, I'll actually toss it. Remember last year when I ate those funnel cakes at the fair and then rode the tilt-o-whirl? Nasty!"

I nodded. "Hopefully you'll hold it down. But just in case, if you think you're going to meet the right one, don't eat funnel cake before getting on anything that spins."

"Gotcha."

"And she said your chest tingles, but it doesn't stop there; it kind of pulses out all over your body, like you've got tiny strings of energy rippling down your arms and legs and straight up into your head. And like you'll die if you don't talk to him. Meet him. Touch him."

"Nope, haven't felt anything like that," Sophie said. "Ever."

"Me either."

"You know, it could be different for different people. I mean, whenever Johnny Langlinais comes back to visit for the footbal games, I kind of feel like the ground falls out from beneath me. You know, like I'm suspended on air and I can't walk or move or anything like that. Almost like the way you feel after you've had your eyes dilated at the eye doctor, and then you try to walk outside. Everything is kind of hazy and lopsided. Oh, and my ability to speak seems to take a hike as well. I think my last conversation with the guy consisted completely of 'uh' and 'well uh'."

I laughed. She'd had a crush on Johnny Langlinais ever since we were ten and he asked me out (that was right after the first Jezze's Man bonfire, and every guy in the school wanted to go out with the *star* of the fiasco. Of course, that'd all died down now, though I did get a bit of extra guy attention each year at Christmas). "You realize that you're fifteen and he's, let's see, twenty?"

"What's your point?" Sophie asked, wiggling her brows and swinging her long, straight blond mane around to flip against her shoulder. (I may have been blessed with more prospects for pride and joy, but Sophie had me beat big time in the hair department. It'd taken Aunt Edna nearly an hour to figure out what to do with my mega-long whacked out spirals for the wedding. Finally, she'd given up and simply pulled the top back into a thick, industrial-sized pearl barrette, leaving a couple of long tendrils to hang in front of both ears. To me, they looked like worn-out Slinkies, but considering the mess normally looked like it hadn't seen a brush since preschool, I didn't complain).

"No point," I said, shaking my head. "No point at all."

"So, what do you think? Do you reckon that means Johnny Langlinais is the right man for me? Cause if he is, I probably need to make my move, huh?" She giggled. Sophie talked real big, but like she said, whenever he came around, she turned to mush, like hoghead cheese melting in a bowl of grits.

"Yeah, Sophie, make your move," I said. "And be sure to tell me when you're gonna do it so I can watch."

"Oh, leave me alone, Jezze," she said, shoving her shoulder against mine. "I could end up with him, you know. Stranger things have happened. And I've gotta admit, whenever I see him, I do feel something strong."

"You realize that most every female who sees him feels something strong."

She shoved me again, and I nearly fell off the log. "Lord, Jezze, don't you go and ruin my dream now. I'll tell him. One day."

"Tell him what?"

"The way he makes me feel," she said. She held up the last bite of funnel cake. "Want it?"

I shook my head, sending those tendrils into another bouncing fit against my cheeks.

"You know, you'll feel something like that too," Sophie said. "Maybe it won't be the same as what your Mama felt, or as what I feel for Johnny, but you'll feel something. Even if it isn't with Cale."

"It won't be," I said.

"We'll see," she whispered, tossing the last bite in her mouth and swallowing. "Hey," she said, pointing toward the street. "Is that her?"

I jerked my head toward the paved asphalt that banked against the levee. Sure enough, a horse and buggy, the same kind that gives the tours on Jackson Square, rounded the curve on River Road.

"Mama," I whispered. Then I hurried down the levee to greet the bride.

CHAPTER FOURTEEN

The bride wore shrimp. And butt budder.

No, she didn't literally wear crustaceans. She wore the hue. But the butt budder? Well, yeah, that was literal.

According to Mama, the prettiest color in the world was that odd pinkish-orange of boiled shrimp. So, being Delilah Thibodeaux, she took some boiled shrimp to her dressmaker and asked for a wedding gown.

Sassy in style, shrimp in color.

The dressmaker, Mrs. Jeansonne (who, consequently, had donated all of the wedding gowns for our bonfires over the past five years), was thrilled to produce a dress in such an *interesting* hue.

As it turned out, it couldn't have been more perfect. Shrimp is definitely Mama's color, bringing out the pink in her cheeks (of course, that could've been the ultra-glitter blush) and accenting the stark whiteness of her hair.

Aunt Edna put tiny pink flowers and baby's breath around her morning glory bun, and her trademark hairdo bobbed on top of her head like a poofy cheerleader pom-pom as the horse and buggy neared.

"Mama," I squealed, hurrying to the door. "You're beautiful!"

"Thank you, sweetie." Holding a bouquet of red, white and pink roses (which clashed with her dress, but that didn't really matter, I suppose), she stepped from the carriage and smiled.

The crowd sucked in so much air at once that it was amazing we could still breathe. So okay, her dress was a bit on the flamboyant side. But hey, this wasn't any ordinary bride.

This was Delilah Thibodeaux.

Aunt Edna had pitched a holy tissy when she'd first seen the gown at one of Mama's fittings. But now, Edna grinned at her sister. "I guess if you've got it, you might as well flaunt it, huh, Delilah?" she said as she neared the two of us.

The hairpiece Aunt Edna had bought for the occasion balanced on top of her head in silver ringlets. She wore a crisp lime green pantsuit that showcased the curves she'd acquired over the past few years. (And yes, her suit also clashed aplenty with Mama's dress, but they didn't seem to care. Then again, there wasn't much that didn't clash with shrimp.)

The bodice of the gown, covered with over a thousand crystal beads that we'd found at a local Mardi Gras shop formed a heart shape. The V of it plunged low—very, very low—exposing a good four inches of cleavage in the center (and two softballs of flesh on both sides).

"At least I've got them covered," Mama said, winking at her sister. "I'd be much more comfortable if I didn't."

"Well, I'm sure the preacher appreciates that, Delilah," Aunt Edna said, "Though I'd say 'covered' is only half true. Really, sis," she whispered. "You do look gorgeous, over-exposed or not."

"I know," Mama said in her most wicked I'm-bad-and-prouc-of-it voice. Then she laughed out loud, causing her chest to bounce and making me wonder if she were about to bare her pride and joy to the entire levee.

After recovering from the shock of Mama's dress (and everything hanging out of it), the guests stopped shaking their pom-poms and moved from the various festival stands scattered around the area to accumulate by the circle of rose petals.

Zip stood at the top of the levee next to the preacher (yeah, yeah, I know. We live in Louisiana and you'd have expected it to be all Catholic and a church and a priest and everything; but Mama worships God. Period. But as far as thinking she has to go to a certain church or that she has to be inside some particular building to be able to communicate with the Great Almighty, well, she says that's all hogwash).

So anyway, Zip said this preacher didn't care if they were Catholic, Baptist, Presbyterian or Martian Green, for that matter. He'd marry them. It was a good thing he didn't care about color, giving Mama's choice of dresses and all.

Seeing Mama, Zip moved his top hat to cover his heart and beamed at his shrimp-wrapped bride.

"Here, honey," Mama said, handing me something that had been tucked beneath her nosegay.

I looked down at the yellow tube. The baby smiled back. I swallowed. "Butt budder, Mama?"

"Good heavens," Aunt Edna mumbled.

"Of course butt budder," Mama said, leaning over and kissing my forehead. "You'll hold it until the nuptials are over, won't you, dear? I'll need it back eventually."

I could tell by the way I suddenly felt the breeze on that damp spot of flesh on my forehead that she'd left a nice big lipstick mark. I looked at her mouth. Sure enough, her flaming lips matched the dress perfectly, and she still had an excess of the glossy hue covering them, in spite of the kiss I'd just received. I decided to wait till she started her walk before wiping it off.

The shiny tube caught the sun's rays, flashed my eyes and made me squint. What did she need it for today? Oh, who was I kidding? Mama equated Babineaux's Butt Budder as a fundamental source of survival. Said she didn't know how folks got by without it. She used it for everything.

And I mean *everything*.

Cuts, scrapes, mosquito bites, you name it. She'd been head over heels with the product ever since Aunt Edna and I had mistakenly brought it home from the pig.

What's more, my mama wasn't content to merely buy butt budder for her own ailments. Oh no, she'd decided the entire parish should know about the wonders of the product. So she actually contacted the company and asked to be a distributor.

Now the Cakery sold pastries, cakes, coffee and butt budder. Seriously. As soon as customers entered our front door, they were met with a big bouncing five-foot-plus baby boy. The Babineaux's display had their mascot, "Boodie the Baby" on the front and he actually bounced up and down while he waited for folks to purchase his wares.

And purchase they did. Everyone in Grand Point, Paulina and Gramercy soon caught on to the wonders of the miracle tube and bought it by the cases. Thibodeaux's could hardly keep it in stock (which was actually good for business, since customers never came in and only bought butt budder; they picked up a couple of sweets too).

Mama had even altered our advertising in the local paper so that each ad for the Cakery included a small picture of Boodie in the lower right hand corner, followed by "Proud Supplier of Babineaux's Butt Budder."

"What do you need it for today?" I asked, wishing I had a pocket in my skirt so I wouldn't have to hold the stuff throughout the entire ceremony. Everyone on the levee would recognize it. They should; they all had at least one tube at home. However, they hadn't brought theirs to the wedding. And if they had, they wouldn't stand there and hold it throughout the ceremony like a moron (or someone with severe hemorrhoids).

"The new lace thong is a bear," Mama said, not even attempting to drop her voice. "Downright crack attacker." And to my horror, she reached to her behind and attempted to pull the invading force from the war zone.

Aunt Edna turned to see the guests that were nearest to us. Their jaws hung down like they were trying to catch flies (or Louisiana mosquitoes). "You'll have to excuse her," Aunt Edna said, while she fought the urge to laugh, "pre-wedding jitters."

"Heck, I don't care who knows," Mama said. "I can't have a raw butt for my honeymoon, now can I?"

A loud, hissing noise filled the air like a helium tank with a bad leak as the group of guests, once again, sucked wind.

"No dear, you can't," Aunt Edna said, patting Mama's arm. "You'll hold it for your mama, won't you Jezze?"

"Sure," I said hesitantly. I'd hold it. But I wasn't going to be happy about it.

We backed away from Mama so everyone could appreciate her gown (as well as her pride, and her joy). Then we listened to the jazz band start the wedding march.

"Y'all head on up," Mama said. "I want you to see me make my walk down the aisle."

"Up the aisle is more like it, don't you think?" Aunt Edna said, huffing her way up the levee and pumping her arms like she was doing a power walk.

I followed along, somewhat dazed at the reality. Mama's wedding. My Mama. Finding her right man. Zip DuBois.

My Daddy.

The clowns extended the strings on their kites so they all climbed an extra twenty feet or so as Mama began her journey to her groom.

There weren't any chairs for the ceremony, but that didn't matter. The guests wouldn't really need to sit down, since Zip specifically requested a "five-minute wedding and a ten-hour reception." So Aunt Edna and I finagled our way to stand at the edge of the crowd and get a good view of the proceedings.

The jazz band, evidently unaccustomed to playing the wedding march, seemed to think that it progressively got faster and faster. And Mama, trying to walk in time to the beat, was nearly at a full trot by the time she reached the top of the levee.

I heard a few snickers in the crowd, but Mama didn't seem to notice or care. She'd found her right man. And in about five minutes, he'd be hers forever.

The preacher said a few words, which all seemed to blur together as my eyes misted over at the vision. Mama, gorgeous in her pink-orange dress (matching heels, earrings, necklace, bracelet and lipstick) holding hands with the man who'd captured her interest at fifteen.

And claimed her heart at fifty-nine.

I swallowed, my throat tight and my chest strained. Bit my lower lip. Sniffed to keep my nose from dribbling.

Was I losing my Mama?

Then Zip looked at me, as if he could absolutely read my thoughts.

And he smiled.

No, I wasn't losing my Mama. I was gaining my Daddy.

"Do you, John-Paul DuBois take this woman to be your wife, to have and to hold from this day forward, for richer, for poorer, in sickness and in health, as long as you both shall live?" the preacher asked.

Zip turned his attention from me to my mama. And I knew the look he was giving her...

Love.

"I do," he said. Then he brought Mama's hands to his lips and kissed her knuckles. The tender gesture caused a wave of "awwwww" from the audience and a wave of goose pimples to waterfall down my arms. I could only imagine what it did to my mama.

The preacher looked at a slip of paper in his hand (apparently he'd brought a cheat sheet) then raised his eyes to Mama. Her back faced me, and I could tell by the way it shook that she'd started to laugh. Now, what had happened to turn Mama's funny box over in the middle of her wedding?

Then I thought about what came next in the ceremony. And I knew. That poor preacher.

He cleared his throat. Took a deep breath.

By this time, Mama was about near hysterics and Zip had joined in.

"Go—on," Mama encouraged the preacher, her breath catching in the middle of the two words. "You can do it."

The old man, whose face had been utter seriousness until this point, broke into a smile. He cleared his throat yet again. And again. Then another deep breath.

I waited, thinking he might do the sign of the cross just to help him get through it (not because he was Catholic or anything, but just for good measure).

But he didn't.

"Do you," he paused, looked up at Mama again, then continued, "Deidre Edna Lucinda Isabelle Laila Ann Hiram Thibodeaux," he stopped, waited for the applause and chants of praise from the audience to die down (They'd brought the shakers back out, and I thought someone might start the wave. I was ready to join in, but they didn't get it going), "take this man to be your lawfully wedded husband, to have and to hold from this day forward, for richer, for poorer, in sickness and in health, as long as you both shall live?"

Again, more cheers sprang wholeheartedly from the audience. Mama waited for the noise to die down, until all we could hear were the sounds of the barges pressing down the Mississippi and the wind whistling through the cane on the levee's edge.

Mama tilted her head for a second, then slowly lifted Zip's hands to her shrimp lips and kissed her right man's knuckles. "You know I do."

Zip grabbed Mama and gave her a kiss that I swear should totally be reserved for the bedroom. Actually, it appeared he would've pulled back after the first little peck, but Mama grabbed him in a death grip and refused to let go. Zip turned so his back faced the audience. I assume he did it to give them a tad of privacy, but it didn't work.

Mama's arms were moving up and down his back and her hands grasped and clutched the fabric of his tux so that it looked like he was alone and hugging himself. You know, that funny thing that people do to make it look like there's someone hugging them, but really it's their own arms doing the wild and wooly?

Anyway, they kept it up for so long that some of the guests got tired of clapping and hooting and hollering and headed off to find something to drink.

I didn't though. I watched in awe and hoped to high heaven that somebody'd kiss me like that one day. Then the slurping, smacking, moaning and groaning finally ended and they thanked the embarrassed preacher. Sighing, I turned to head toward the lemonade stand.

And saw *him*.

Standing on top of the levee with the wind rippling his brown waves, he was...perfect. Made my breath catch in my throat. A Greek god couldn't look better. Tall, an easy six feet, he stood a few inches above all of the other guys. Guys who looked to be hanging on his every word as he gestured with his hands and laughed throughout the story he told.

I strained to hear his voice, but the ripping wind kept it from my ears. Was it deep? Husky? Sexy? Oh yeah, I knew it was sexy. I just knew.

He held up a hand in description. Long fingers. Nice palm. Rough? Callused? Smooth?

And his eyes. Blue? Brown? Green? I was too far away to tell, and I had to know.

Had to.

My feet moved of their own accord without any conscious participation by the rest of my body and headed in a direct path toward the gorgeous male.

He wore a white shirt and pleated khakis. The top two buttons of the shirt were undone and a sprinkle of brown hair peeked from the open V. I'd never cared for hair on a guy's chest (not that many guys my age had any), but on his chest, it looked mighty nice.

He had a muscled, athletic build. Thin, but not too thin. Like a baseball player.

I could picture him wearing a baseball cap, standing on the pitcher's mound, chewing a wad of gum and nodding his head to accept the sign from the catcher. Yeah, I could marry a baseball player.

My stomach started cramping, got stronger with every step, but I didn't stop. I couldn't. I was on a mission, and I wouldn't stop till I accomplished my goal.

To meet him.

Hear his voice.

Learn the color of his eyes.

The sounds and images of the crowd faded together, becoming a myriad of colored swirls, like my favorite tie-dyed shirt. Voices were indistinct and muffled, like that low humming that you hear after you've left a loud concert and sat too close to the speakers.

Everything else faded together in the background, became a marbled mess around the one thing that stood in the center. The one vision that was so perfect, so crystal clear.

Him.

In the back of my mind, I heard my name, as if called from a land far away. Jezebel...Jezebel...Jeze...

My skirt tangled, whipped wildly in the wind, slid up my legs and exposed my thighs. I paused to straighten it, but my hands were too fidgety to perform the simple task. So I let it fly and continued my trek.

When I'd nearly reached the group, he looked up. Stopped talking. And stared directly at me.

Brown. His eyes were Hershey brown. So rich and dark, in fact, that I couldn't tell where the iris ended and the pupil began.

Wow.

Deep dimples. Deep enough to make me wonder if my tongue was still in my mouth. Deep enough to make me drool. Deep enough that my finger burned to trace the sexy crevice.

I was barely aware that the group's attention had turned toward me and totally aware of his attention doing the same.

What to say? I should have thought of that by now, but my brain refused to cooperate.

What to say. What to say.

And what would he say to me? This right man? Oh, I knew. I knew from the way my body burned all over that I'd finally found the one. What would the first words from the mouth of my soul mate be? What would my first words be to him?

We'd remember this forever. We'd tell our children, our grandchildren. The words I said now would forever be a lasting memory in my life. As would the words he said to me.

Evidently, we both knew how important this moment was, because we stood there for a second, waiting and preparing for that pristine moment when the world would stand still.

And we'd speak.

Finally, we decided simultaneously that the moment was right.

"Do you play baseball?" I blurted at the exact same moment that he informed me, "Your butt budder is leaking."

CHAPTER FIFTEEN

"Jezebel!" Mama yodeled from her stance behind the three-tiered cake. "Come on, sweetie, you're missing everything. We're about to cut the cake."

I stared at the offending hands connected to the ends of my arms. I'd known they were fidgeting during my entranced hike up the levee, but I hadn't dreamed that I'd somehow removed the top from Mama's butt budder. And I sure didn't know I was squirting the stuff in my wake, like Gretel's path of breadcrumbs. Only messier.

I looked down at the tube, squished nearly empty. Then I ooked up. Big mistake. The crowd of hunky, obviously older guys laughed.

And he—smiled. Was he smiling because I'm so cute? Or because I squirted a month's supply of butt budder down the side of the levee (and my skirt, for that matter).

"Good stuff, huh?" he asked, indicating the mashed tube that dangled from my fingertips as though it were a dirty sock I didn't care to touch.

The funnel cake I'd shared with Sophie started a lazy path from my stomach to my throat. And every ounce of blood near the vicinity of my face pooled into my cheeks, crept into my forehead, my ears, my neck, burning hot as a Cajun bonfire as it spread.

"Jezebel!" Mama called again.

I turned from my right man.

And ran.

Thankfully, Mama insisted that I be in most of the pictures and even more thankfully, it took quite a while to take them. Of course, I knew my face would be beet red in every dang one of them, but I didn't care. At least the picture-taking kept me occupied for a while and stopped me from making an even bigger fool of myself.

What in the world had I been thinking? Waltzing up there to talk to the guy, a complete stranger, and standing there like a dimwit while I tried to think of the perfect thing to say.

"Do you play baseball???"

Where the heck had that come from? I mean, yeah, I was wondering if he did, but still, I should've at least asked his name, or if he enjoyed the wedding, or if he wanted to help me have beautiful children (not anytime soon, mind you, but when the time got right).

And the butt budder. Good Lord.

I shook my head. No, I wouldn't think about *that* anymore.

Mama unwrapped herself from her husband and walked toward me. She brought both palms beneath my chin and cradled my face. "You okay, sweetie?"

I nodded, bit back my tears. "Yes, ma'am."

"It was beautiful, wasn't it? I tell you what, precious, marrying your right man, there's nothing quite like it."

Hearing her comment, Zip called, "Sure took you long enough to do it, though, didn't it?"

Mama chuckled low in her throat. "He's right, you know. I should've married him years ago. But I've got it right now. And one day, when you're a bit older, I know you'll find someone who'll make you feel the way I feel today."

I couldn't stop the tears this time. Should I tell Mama that I'd found him a few minutes ago and that I'd blown it with butt budder?

"Oh, Jezebel," Mama murmured, pulling me close and smashing my face against her boobs. The top of her dress shifted beneath my cheek, and I prayed that when she freed me, I wouldn't be staring at her flowers. She kissed the top of my head. "Nothing will change between us, baby. You will always, always be my little girl. And now you'll have your Daddy too."

Well, shoot. I should've known Mama thought my tears were unhappy ones. And now would be the perfect time to tell her the truth. I wasn't unhappy at all with her marriage. In truth, I'd been waiting on it since that night on the levee five years ago, before I even knew that it'd been Zip gave my mama the gift of me. But I didn't exactly want to explain what had just happened either. So I waited until she released her grip, then I leaned back and nodded.

"I know, Mama. Everything's going to be great," I said, and I meant it. "I love him too, you know."

Her glittery cheeks pushed up high against her eyes and sparkled beneath the brilliant blue. "Oh, Jezebel, you make me so happy, angel," she whispered. She looked at me with love, not the "I'm glad you're my daughter" type of look, but the look that says "Jezebel Thibodeaux, you make my life complete."

I smiled then watched her eyes center on a spot on my forehead.

"Oh, baby," Mama said, then she laughed softly. "I'm afraid I left my mark." She rubbed the spot that she'd kissed before the wedding began.

Well great. That's just great. Not only had I met my right man with butt budder dripping from my hands and my speech completely MIA, but I'd had big, plump shrimp lips on my forehead.

If that didn't keep him away, I couldn't imagine what would.

Mama said something about flying a kite, though I wasn't really listening. Then she turned, found Zip and the two of them headed toward the clowns.

Unsure whether I really wanted to see my right man again (at least until I got the butt budder off my skirt), I scanned the levee. It crawled with Cajuns, dancing, eating and partying in Mama and Zip's honor. But *my* right man apparently had gone.

Super.

"Hot as the devil out here, huh?" Sophie said, walking toward me and eating another funnel cake.

"Did you ever eat any real food?" I asked.

"This is real food," she said, and she stuck another hunk in her mouth. "Hey, I heard about the butt budder thing. I've got some shorts in my car, so why don't we go change?"

"You heard?" I asked, shocked. I darted my eyes around the crowd, which included practically everyone in the parish, as well as a few tourists who'd simply joined the party because—well, just because. "Does everyone know?"

"Probably," she said. "But I have good news. Or, I think it's good news."

"I could use some," I said. "Shoot."

"Cale wanted me to tell you that he's breaking up. Seems he doesn't want to date the girl known for the butt budder incident."

"And that's good news?"

"Well, you said that you didn't want to have to speak to him again, didn't you? Now you don't have to." She scooped up some whipped cream and blueberry topping (at least she had changed her fruit intake) and stuck it in her mouth.

"Yeah. Now everything's just great." I filled my hand with a glob of cake, fruit and cream, held it to my mouth and chowed down, like a little kid eating a mouthful of popcorn at a movie, you know, when they kind of stuff it inside but lose most out the edges. Blueberry gunk dripped from the sides of my mouth and fell down the front of my top. And I didn't even care. I mean, why did I have to worry about impressions? What could be worse than being known as the butt budder queen?

Wide-eyed, Sophie gawked at my cake attack.

"Goodness," she said, grinning. "All right, that does it." She stomped over to the nearest trashcan and dropped the half-eaten funnel cake inside. Then she marched back to me, grabbed my hand and yanked me behind her as she headed toward the street.

"Where are we going?"

"It's too dang hot out here, and we're going to get out of these clothes," she said.

"Listen, it's bad enough I dribbled butt budder all over my skirt and had shrimp lips on my forehead when I met my right man. I will not go parading around this levee naked, even if I do think I'd feel a whole lot better in the buff."

She stopped walking, and I nearly slammed into her from sheer momentum.

"What?" I asked.

"You met your right man?" she asked, eyes big with excitement.

"I scared him off."

"Who is he?"

"Dang if I know," I said honestly. "But he made me all, I don't know, funny feeling inside."

"You don't know who he is?"

"Uh-uh." I looked over my shoulder at the crowd. "And I think he left. I haven't seen him or any of the guys he was with since we finished taking pictures."

"A bunch of good-looking guys?" Sophie asked. "Looked like a herd of mouthwatering studs? And every last one of them hunkalicious?"

Okay, now she had my attention. Did Sophie know my right man? "Um, yeah."

"They left about ten minutes ago. I practically had to hold myself back to keep from asking them if I could tag along," she said with a giggle.

"You don't know them?"

"Nope," she admitted. "But I know where they're from."

"Where?"

"Lutcher High. Or at least that's where they *were* from. All of them have graduated, according to Rooster."

"Rooster knows them?"

"Just from sports, I suppose. He recognized them when they got here. He introduced me, you know. It was right after you headed down the hill to meet your Mama."

"The tall one," I said, and I didn't even fight the quiver in my voice. "Brown hair. Brown eyes. Dimples..."

Sophie laughed. "Yeah. Pretty gorgeous, huh?

"Do you remember his name?"

"Sure do," she said. Her eyes glittered. She was having way too much fun with this.

"Tell me."

"Say the magic word," she teased.

"Now," I deadpanned.

"Oh, all right, spoiled sport. His name is T-Roy. T-Roy Bertrand."

"T-Roy? You're sure?"

"He was the tall one. Gorgeous hair. Eyes that you could drown in. And a ripped body that—"

"That's enough, Sophie."

She laughed. "I thought so. Now, let's go change out of these hot dresses. Then we can talk about your right man. And how we can make sure you see him again."

Within minutes, we'd swapped into shorts and T-shirts in the backseat of Sophie's Mom's Lincoln. Then we headed back toward the reception, where more than a few Cajuns were steadfastly working their way toward getting smashed. We ate some jambalaya (even though Sophie said she'd rather eat desserts) and we talked about T-Roy Bertrand.

There really wasn't much we could say about the guy, since neither of us knew more than his name. And we didn't have a clue how to find out. We took turns flinging out questions about the fellow, and then we sat in silence while we wondered about the answers.

"Do you think he's in college?" Sophie asked.

"Or do you think he's working already?"

"What about a girlfriend. Surely he's got a girlfriend, don't you think?"

"Reckon she's older?" I asked, picturing a tall, leggy blonde on his arm. "Hmph. Probably has great hair."

"How old do you think he is?" Sophie asked.

I shrugged. "I don't know. Do you think he's twenty? He didn't look twenty, did he?"

"I thought he looked eighteen, didn't you?"

"What about brothers? I mean, he could have a brother and you could date him. Then we'd have found both of our right men in the same family. Wouldn't that be cool?" I asked.

"My right man is Johnny Langlinais," Sophie said, breaking the question/silence pattern.

"Well, my right man is T-Roy Bertrand," I said, then I added, "I think."

Additional questions zipped through my mind as we quickly downed two fluffy plumes of cotton candy. The pink and blue sugar crystallized with our touch, sticking to our fingers and lips like tiny pellets of concrete.

"We're going to have to take a dip in the river to get this stuff off," I said, licking my fingers.

"A dip doesn't sound so bad in this heat," Sophie said. "As a matter of fact, it'd be fun." She shoved me in the shoulder and pointed across the levee. "You up for it?" Then she took off running.

Before I'd determined what she had in mind, she had crawled into the dunking booth and started heckling the kids lined up to throw. I ran toward the section of the levee that housed the big water tank. Water sloshed over the side and drenched the earth below, creating a mini swamp.

"Yeah, you can't hit!" Sophie screamed. "Come on, is that the best you've got? My grandmother throws harder!"

Sure enough, the kid tossing the pitches, who appeared about ten, gritted his teeth, reared back, and flung the cabbage ball as though he were pitching for the Braves.

He hit the target dead center.

Sophie dropped into the blue depths of the tank and made hideous underwater faces at the kid through the clear glass.

"Oooh, you're gross," the boy said, scrunching up his face like a prune.

Sophie climbed back up to the suspended seat and started back up again, swinging her legs and taunting the little boy's friend, who was next.

"Hey, noodle-arms, think you can sink me?"

"We're gonna drop ya!" the boy yelled. He was younger than the first, maybe six or seven, and wore glasses. He had a big hole at the front of his smile where he'd lost a few of his teeth, and he stuck his pink tongue through the gap and wiggled it at Sophie.

Sophie stifled her giggle, then she yelled, "We? What do you mean— we? You gotta flea in your pocket?"

The boy doubled over and held his tummy while he laughed. "You're funny, lady," he said. Then he straightened up, took aim and fired.

Sophie dropped, flailing her arms and legs for drama.

It worked.

Within minutes, the two boys had gathered every other kid in the place to come dunk the funny girl.

After a good twenty plummets into the tank, Sophie declared mercy and informed the crowd that her friend would take over.

"Gee, thanks," I said, climbing inside to take my place on the wet bench. It was covered in Astroturf, or perhaps another type of outdoor carpet, and the cold, stubby spikes prickled my legs and my butt. My feet dangled in the water and I swung them, partly to test the sturdiness of the seat and partly to feel the slick, blue wetness between my toes.

"Don't mention it," Sophie said, accepting a towel from the booth's assistant and drying off.

My first plunge into the turquoise liquid was pure bliss. For a moment, I thought I'd merely stay down there, beneath the surface, enjoying the feel of complete tranquility that the water provided. No screaming children. No laughing Sophie. No memories of embarrassing butt budder.

But, eventually, I needed air.

I shot up from the water and hauled my drenched body back on the plank. Unlike Sophie, I couldn't bring myself to taunt the youngsters who were sending me to a watery grave. For one thing, they were too dang cute and excited for me to tease them. For another, I actually wanted to fall, to experience the rapture of the water once more.

"Come on, you can do it!" I yelled, as a little girl with pigtails gave it her best shot. She tried three times and missed three times. I called, "Oh, come on up here and hit the button."

She wasn't quite tall enough to manage the feat alone, so several of the young boys decided to help. They hoisted her little body up until she slapped a flat palm against the red circle.

And I fell in.

The tiny crowd (tiny in size, not in number) howled with laughter, then each of them took a turn at knocking me in with their hands.

When they finally became bored with seeing me fall, they gathered in a huddle and discussed what they'd do next, unanimously deciding that they were all due a turn at the kites. I watched them run away up the levee. Sophie had long since gone, probably to buy another funnel cake or some other fattening treat.

"Miss Thibodeaux, do you need some help getting out?" the dunking booth attendant asked.

I looked toward the man, shook my head. "Would it be okay if I sat here a few minutes?" I asked. "The water feels so good on my toes."

He laughed. "Stay as long as you want. I'm gonna go grab me a bite to eat, though, okay?"

I nodded. Sophie and I had sat in the booth for so long that the sun had started to drop and the breeze from the Mississippi actually started feeling cool. I closed my eyes. Thought about the day.

Mama's wedding day.

She'd looked so gorgeous in her wild-colored dress with her flashy makeup and her pom-pom hair. One thing about Delilah Thibodeaux...when she set out to make a statement, she made it. And today, she'd made it with pizzazz.

Folks would be talking about this wedding for years, about the incredible event that took place on the levee at the site of Jezze's Man.

Jezze's Man.

Had I met him today? Or was the feeling that ricocheted through my body when I'd seen T-Roy Bertrand merely part of those raging teenage hormones that Aunt Edna was always talking about.

And how would I know the difference?

Aunt Edna. I'd seen her heading back the levee with Will LeBlanc. Had she finally admitted that she may have found her right man during one of those trips to the pig? And if she had, how long would she wait before declaring him hers forever?

Fifty-two. Goodness, she's fifty-two. How much longer would she wait? And would I end up waiting that long too?

Frowning, I tried to take my mind off the pressure of finding my right man. I swung my feet through the water, lost myself in its coolness. I could sleep here, I thought. Simply keep my eyes closed forever and let the water soothe me to happy dreams. Dreams of me and my...

My brain barely had time to register the sound of the cabbage ball hitting the target, the shock of the bench dropping away from my behind, the iciness of the water as it entombed my body.

Trying to scream, I ended up swallowing half the tank. I came up coughing and hacking and blinking, trying to focus in the dimness of the afternoon so I could identify the villain who'd caught me unaware.

"What the devil were you—" my voice lodged in my throat. I pushed the tangled, wet brown curls off my face to make certain I wasn't hallucinating. Then I dunked back into the water, tilted my head back and came up again with my hair billowing behind me, and my face not withholding a smile. "What were you doing?" I whispered.

He walked to the tank, stepped up on the ladder and placed his hands on the rim.

On top of mine.

"I'm sorry," T-Roy Bertrand said, his voice low and husky and his dimples even deeper than I remembered. "I thought you were ready."

"I am," I whispered, melting beneath his chocolate gaze. "I am."

CHAPTER SIXTEEN

If my hands were struck by lightning at that very moment, I wouldn't have felt it. I looked down at them, completely covered by his warm palms, and thought, *If I died right now, it wouldn't be such a bad thing.*

"I thought you left," I mumbled, feeling prickly from my fingertips to my toes in spite of the cold water surrounding most of my body.

His straight white teeth practically sparkled as his grin grew broader. "I didn't realize you noticed."

I blinked. Probably shouldn't have told him that, but it was too late to drag my foot, ankle, shin and knee out of my mouth now. "I did," I said.

"Hank rode with me and he needed to get home. He had a date," he said. "By the way, I'm T-Roy. T-Roy—"

"Bertrand," I whispered dreamily, completing his statement. "I know. And why don't you have a date?" I figured my knee was already lodged in my throat, might as well push the thigh in too.

This time, he laughed. It was a robust, head-thrown-back all-out rumble that pulsed through the air and joined beats with my heart. "Jezebel Thibodeaux, you are a treat."

Okay, my brain might have been hazy, but I didn't remember introducing myself. "You know me?"

"My father and Zip have been friends since college, and Zip never fails to talk about Delilah, Edna and you when he visits."

"So you know me from Zip?" I asked, thinking I'd have to thank my father profoundly.

"That, and I never miss the bonfires."

"Oh yeah, there is that," I whispered, giving him an embarrassed grin. So, he'd watched Jezze's man progress up the side of that cake along with the rest of the town (and most of the state of Louisiana). Was he impressed by it, or did he put me in the "Crazy Thibodeaux" category?

"And your Aunt Edna mentioned you a few times when I came into Thibodeaux's with my father."

"You've been to the Cakery?" Dadgummit, Aunt Edna and I were going to have a serious talk about basic etiquette involved with having a teenage niece. Surely she knew protocol required her to announce the presence of hot hunks in the store. Heck, was I in the kitchen, cooking topless with Mama, when this masterpiece was buying treats out front?

"I spend my summer breaks riding with my father and learning the ropes, since I plan to take over his business one day. The Cakery, of course, is one of our stops, since your mother is the—"

"Jezze!" Sophie screamed. She jogged toward the dunking booth with another plume of cotton candy, this one lime green, pumping through the air with her strides.

"They're getting ready to throw the birdseed and your Mama wants to see you before they leave," she panted, her sugar-coated mouth forming a wide O at the sight of me and T-Roy. "Um, can you come?" she asked.

"Sure," I said. Regretfully, I slid my hands out from under his palms, climbed out of the tank, and immediately started shaking. No, I wasn't really cold. Or at least I didn't think I was.

"Oh, Jezze," Sophie whispered, "Um, oh, my," she continued. I followed her gaze, which had landed on my chest.

Okay, so the T-shirt she loaned me was thin, but that wouldn't have been a problem if that unseasonal chill hadn't piped through my body when T-Roy's hands left mine. And if the strapless bra that I'd worn for my dress hadn't slid down past my bellybutton.

"Well, shoot," I said. I was really batting a thousand now. I'd squirted butt budder all over my skirt, had shrimp lips on my forehead, and had my own private wet T-shirt party at my mother's wedding. Even worse, my high beams were in true form. I could hang a Christmas ornament on each one. Yep, after tonight, he'd be breaking the door down to ask me out, for sure.

"Here," he said, his voice a tad lower than before.

My eyes about popped right out of my head as I watched him. Working the buttons free of their holes, baring his chest as he progressed. Was he going to take his shirt off to make me feel better about my predicament?

Because if so, it was working.

He slid out of the lucky white fabric (anything touching that body would have to be considered lucky)...and draped it around me.

"Thanks," I mumbled, analyzing the additional hair exposed by the removal of his shirt. A tapered V that started in the center of his chest and sprinkled down ripped abs like a faint waterfall, curling around his navel, then...

"Here," he said, withdrawing something from his pants pocket.

I accepted the item. What would it be? He'd given me his shirt, so what other wonderful treat did my right man have in store for our first night together. Looking down, I saw...

Butt budder.

"I thought you might want another tube, since you emptied the other one. Good stuff, isn't it?"

I blinked. This could not be happening. "My mom's," I mumbled. "It was my mom's."

"Well then, you can give it to her," he said. Then he smiled.

And I melted. Again.

"Now go on!" Sophie squealed, pushing me down the levee toward Mama and Zip. "You better hurry if you want to see her!"

I grinned dopily at T-Roy, bare-chested and glorious, and headed away. But not before I heard Sophie start her one-on-one interrogation. "She's fifteen. How old are you? Where do you go to school? What are your thoughts regarding marriage and kids?" her high-pitched voice followed me as I ran, and I held my shock in check. In her own peculiar way, she was trying to help. Maybe, if I hadn't scared him away already, she wouldn't either.

Lanterns dotted the levee, but it wasn't enough to help Mama spot me in the crowd. "Where is she?" I heard her say, squinting through the night and refusing to budge from her stance. Both knees were locked firmly in place and her arms were crossed under her bodice, pushing pride and joy clear up to her neck. "I'm not leaving until I see Jezebel."

"I'm here, Mama!" I yelled, pushing my way past the fat guy in the overalls to get closer.

"Oh, sweetie," Mama said, her eyes glistening as she leaned over and hugged me. "I love you."

"I love you too, Mama."

Then she leaned back and cupped my chin. "Jezebel?"

"Yes, ma'am?"

Mama shifted her hand, so that my head tilted to one side, then the other. Wet droplets of dunking booth water trickled from my temples down my cheeks. She lowered her voice and put her lips near my ear. "I know that look, darling, don't I?"

"What look?" I asked.

"When did you find him?"

My heart pitter-pattered harder than Aunt Edna's kill-the-cockroach move. "I'm not sure I did," I admitted. "But maybe a few minutes ago."

"Oh, my little angel," Mama said, kissing the shell of my ear. "You found him."

"Delilah, it's time to go," Zip said, stepping from the shadows behind Mama (whose shrimp dress practically glowed in spite of the dark). He wrapped an arm around me and squeezed. "We're going to call you everyday while we're gone, kiddo, okay?"

I nodded, my throat all lumpy and dry at the same time.

"Hey now," he added, pulling me close. "I'll bring her back safe and sound, and you'll be with Aunt Edna while we're gone. She'll take care of you."

"Shoot, who're you kidding, Zip?" Mama asked. "You'll take care of your aunt, won't you, sweetie?"

I smiled. "Sure I will, Mama."

"By the way, where is Edna?" she asked.

"Last time I saw her, she was headed back the levee with LeBlanc," Zip said.

Mama giggled, whispered in my ear, "Looks like maybe someone else found her right man tonight too, huh?" She moved a wet curl from my cheek and tucked it behind my ear. "Took a turn in the dunking booth, did you?"

"Yes, ma'am."

"Lord, you're mighty drenched," Mama said.

"I'm afraid that's my fault."

I turned toward the voice that reminded me of cocoa butter dripping down my skin. Nice. Thick. And hot.

"Your fault, T-Roy?" Zip asked.

"Yes, sir. I'm a fairly good shot with a cabbage ball and a target."

"I see," Mama said, and the look in her eyes said she did see. Everything. She held out a hand. "I don't believe we've met."

"Thaddeus Royce Bertrand," he said. "But folks call me T-Roy."

"And I'm assuming you prefer that," she said. "In the same manner as I prefer Delilah over Deidre, Edna, Lucinda—well, heck, if you heard the ceremony, you get the picture."

"Yes, ma'am."

"Bertrand?" Mama repeated, realization dawning. "Your daddy isn't Fenton, is he?"

"Yes, ma'am, he is."

"You know, most times he comes in Thibodeaux's, I'm in the back cooking, but I have met him a time or two. He's a good man. You must be the son he spoke of, said you were taking over his business one day, and that you'd do a fine job."

"I'm at LSU now, Ms. Thibodeaux, working on a degree in business administration. When I graduate, he plans to retire and turn everything over to me. Hopefully, I'll do as good of a job as he's done."

"You can call me Mrs. DuBois now, T-Roy," she said, and w nked at her new husband. "And I'm sure you'll do a fine job following your daddy's footsteps," Mama said. She smiled at him, then at me.

I could almost see her mind clicking. She hadn't even left for her honeymoon and she was already planning my wedding. Obviously, she saw no problem at all with the fact that this guy lived in a dorm in Baton Rouge (I assumed), that I barely knew more than his name (actually, I'd learned it only a few minutes ago), and I didn't know his age, his likes, his dislikes, or anything else. In other words, I didn't know diddly-squat about T-Roy Bertrand. But I knew that he made my insides go hot and liquid. And I knew that I wanted to spend more time with him.

I just wasn't sure how.

But wouldn't you know it, Mama wasn't about to leave for her honeymoon before she helped me out (and I hadn't even told her my problem). "Is this your shirt?" she asked, nodding from the del cious smelling shirt covering my wet clothes to his bare chest.

"Yes, ma'am. I thought she might need it."

"You know, T-Roy," Mama said. "In a second, we're going to be running out of here in the royal bombing of the birdseed. And then we'll be heading straightaway to Mexico."

T-Roy nodded.

"And with Jezebel so wet and all, she's liable to catch cold out here on the levee if this temperature keeps dropping. I mean, this shirt is fine, but she really needs to get home soon. To get out of this wind."

All right. Mama was really heading out on a limb with that one. Louisiana in September, even at night and with a Mississippi breeze, was about the same as July anywhere else. Hot. Hot enough to fry bacon on River Road. Mama knew it. Zip knew it. I knew it.

And T-Roy knew it.

But he nodded his head as though she were speaking the gospel truth, so I didn't argue.

"I believe Edna will need to stay here a while to take care of the cleanup, and I don't want Jezebel stuck here in the cold for all that length of time," Mama said. She let the last word kind of hang there while she waited to see how long it would take this boy to complete her thought.

It didn't take long. At all.

"Well, I was planning to offer her a ride home anyway, Ms. Thibodeaux—I mean, Mrs. DuBois," T-Roy said, and his dimples pierced his cheeks with the words. "I figured since I'm the reason she's all wet, it should be my car that she sits in on the way home. You know, I don't want to mess up the seats in her aunt's vehicle, particularly since I'm the reason she's soaked."

"That's a good idea," Mama said. "And quite noble of you. I'm assuming you're that conscientious about everything. You try not to hurt things. You don't mess anything up."

"I take extreme care with things, Mrs. DuBois," he said. "Particularly when something's not mine."

"Why, that's downright thoughtful of you, T-Roy," Zip said, not even attempting to masque his amusement with the dual conversation taking place in front of him. Of course, Zip hadn't been fooled. He'd heard the same thing I did...

Delilah: "You seem to be a responsible boy and you come from good stock."

T-Roy: "I do come from good stock, and I plan to be just as successful as my father. Or more."

Delilah: "I believe my daughter has her eye on you, so I'm allowing you to take her home."

T-Roy: "I'd be happy to take her home. And I know better than to try to hurt her."

And then, the finale, Mama's last question, directed to me…

"Is this okay with you, sweetie?"

Which, translated, is "Is he the one who put that look on your face, my darling daughter?"

And my answer?

"It's fine, Mama." Absolutely fine.

T-Roy and I got in line with the rest of the guests and flung birdseed at Mama and Zip as they dashed wildly to the limo. Mama made quite a display of shaking the excess seed from her cleavage before hopping in, which garnered another shocked gasp from the crowd.

And an excited growl from her husband.

"How long will they be gone?" T-Roy asked as the limousine wheeled down River Road.

"Two weeks in Playa del Carmen," I said, grinning from ear to ear. Mama and Zip. Mama and *Daddy*. Married. On their honeymoon.

And me. With my right man.

"So, we should go find your aunt and tell her I'm taking you home."

I turned to face him and realized I was eye-level to the flat, brown circular disks on his chest. Personally, I'd never found much appeal in guy nipples, but right now, I begged to differ. Rather, my tongue and my lips begged to differ, because all they wanted to do was take turns hitting each bull's eye.

"There she is," he said.

Lordy, I was glad he'd been looking for Aunt Edna. No doubt if he'd been looking at me, he'd have seen my tongue lolling out like those begging dogs that hang out at the Cakery's back door.

Or worse, foaming at the mouth.

Aunt Edna had topped the levee and was patting her spiral hairpiece in place. Problem was, it was hanging lopsided over her right ear and she looked like Princess Leia from Star Wars (minus one ear bun thingy). And her pantsuit had more wrinkles than Jabba the Hutt.

William LeBlanc came up behind her, wrapped an arm around her waist and pulled her against him. Even in the darkness, I could see Aunt Edna's face. It looked peaceful, content, happy.

She whispered something to Mr. LeBlanc, then turned and started down the levee. Her eyes lit up when she spotted us. "Jezze," she said. "I'm afraid I missed their exit."

"It's okay. Mama was glad you were," I paused, "visiting."

She giggled. Aunt Edna *giggled?* Then she grinned at T-Roy. "Well, how've you been, Mr. Bertrand?"

"Just fine, ma'am."

"And loaning out your shirts, I assume?" she asked, doing the same take on the situation as Mama, flashing a gaze at his chest, then my shirt-clad body.

"I reckon I am," he said.

"I sure miss your smiling face in the shop," she said. "I suppose your Daddy will be on his own again until next summer, huh?"

He nodded. "Probably so."

I waited for him to tell Aunt Edna that he was taking me home, but he didn't. Instead, he looked at me. Could it be this hunky fella was shy? And, could he be any cuter if he tried?

"Aunt Edna," I said, deciding to give him a break, "Mama said T-Roy could take me home, since I'm wet and all."

"Oh, she did, did she?"

I nodded. "If that's okay with you, of course."

"Well, I'll be," she whispered.

"What is it?" I asked.

"Oh, I was simply realizing how blind I am nowadays. You know," she pretended to be searching the crowd for someone, but I couldn't imagine who, "Sometimes I just can't see things like I used to."

I couldn't figure out why her mind had shifted gears so quick. "So, is it okay if we go ahead and head home?" I asked.

"Sure, Jezze," she said. "It's fine."

"Thanks." I gave her a hug and was surprised when she held me there a moment longer than usual. Long enough for my wet body to soak the front of her green suit, but she didn't seem to mind.

"I do believe you've found him, child," she whispered. Then she released her hold, and I watched her eyes mist over and sparkle in the moonlight. "You be careful driving home, T-Roy. You understand?"

"Yes, ma'am." He jingled his keys in his hand as he led me toward his car. And I replayed Aunt Edna's words with every step. Not the words she'd actually spoken, but the words her heart had conveyed.

"You take good care of our Jezze."

CHAPTER SEVENTEEN

By the time we'd made the short drive (way too short, especially when trying to learn more about a future husband) to Grand Point, I'd learned that he's a sophomore at LSU who rarely comes home for visits (since his father typically sees him whenever he's working in Baton Rouge). And that he and his dad enjoy LSU football, basketball and baseball, and go to as many games as possible throughout the year.

No mention of a girlfriend, and no, I didn't ask. I figured I'd simply remain optimistic. He's too busy studying and spending time with his dad to have one. Surely. (Okay, I know, what are the odds a total hottie like T-Roy Bertrand would be single? About a million to one? But I'm not going to think about that now. I'm not. Really.)

But, girlfriend or not, I learned quite a bit of valuable information during our chitchat from the levee to home. Mainly that T-Roy Bertrand wasn't going to be home all that much until he graduated. So he probably wouldn't be a prime candidate to say, meet the hometown girl, fall in love, ask her to marry, and then get started on a dozen or so children.

At least not until the end of his senior year.

And consequently, since I'm currently a sophomore as well (albeit high school rather than college), my plans to go directly to Southeastern and get a degree in Nutrition would add a few years to the scenario (unless, of course, we married before I graduated and I commuted to school, which might work, as long as I didn't get pregnant too quick and all). But no, if I got married I'd want to go ahead and have children, and I'm sure he would too, since we're going to want so many and all, so we should wait.

Definitely. We'll wait until I get my degree and follow through with my plans, running the Cakery and expanding it to include a small restaurant. Of course, that would most certainly require an employee or two, which Aunt Edna totally opposes, but I figure I'll cross that bridge when I come to it.

In any case, my brief talk with T-Roy highlighted two obstacles in our marriage plans. A) He lives in Baton Rouge and doesn't come home much. Granted, I don't know if he'd be willing to change this for a girl he was going out with, but I'm merely putting things in perspective here. And B) He would graduate LSU at the same time I graduated high school, then he'd take over his father's business and start working locally, while I'd take off to Southeastern University in Hammond.

For four years.

So, doing the math, I calculated our earliest possible wedding date to be—let's see—two and a half years to graduation from LSU (h m) and from Riverside (me). Then four years while I get the Foods and Nutrition degree to help me better run the Cakery (specifically, a degree in Family and Consumer Sciences with a concentration in Foods and Nutrition, but that's a whole lot to say, don't you think?)

For a grand total of six and a half years, age twenty-one for me (three years shy of the target date for Jezze's Man—oy!) and...

Shoot, I haven't found out how old he is.

"How old are you?" I blurted.

He'd turned onto the blacktop drive that led beside the Cakery and extended to the two houses on the back of the property. The house Mama, Aunt Edna and I had shared my entire life and the new house that Mama and Zip had built. It took me a second to realize that he'd been talking the entire time I'd been calculating our wedding date. Dang, had I missed some vital information while I was working out our future? Could he not tell that I was preoccupied? Surely my soul mate should know such things.

Shouldn't he?

He stopped the car and turned in the seat. I wouldn't have minded if he'd have been bare-chested at this moment, but unfortunately he'd put on a purple LSU T-shirt before we left the levee. He said it'd been in his car since his last workout, which made me wonder how often he worked out. And also if the fabric smelled like him, post workout. Which, in my opinion, was probably a pretty awesome smell.

The streetlight in front of the Cakery cast bright white beams that bounced off his face and made his smile sparkle.

"Does anyone ever have to wonder what you're thinking?" he asked.

Evidently, you do. Or you'd simply tell me your age, how many kids you want, and precisely how long you want to wait before we have the official gathering of family and friends. Do you want a church wedding? Or a levee? Cause I really enjoyed Mama and Zip's wedding today, so a levee wedding would be fine. And what about the reception? Mama and Zip had everything I wanted. Except the money dance. They didn't have one, and I really want a money dance. Don't you?

"Jezze?" he prompted, and I realized I hadn't spoken.

"Yes?"

"I asked you a question," he said, grinning.

"I asked you one first," I said then I stuck my chin out a notch. No need to let him think I was going to be a pushover wife. I asked about his age a good second before he asked about my thinking habits.

"Nineteen," he said, smirking. "I'm nineteen."

"All right," I said, satisfied. Four years older than me. That'd work. "Yeah, sometimes people have to wonder about what I'm thinking."

"So, I've got a question for you, Jezebel Thibodeaux, since I wouldn't mind learning some of your thoughts." He draped his arm across the seat and touched my hair. Barely. But enough that a frisson passed from the top of my head down my eyelids, my nose, my mouth, the spot right behind my ears, my throat, my pride, my joy, my belly...and everywhere.

Goodness, if a touch could do this, what would a kiss do? I bet he didn't slobber like Cale. Or inhale like Derrick Walker. Or try to bruise your lips like Sid Lambert (the first guy I ever kissed, in one of those spin-the-bottle games when we were twelve). No, I bet his kisses were...

Perfect.

"Jezze?" he prodded.

"What ya wanna know?" I asked, or at least that's what I attempted to say. It came out as more of a choked kind of gurgle thing that made him laugh. I cleared my throat, tried again. "What?"

"If you're not ready to call it a night yet, we could spend some time together."

All right. I could nearly hear Mr. Miyagi from Karate Kid. Breathe in. Breathe out. Wax on. Wax off. (Okay, the wax on and off deal didn't apply in this situation, but I couldn't very well stop Miyagi when he's coaching. I mean, the man could catch a fly with chopsticks!) I cleared my throat, slowed my heart rate. "What did you want to do?"

"Believe it or not, I never got a piece of wedding cake at the reception. And I've got a killer sweet tooth."

"Me too." Oh Lord. He had a sweet tooth. Like me. And we'd have kids with sweet teeth too. I smiled, wide, showing each and every one of my sweet teeth. And I fought the urge to propose.

"So, you think the Cakery might be able to spare something for a couple of sweet tooths?" he asked.

"I suppose so."

He parked behind the shop then followed me in.

Within minutes, we were sitting at the breakfast nook, my own private haven, sipping coffee and eating beignets with extra sugar. I'd sat here plenty of times before, pondering the mysteries of my right man. And now that he sat here with me, it felt very *right*.

"So, tell me about you, Jezze," he said, then he bit into his beignet.

"What about me?"

"What do you like? What do you do? What are your plans?"

Okay, he about covered it all. And now I had to decide how honest I wanted to be. What do I like? *You*. What do I do? *Um, dream of my right man, which, of course, is you*. What are my plans? *Let's see...that'd be marrying you, having a house full of kids with you and running the Cakery, again, with you.* Te-dah.

"Jezze?"

Dang it, I hadn't said a word. Again. I decided I wouldn't go for blatant honesty. Didn't want to scare him off, or anything like that by asking him if his mother smoked during pregnancy (Aunt Edna had read an article that said that mothers who smoked during pregnancy decreased the sperm count of their sons, which mght limit our ability to have all those babies we want).

"Okay," I said. "I like working at the Cakery. I plan to run it one day, but I'm going to build on, add a restaurant and possibly a gift shop. I'll start college at Southeastern after I graduate from Riverside and I'll get a degree in Nutrition to help me run Thibodeaux's. What about you?" I asked, rattling off the entire shebang in two seconds flat.

"There's not much more to tell that I didn't cover already in the drive over."

Uh-oh. What the heck did I miss? Thankfully, he was willing to provide a do-over.

"I'm getting my degree in Business Administration so I can take my father's territory when he retires. I do plan to increase our coverage, though. Expand through northern Louisiana and possibly western Mississippi."

"That sounds great," I said. So, he had big goals for his family business. So did I. And he knew my family and they liked him, which was good.

But, shoot, I hadn't met his.

A little sting of panic pinched my temples. What if they didn't like me? What if they thought I was crazy, like Mama and Aunt Edna? (And no, I'm not calling them anything that they don't call themselves.) What if I *am* crazy? Not bad crazy, but Thibodeaux crazy. And would they mind if I was? Lord, I needed to meet his parents, needed to make that happen. And quick.

"Were your parents there tonight?" I asked. "At the wedding? Did I meet them?"

He finished chewing his beignet, swallowed some coffee. Then his face altered a bit, went kind of serious, like I'd said something wrong.

"No," he said.

"Oh." I could tell I'd hit a sore spot, and I didn't know whether to keep prodding or let it be. Right now, letting it be seemed the smart move.

T-Roy sat there a minute, sipped some more coffee and looked out the back window of the shop. I turned my eyes in the same direction. Nothing. Total blackness, except the porch light of Aunt Edna's house.

"I shouldn't have asked," I said, though I wasn't sure why I was apologizing.

He looked back at me and his heavy, lower lip pulled to one side, made his left dimple dip in. "Weddings are tough for my father," he said, his voice much quieter than it had been all night.

"Want to talk about it, or would you rather not?"

When he didn't answer immediately, I added, "You don't have to."

That luscious lower lip rolled up a bit, providing me with an I-really-do-need-to-talk half-frown/half-grin. "My mother passed away three years ago. A car accident on River Road."

I bit my inner cheek, stretched my hand across the table and placed it on top of his. Although I did feel that zing of energy as my skin met his, it wasn't that same, tense, sensual zing that I'd experienced earlier in the dunking booth. This was more of an I'm-sorry-and-I-want-to-help zing. The kind of close compassion that you experience at a wedding, when you hug the sobbing mother whose daughter is moving on to her life with her new husband. Or at a funeral, when you hold an elderly man who's just lost the woman he's loved for over fifty years.

I'd experienced both, since the residents of Grand Point were basically an extended family for Mama, Aunt Edna and me. We attended all weddings, where we felt the happiness of lovers uniting and the sadness of parents letting go. And all funerals, where we felt the joy of a full life lived and the sorrow of a full life lost.

Right now, I didn't sense any joy at all in what T-Roy Bertrand recalled. He wasn't remembering his mother's full life. He was simply remembering how much it hurt to lose her.

I didn't say a word, simply held my hand on his and waited. Waited to see if he wanted to tell more and needed someone to listen, or if he simply needed a comforting hand. Either way, I wanted to be there.

"He hasn't driven down River Road since that night. Can't get near it without seeing her car, crumpled and mangled and completely entombing her body."

"I'm sorry," I whispered, amazed at how quickly the conversation had turned solemn. Very solemn. And touched beyond words that he was willing to talk about it to me.

"He hasn't been to a wedding since," T-Roy said. "But he wanted Zip to know how happy he was for him, and he asked me to go. He truly wants everyone to experience what he shared with Mom."

T-Roy turned his hand, squeezed my palm and grinned. "More than you bargained for, huh? Oddly enough, I've never talked to anyone else about it."

I was about to tell him that I was glad that he trusted me enough to talk about it. And I was about to tell him that he could trust me forever. As long as we both shall live. But at that very moment, Aunt Edna came barreling down the driveway in her new Buick (a Regal this time) and sped past the Cakery fishtailing as she headed toward her house.

"Something wrong with her?" T-Roy asked.

"Nope," I said, "That's the way she drives. She used to trudge along like a turtle, but for the past few years, she's converted to Speed Racer."

He laughed out loud, and I was glad to see it. Crazy Aunt Edna had done the impossible, lightened our mood. With the mere stomping of the accelerator.

"Hang on," I said, standing and making my way toward the telephone. "Watch this."

He turned in his chair to see me pick up the cordless phone and wait.

I watched her grab a bunch of stuff from the trunk of her car, slam it shut then totter to the house. "Three, two, one," I said.

And the phone rang.

Walking toward T-Roy, I turned the receiver so he could view the caller id.

Thibodeaux, Edna.

He laughed again.

"Hello, Aunt Edna," I said in my best singsong voice.

"Oh, child," she said, panting. "I was making sure that was you down there. You with T-Roy Bertrand?"

"Yes, ma'am."

"He treating you right?"

"Yes, ma'am."

"Tell me something. What kind of car is that he's driving? It was too dark for me to see it under the shade of that oak tree down there."

"It's a Mustang, Aunt Edna," I said. "It's an older one. Hang on. I'll check the year." I put a hand over the mouthpiece on the telephone. "What year is your car?"

His thick brown brows raised a hair, but he answered, "It's a sixty-five fastback, but I only drive it when I'm home. At school, I drive a Saturn."

"A sixty-five fastback," I said into the phone. "But he only drives it when he's home. When he's at LSU, he drives a Saturn."

"Well, a Saturn isn't a Buick, but they're both made by GM, right?" Aunt Edna asked.

"Is Saturn made by General Motors?" I asked T-Roy.

His face showed genuine astonishment, though I didn't know why. Didn't everyone's aunt have a Buick fetish?

"It's a GM," he said. "They've stopped making them now, but mine runs great, and I like it for traveling around school."

"Yep, it's GM," I repeated, stating only the part Aunt Edna was interested in knowing.

"Fine then," she said. "That'll do, I suppose. All right, child, I'm heading to bed. You're staying over here tonight, I reckon, right?"

Mama and Zip had fixed a room for me in the new house, but I still had my room at Aunt Edna's too. They had all informed me repetitively that I was welcomed at each home, and in truth, I planned to stay at both.

"Yep, I'll be there."

"All right, honey. I'm turning on in then, okay? It's been a heck of a day, hasn't it? Heck of a good day, I'd say."

"Heck of a day, Aunt Edna," I whispered, and I gazed at my right man. I hung up. And yawned. Big.

T-Roy saw and chuckled. "I bet you're beat, aren't ya? You probably got up and helped your mom with all the wedding prep."

"I did, but I'm not really ready to—" I couldn't even finish the sentence before I yawned again.

"Come on," he said. And then *he* picked up the dishes and took them to the sink.

I could really get used to having T-Roy Bertrand around. A sensitive hottie who doesn't mind helping out a tad in the kitchen. So, how long do I wait before I propose?

"Let me walk you home, Miss Thibodeaux," he said.

Miss Thibodeaux. Did he know that the way he said it made goosebumps trickle down my arms and made my pride and joy salute? Probably not. Someday I'd tell him. But not tonight. There's only so far you can go on a first date. Which this wasn't, technically, since he hadn't picked me up.

Or was it?

Did it count if the guy only took you home? Or did you have to start with him at your front door for it to count as a full-fledged date?

We closed the Cakery and walked down the stone path that led to Aunt Edna's (the path actually formed a Y now, where it branched out to the new house on the left, but T-Roy and I kept right). As we progressed down the path, he reached for my hand, clasped his fingers with mine. Another zing shot up my arm. This one, like the one in the dunking booth, was strong. So strong that it made me laugh out loud.

He stopped walking.

"S-sorry," I whispered.

"What is it?" he asked. We were a few steps shy of the porch, close enough for the shadow of the roof to kiss his face. Adding mystery. And increasing my infatuation.

"I guess I'm just happy," I said honestly.

He put his finger on my lower lip, held it there for a brief moment of time. But a moment that I'd remember forever. "Being happy is a good thing," he said.

"Yeah, it is," I admitted, enjoying the feel of my lip moving against his fingertip with each word.

He ran the finger down my chin. "I've enjoyed this," he said. "You're as unique as I suspected."

Okay, that was a compliment if I ever heard one. So, go on. Kiss me. Kiss me now.

"Sweet dreams, Miss Thibodeaux," he said. And he removed the finger. Released my hand.

I started to shiver. It wasn't over yet. This couldn't be it. But he took a step back and waited for me to go inside.

No way. No freaking way.

"When do you go back to LSU?" I asked, trying to disguise the panic in my voice, to make it sound like mere curiosity.

I failed.

"Tomorrow afternoon."

"Oh."

He stood there, still waiting. Did he have a girlfriend? Was that it? Someone in Baton Rouge that he wouldn't cheat on, or something like that? Cause I have a phone inside. He could call her and break up over the phone. Hey, it happens. And then, we could pick up with that finger on my lip thing and see where it led.

I waited.

He waited.

And so...I blurted.

"Can I kiss you?" Well, shoot. So much for keeping my cool.

His mouth spread into his cheeks. Dimples dipped. Eyes twinkled (yeah, I know, twinkle isn't typically an adjective for guys, but in this case, it fit).

"Can I?" I asked again, and I tried not to listen to the tremble in each word. I would *not* say please. I wouldn't.

Unless he didn't answer me soon.

"Do you know how hard that would be, Jezze Thibodeaux?" he asked, and he stepped back toward me, his finger blessedly returning to my lip.

"To kiss me?" I asked. Oh, please please please don't say it'd be too hard. Cause I can help. It'd be easy. I swear!

"No, Miss Thibodeaux," he said, his face coming closer to mine, until his finger slid down and tilted my chin and his last words feathered across my lips, "To resist."

CHAPTER EIGHTEEN

I pulled my down-filled pillow to my chest and squeezed, trying to replay the intensity of last night's kiss.

"No, Miss Thibodeaux," I whispered into the stillness of my bedroom. "To resist." Then I giggled and burrowed into my comforter, thrilled at the memory that I was certain would last a lifetime. "T-Roy Bertrand," I declared aloud, "You sure know how to kiss."

"Is that so?"

I kicked the comforter, sheets and blankets away to view Aunt Edna, wearing her robe (lavender with frowning coffee cups) and leaning against the doorframe, with a sneaky smile creeping into her cheeks.

"Yep," I said, sitting straight up in the bed and bobbing my head for emphasis. "That's so."

"And to think, he's been in the shop umpteen times when you've been in the back cooking with Delilah. If I'd have only known..."

"Well, you should've known," I said, wagging a finger at her. "I mean, can't you see it? The two of us. Me and T-Roy Bertrand. Mrs. T-Roy Bertrand. He's the one, Aunt Edna. I finally met my right man."

"So, did you enlighten him to that fact, or are you leaving him to figure everything out on his own?"

"He doesn't know it yet, but we've got time. Nine years to be exact."

She laughed out loud. "You realize that your bonfire can be altered. Your groom can hit the top of that cake earlier. Or later, as the case may be."

"Well, by all means, don't make it later," I said. "I don't think I could stand it. But earlier...now, that could be a possibility, depending on how long it takes me to finish up at Southeastern."

She stepped into the room, leaned against the wall, and stared at me in shock. "The two of you talked about marriage?"

"Not yet, but we will."

She grinned knowingly. "And when do you suppose that'll be?"

I shrugged. "Don't know. Doesn't really matter though, does it? I mean, I know we're going to get married and all. As soon as he figures it out too, we'll be set."

"Make sure you keep your mama and I aware of the date, whenever you set one. I expect you'll want Thibodeaux's to cater the blessed event."

"Will do," I said, fluffing my pillow in my lap. "And Aunt Edna?"

"Yes, child?"

I loved the way she called me "child," even though at five-foot-six, I already had two inches on my aunt.

"You said I could tell you anything, right? Ask you any questions, confide anything I want to, and all that."

My white wicker vanity sat cattycornered on one side of the room. It took Aunt Edna three paces to reach it and half a second to plop down in the seat. "Good Lord, child, what did you do last night? Not that I'm going to be upset or anything, mind you, cause you can talk to your Aunt Edna. Then she crossed herself, but if my memory is right, she did it backwards.

I laughed. "No, Aunt Edna, we didn't do that."

She expelled a puff of wind that had to have started in her toes. "Thank God."

"But..."

"But what? You can't do this to me, Jezze Thibodeaux. I swear my heart isn't near as spunky as it was in my younger days."

"Aunt Edna, you're even more spunky, and you know it," I corrected. "But what I wanted to tell you about was his kiss."

Her entire body relaxed in the chair like a limp noodle. "Well, by all means then, spill it. I can handle a kiss."

"That's what I thought to," I said, flopping onto my belly and propping my chin in my palms. "Then I kissed T-Roy." I rolled over on my back, stretched my arms above my head and moaned.

"That good, huh?"

"That good. Of course, it probably wouldn't have been as spectacular if I'd let him stop when he wanted to." I flipped back over and grinned.

"Now, what the devil does that mean?" Aunt Edna asked.

I giggled, or at least I planned to. The sound I made sounded downright sinister. And that made me laugh even harder. Had I really attacked him?

Yep, I did.

And I liked it.

"What did you do, child?" she asked, examining my guilty face.

"He was trying to be too nice," I explained, shrugged. "You know, a sweet, soft kiss. On the lips, of course, but still, way too sweet."

"And?"

"And so when he started to pull away, I kind of followed Mama and Zip's example from the wedding."

"Lord Almighty," Aunt Edna declared. "I'm gonna kill my sister."

My chest tingled at the memory of T-Roy Bertrand's surprise, as I pulled him as close as possible and practically crawled up his strong body to invade his mouth. "Oh no, Aunt Edna, don't kill Mama. I think, thanks to her, I finally got it right."

"Have mercy."

"That's what I was thinking," I said, "the whole time I attacked him." Remembering the way his hands had bunched in my shirt—in *his* shirt—I scanned my room and spotted the white garment in the chair beside my bed. I rolled over, scooped it up, put it to my face and inhaled. "Never, ever wash this shirt," I said.

"Noted," Aunt Edna said. "And what did he do? I mean, when you *attacked* him?" Then she shook her head, mumbled, "I can't believe we're having this conversation."

"Well, he sure enough didn't fight me."

"I guess not. What red-blooded male would? But how did you get him started and then not—well, Jezebel Thibodeaux, you best tell your aunt what happened right this very second, before I go clear out of my mind with wondering."

"You called me Jezebel," I said, realizing exactly how much I'd shocked her.

And enjoying it.

"Heaven help me, you're gonna be the death of me, child."

"Oh, all right. To tell the honest to goodness truth, I got so carried away that I might not have stopped if he hadn't put on the brakes." I smiled confidently. T-Roy had looked like he wanted to die right then and there. And he'd wanted me as much as I wanted him.

Maybe even more.

"*He* put on the brakes?" she asked, disbelieving. "You're kidding."

"Nope," I said triumphantly. "He said that he didn't want to take advantage of me, and he felt like I was probably caught up in the whirlwind of Mama's wedding and all. But, I bet if I tried again…"

"Jezze!"

"Oh, come on, Aunt Edna," I said, laughing as I threw the feather pillow at her, "I'm messing with you."

"So you didn't attack that boy last night?"

"Sure I did, but I don't plan on doing it again."

She crossed herself again, and I think she got it right this time.

"Next time, I plan on him attacking me."

"Enough, child," Aunt Edna said, fanning her hand in front of her face. "I want you to talk to me and all, but the rest of this conversation is going to happen with your mama. I swear you're killing me. Now, when are you planning to see him again? Delilah won't be back for two weeks and if it can't wait that long, then I suppose I'll have to handle this heat on my own"

"He's leaving today," I said, and I didn't even try to hide my disappointment. "And he probably won't come back until Christmas."

"Good," she said. "I mean, not necessarily good, you know, but at least that will give your mama and Zip time to make it back home." She stood from the chair, evidently too fast, because she swayed a bit and held her head.

"You okay?" I asked.

She nodded. "I'm fine. Just can't get used to you growing up."

I scrambled off the bed and grabbed some clothes from my dresser. "I'll take a shower and then we can get started cooking. You need help since Mama's gone, don't ya? And I won't be here during the weekdays, so we better make the most of today," I rattled, glad that we'd had a chance to talk, even if she had acted like she'd rather had her teeth pulled. *All* of her teeth pulled.

"Quite a bit of energy you got going today, huh?" she asked.

"It's called," I started, sighed deeply, leaned against the wall and put my palm over my heart, "the energy of love."

"Mercy, you've got it bad."

I stepped into the bathroom, shut the door and yelled, "From what I saw of you and Mr. LeBlanc last night, I'd say you do too!"

I heard a faint "hmph" from the other side, but I'd bet my last beignet she was smiling.

CHAPTER NINETEEN

Within an hour, we were busy in the Cakery, cooking up the sweets that had been ordered for pickup on Monday. Aunt Edna worked on a batch of pralines while I mixed boiled cookies on the stove.

"Look Aunt Edna," I said, staring into the deep Magnalite pot that held the boiling mixture of milk, sugar, butter, and cocoa. Big, fat chocolate bubbles formed on the surface, then exploded with gusto. At the points where the large bubbles hadn't formed, tiny, pulsating pops occurred, as though the concoction was alive. And excited.

"What is it, Jezze?" she said, thinking something was wrong with the mix. "Too much cocoa?"

"No, ma'am," I said, mesmerized by the wild chaos of chocolate.

"Then what is it?"

"That's the way it felt. That bubbling, wild, frenzied, out of control feeling. Like my blood gyrated through my veins. Just like this chocolate." I ran a wooden spoon through the mass, noticing that the stroke wasn't even acknowledged by the mixture. It was too strong.

Too powerful.

"The way what felt?" Aunt Edna asked.

"T-Roy's kiss."

She touched my cheek then returned to her pralines. "Lordy, when you got it, you really got it, huh child?"

I nodded. "Yeah, I do, and if he and his daddy ever show up again out front, you best dang send him on back." I slid the pot off the eye, plopped in the peanut butter and oats and stirred. Then I dropped big spoonfuls on a long, stainless tray to cool.

"Don't worry, child," Aunt Edna said. "Whenever they come restock the Babineaux's, I'll make sure to let you know."

My hand stilled, suspended in mid-air, holding the wooden spoon as the next cookie blob slid messily onto the tray. "The—what?" I whispered. She *didn't* say it. Surely not. And why hadn't I asked T-Roy which product they distributed to the Cakery.

No, no, no. My right man was *not* the future butt budder rep.

No way.

Uh-uh.

"The Babineaux's," Aunt Edna said, taking the pot from me and finishing up with the cookies. "What is it, Jezze?"

"B-butt budder?" I whimpered. "His daddy is the butt budder rep?"

"Well, sure," Aunt Edna said then her thin brows shot up. "Oh, Jezze, what did you think he sold?"

"I didn't know," I said, swallowing thickly. "I thought maybe our cake decorating supplies, or our books, or even the boxes. Anything but the butt!" I took off my apron, tossed it on the desk.

"It's a good business he's got," she said. "Shoot, he covers all of southeast Louisiana, and he makes good money, I'm sure. Babireaux's is good stuff."

"I know that, Aunt Edna," and I recalled T-Roy's words last night.

"Good stuff, huh?" he'd said, when I'd squirted the entire tube down my front. Now it made sense that he brought me another tube. I bet the trunk of his Mustang had been filled with them. Cases, in fact.

"Oh my," I said, dropping into the desk chair. I'd kept my shirt on for the cooking, because I'd wanted to keep Aunt Edna happy. But I couldn't worry about that anymore, and I felt like I was suffocating in the kitchen.

The shirt came off.

Then the bra.

"Have mercy," Aunt Edna said. "Let me at least close the blinds." She darted across the room and quickly worked to twist the rod that controlled the thin slats. "That boy will be set for life when he takes over his daddy's territory, Jezze. He'll make good money, and he'll take good care of his family. What in the devil is wrong with you?"

"My right man," I whispered. "He's a butt budder rep in training."

"Vain," Aunt Edna spouted. "Since when did we ever teach you to be so vain?"

"I don't know, Aunt Edna," I said, dropping my head to the desktop and refusing to look at her. "It's ridiculous, I know, but I never planned to be married to a butt budder guy. It doesn't feel right."

"Pardon me, child, but aren't you the same girl who showed me just how right it felt a few minutes ago, courtesy of that chocolate in the pot."

"That's before I realized he was Bertrand the Butt Man."

"Good heavens," Aunt Edna said, clucking as she put the pot in the sink and filled it with hot water. "T-Roy Bertrand is a promising young man, the kind who spends time with his father cause he knows the man is lonelier than any poor soul should be since he lost his sweet Sylvie. You'd be blessed to have him, let me tell you."

"Yeah. No. I don't know," I mumbled into the desk. I thought back to last night. He'd tried to mention his father's job several times, and I'd cut him off each and every one.

The ringing of the phone on the desk sent my head straight up. I glared at it and at the displayed identification on the back.

Bertrand, Fenton G.

I'd been caught up in everything last night that I'd forgotten to give him my cell number. But the business line was in the book, and he'd obviously found it. "Oh no," I whispered then turned to gawk at Aunt Edna.

"That's his Daddy's name," she said. "And I bet your young fella is on the other end." She reached for the phone.

"No," I gasped. "I don't want to talk to him."

"The boy's done nothing wrong," Aunt Edna said, wrapping her fingers around the side of the receiver.

"I'm out," I mouthed. Then I grabbed my shirt, flung it on and headed out the back door, slamming it in my wake. It bounced against the facing, then cracked back open. I didn't bother shutting it completely.

I had to hear.

Standing on the back deck, I listened to Aunt Edna's end of the conversation. A conversation with my nearly-right-man.

"Hello, T-Roy, how are you?" she said. "Yeah, I heard you were heading back today...When ya planning to leave?...Yeah, um, she stepped out." Then Aunt Edna's voice lowered to a quiet hush, but I heard. "I can't lie to you, son, so don't ask me where. Yeah, I'm afraid she overreacted a bit about...uh-huh...uh-huh. I see. Well, I can't blame you, T-Roy. Not one bit...I'll tell her...You too, hon. Tell your daddy hello from me, and you be safe driving back to school." Then she disconnected.

I cracked open the door, stepped timidly back into the kitchen. "He knows, doesn't he?"

"I didn't tell him, but I won't lie for you."

"He asked?"

"He did. Seems he's used to people judging his daddy for what he sells, in spite of how awesome of a product it is or what a great job he does. I tell you one thing, I sure can't live without Babineaux's, and neither can your mama."

"I have a tube in my purse for my chapped lips," I muttered.

"So what's the problem?"

"I don't really know."

"Well, I don't either. But I can tell you right now that T-Roy Bertrand isn't the kind of fella to sit around and beg for your attention. And he sure as heck ain't the type that will go looking for a woman. Shoot, there're lots of girls out there who are smart enough to know that the boy's future is set and has a smart, and sweet, head on his shoulders."

"What else did he say?"

"He said if you want to talk to him, he'll be home for another hour. If he doesn't hear from you, he won't call again." She paused to let it sink in. "So, you gonna call him?"

I left the kitchen, walked the short distance through the hallway and peered at the front of the store. Bouncing Boodie bobbed at me while he showcased the Babineaux's Butt Budder. The display was nearly empty, as usual. The stuff was so popular we could hardly restock fast enough. Everyone in the whole parish loved it, including me.

I just didn't want to be married to it.

"Are you?" Aunt Edna asked. She'd obviously followed me in my journey to the front. "Are you gonna call him, Jezze?"

"I'm sorry, Aunt Edna," I said, my heart crumbling like an overcooked praline. "I can't."

CHAPTER TWENTY

True to his word, T-Roy Bertrand didn't call back. As a matter of fact, during the next three years, I only saw the future butt budder rep at the bonfires on Christmas Eve.

Each time we looked directly at each other. Each time we didn't speak. And each time, he brought a date.

A date. Not any ol' date, mind you, but a date that made my throat close in. Caused my hands to clench into tight fisted balls. Forced me to contemplate the decency of tossing the leggy blonde (year one), the buxom brunette (year two) and the black-haired beauty (year three) over the side of the levee. To be beaten by the cane. Then squashed by a barge.

Not that I was bitter.

Or that I even cared who T-Roy Bertrand dated. He wasn't my right man, after all.

And maybe if I kept telling myself that, I'd start believing t.

As it was, I'd gone out with approximately three guys since that wild and wicked kiss I shared with the butt man. And as it was, I'd traded the opportunity to date the official butt budder guy for the chance to date...royal butts.

But hey, college would start soon. Very soon. In two weeks, to be exact (though I suppose you could count it as starting today, since I was about to go ahead and move into the dorm). Surely, Southeastern Louisiana University sported its share of hunky hotties. And one of them, of course, was my right man. My *real* right man. The one who didn't deal with the phrase "jock itch" on a daily basis.

Hopefully.

I carried another laundry basket filled with clothes to the trunk of my car. Yes, *my* car. Zip, Mama and Aunt Edna surprised me with a 2002 Buick (what else?) for graduation. And yes, they did buy the biggest Buick possible, a Park Avenue. Aunt Edna insisted, saying that she wanted to make sure I'd be safe in case of an accident. She didn't seem to care that driving a land barge to college wouldn't do much for my social status.

Anyway, I put the last of my things in the gigantic trunk and slammed it shut. Mama and Zip stood on the porch, Zip smiling, Mama bawling.

"Geezum, Mama," I said, crossing the yard in nothing flat and flinging my arms around her. "I'll probably come home every weekend. It's not like Hammond's all that far away."

"It's only an hour, sweetie," Zip said, patting Mama's back. "Heck, we can drive over and have dinner with her during the week if you want."

"Sure you can," I said. "As long as you bring beignets."

Mama sniffed loudly and attempted a little laugh. "Deal," she whispered.

"You gonna be okay, Mama?"

"Sure, honey, I'll be fine. Takes some getting used to, that's all. Seems like we should still be in that hospital, you know, watching that nurse bring you in and put you in my arms. You were such a beautiful little thing."

"You're saying I'm not gorgeous now?" I asked, backing away from her and fluffing my hair with my palm.

"You know you are," she said, and blessedly, her tears slowed. "You're a Thibodeaux. Of course you're gorgeous."

"And a DuBois," Zip added, "Which isn't at all a bad thing." He grinned at me lovingly, white teeth against a tan face. Even now, those looks of his, the I-love-my-daughter looks, made my heart swell.

I hugged him, then turned and started toward Aunt Edna's house.

"Oh, honey!" Mama yelled, "You can't." She frowned, looked to Zip for help.

"Your aunt said for us to tell you goodbye," he explained.

"She doesn't want to see me?" I asked, and I knew that couldn't be further from the truth. Aunt Edna wouldn't dare let me leave without saying goodbye.

"She's been real upset about you going," Mama said. "And she was afraid she'd bring you down."

"That's ridiculous," I said, continuing my trek across the yard and up on her porch.

I hadn't been able to spend as much time with Aunt Edna this summer, since every spare moment she had was spent with Mr. LeBlanc. But I didn't mind. She'd finally found her right man, and I expected the two of them to tie the knot real soon.

"Aunt Edna," I called, entering the house. All of my college things had been stored at Mama and Zip's; consequently, I'd spent most of the summer over there. Now, entering this house and noticing that something seemed *different*, I realized how long it had been since I'd stepped one foot inside. All of my time with Aunt Edna this summer had been at the Cakery. None of it here, in the house that didn't have its usual sounds and smells. No spicy Cajun cooking or lavender bath salts. No Zydeco music pulsing through the living room. As a matter of fact, the house didn't even resemble what I remembered.

Too quiet. Too lonely. Too sad.

"Aunt Edna?"

I walked down the hallway, entered the kitchen.

And saw her, her entire body slumped over the kitchen table as though she'd passed out, but her eyes were open and her right hand fumbled with the edge of a teacup, making the contents slosh over the side.

"Aunt Edna!" I screamed.

"I told them I couldn't see you today," she mumbled. "Supposed to tell you," she paused, swallowed, "I'm with Will. You need to go to school."

I crossed the room and squatted beside her, then gently lifted her so that her body slumped against mine, her tired head resting on my shoulder.

"Sorry, Jezze."

"I'm going to get Mama," I said. "Let me get you to the couch. We'll call a doctor and get some help."

"This is help," she muttered, and she waved toward the tea.

I helped her stand and walked her down the hall.

"They help any more I'll be dead," she mumbled.

I lowered her to the couch, placed a pillow behind her head. "What is it, Aunt Edna? What's going on?"

"Nothing a little chemo and radiation won't fix, or that's what the doctor says. Course, I gotta agree to it, now, don't I?" Her lip quivered, making me notice the lack of color in its usually vibrant curves. The washed out flesh of her face. Dark, tired gray circles under her eyes. Did she not plan on telling me? And how long had she been hiding the truth?

I started to speak, but stopped. I couldn't.

I just couldn't.

"Cancer, sweetie," she said, knowing that I wasn't able to ask. "Awful stuff."

"But they can treat it, right? You need to let them, Aunt Edna. You have to try," I said, not fathoming that the toughest lady I knew would ever give up on anything. The last time we went to the pig, she was still trying to beat her right man at the checkout counter, in spite of the new high speed scanners the Piggly Wiggly had installed. Aunt Edna wasn't a quitter. About anything. And I wasn't about to watch her do it now. I wouldn't let her quit on life.

She shrugged, and the movement started a bout of coughing that seemed to shake her very core. Tears dripped down her sallow cheeks, crossed her lips. She didn't bother to wipe them away.

So I did.

"Let me get Mama," I said. "And Zip. I'll call Mr. LeBlanc and have him bring you something."

Aunt Edna's entire body went rigid, jerked in my arms. "No. Not Will. He doesn't know. I can't do this to him."

My mouth dropped open. Aunt Edna and William LeBlanc had been inseparable since that night on the levee at Mama and Zip's reception three years ago. She'd actually confessed her love for him and had told me as recently as this past spring that if he asked her, she'd marry the man. "He doesn't know?" I asked.

"I ended it. Last month," she said. "When I first suspected the reason for my dizzy spells. He doesn't deserve to go through this again. His first wife died with it. That nearly killed him. I won't do it to him. I love him too much for that, Jezze. And you won't tell him."

My heart cramped with pain. She'd found him, her right man. And now she couldn't have him, because she refused to hurt him. "But Aunt Edna—"

"Swear to me, child."

I swallowed. She was letting herself die. And I wasn't going to stand for it. "On one condition," I heard myself say, and I hoped that she believed me (in truth, I'd never do anything she asked me not to, but I couldn't let her know that now). Tough love. That's what she'd given me plenty of times. And that's what I'd give her now. She had to let herself get better. She had to try whatever the doctors said.

Had to.

"What?" she asked, her eyes squinting as she pondered my request.

"You try the treatment. Let the doctors help."

"I'm drinking the tea. That's not helping."

I knew of Aunt Edna's partiality for the voodoo healers. A cancer-fixing tea would be right up their alley, and certainly nothing a real doctor would recommend. "That tea came from a doctor? A real one? One who works in a hospital or an office and has honest-to-goodness patients?" I asked.

She cut her eyes at me. "Close enough."

"You promise me you'll go to a doctor and try the treatments, and then I promise you I won't tell Mr. LeBlanc. But if you don't, I'll tell."

She shifted on the couch, scooted up on her elbows so that her eyes met mine. Then she licked her parched lips. "On one condition," she said.

At this rate, we'd have a new president before Aunt Edna and my conditions ceased. I grinned. I couldn't help it. Aunt Edna had to have things her way. Always. Now was no exception.

"What's that?" I asked.

"That you'll go on and head for school today. You won't let a little thing like my cancer stop you from reaching your goal."

"I have two weeks before school starts," I informed.

"But you'd planned to go on up, get settled in, and if you change that plan, I won't go to the doctor. I swear."

I kissed her cheek. "You're gonna let Mama and Zip take care of you?"

"As long as they don't smother me."

"You can always take your shirt off whenever you're feeling smothered," I said. "It works for me."

And then, my real Aunt Edna crept into the frail frame on the couch. And slammed a pillow into my face. "Don't know what to do with you, child."

"Love you, Aunt Edna," I whispered, hugging her.

"Love you too." Her thin arms squeezed against my back as though she expected this to be our last hug. But it wouldn't. And I had to keep telling myself that, or I'd never walk out that door.

"Love you," I repeated, before finally gaining the courage to leave. And praying that I would, in fact, see her again.

Mama and Zip were waiting for me when I exited her house.

"Sorry, kiddo," Zip said. "She made us swear not to tell you."

"I've never broken a promise to her, Jezebel," Mama whispered. "I hope you'll forgive me."

"I understand." I took a deep breath. Exhaled. "I got her to agree to try the treatment. You'll have to make sure she gets to the doctor though."

"We will," Mama said.

A black pick-up truck started up the asphalt beside the Cakery. I recognized the truck immediately, and walked toward it as the driver neared.

The window slid down and I viewed the same dark chocolate eyes that haunted my every dream. Only the ones in my dream were missing the surplus of wrinkles framing their depths. "Hello, Mr. Bertrand," I said.

Fenton Bertrand had classic features, wavy dark hair in spite of his age, tanned skin, a bright smile, straight jaw. Everything that T-Roy had.

Only older.

And, incredibly enough, the elder Bertrand had found it in his heart to accept me as a potential daughter-in-law, regardless of A) his son and I had barely spoken in the past three years, and B) I had made no attempt to hide the fact that I didn't plan to marry a butt budder man.

"I heard you were leaving today," Fenton said, climbing from the truck.

"Yes, sir," I said.

"Don't suppose you told that son of mine, did you?"

"We haven't exactly been on speaking terms," I said. "And I heard he's dating that girl that got Miss St. John. What's her name again, Clarise?"

"Denise," he said. "That's temporary. They're all temporary."

I shrugged. "He can date whoever he wants."

"I'd have to disagree," his daddy said, "But he passes the time all right, I suppose."

Grinning, I asked, "Did he know you were coming to see me?"

"I'll never tell," he said, holding his palms in front of him in defense. He'd been visiting me regularly ever since that first night, the night that T-Roy had turned me boneless with his kiss. In this very spot.

I looked down. My knees started to feel week at the memory. Would I ever be kissed like that again?

"You okay, dear?" Mr. Bertrand asked.

"Fine," I said. Not as fine as I was that night, and maybe not as fine as I'd ever be again, but fine.

A loud creak echoed behind me and I turned to see Aunt Edna, her hand clutching the handle of the screen door on her porch as though she'd crumble if she let go.

"You said you'd leave," she accused.

"I am," I said. "I'm keeping my part of the deal, but you have to do the same."

"Then why ain't ya gone?" she asked, cocking her head in true Aunt Edna style.

"Mr. Bertrand came by, and I thought I'd be polite and visit for a minute," I said, trying to act as sassy as I normally would with Aunt Edna. I didn't want her to think I wouldn't treat her the same as always even though, deep inside, I wanted to run across the yard, grab hold of her and never let her go.

"Actually," Fenton Bertrand said, "I came to see Jezze before she left, but I also came to see you, Edna."

"Me?" Aunt Edna said. She moved slowly across the porch and sat down on the swing. "What for?"

Mr. Bertrand returned to his truck, withdrew a shiny purple box with a hot pink bow. "I brought you something."

Aunt Edna smiled. It was a lopsided, in pain kind of smile, but it was a smile, nonetheless. "Well, bring it on over, Fenton. I can't very well run and get it."

He laughed, crossed the yard and handed the gift to my aunt.

She gained a burst of energy (presents always excited her) and ripped it open like a kid on Christmas morning, flinging the bow behind her and peeking beneath the lid. "You're too much, Fenton," she said.

Mama, Zip and I moved closer to see the items she'd removed from the box and placed beside her on the swing. Three tubes of Babineaux's Butt Budder, a Babineaux's Butt Budder baseball cap and another baseball cap that was covered in shiny, lime green sequins.

"What's it all for?" Aunt Edna asked.

"Well, Zip told me about what you're going through," he said. "He thought I might be able to help."

Aunt Edna glared at her brother-in-law. "Zip?" she accused.

"I swear, Edna," Zip said. "I told him before you warned me not to say anything."

She looked skeptical, but she nodded. "All right. So, what's all this for?"

"For the treatments," Fenton said. "You can use the butt budder on your head when," he paused.

"When my hair falls out? Don't worry, Fenton. I know what'll happen," she said.

"Well, yes. It's supposed to help. You put a light coat on the skin to keep it from becoming irritated."

"And the hats?" Aunt Edna asked.

"Why, that's to make certain you can advertise our awesome product, if you're so inclined," he said, lifting the baseball cap with Boodie on the front. "And to let you go sassy when you're in the mood," he said, indicating the green sequins.

"You're a good friend, Fenton," she said. Then she raised her arms and waited for Mr. Bertrand to climb on top of the porch and accept her embrace. Her hands trembled against his back, and when he stood, we watched her teardrops fall. "I suppose I'll give it a shot," she said. "The treatments and all. But, you know, they don't make any promises. I still might not make it."

"Oh no you don't, sis," Mama said. "You're too tough an ol' broad for a little thing like cancer to bring you down."

Aunt Edna smiled, which looked kind of odd with all the teardrops streaming down her face.

"You know, Edna," Fenton said, squatting in front of her on the porch. "I realize you don't want Will to know."

"You didn't tell him, did you, Fenton?" she asked. "Tell me you didn't."

"No, I didn't," he admitted. "But I can tell you that I went to his store today and the poor guy is miserable. Personally, I think what you're doing by not telling him is much worse than if you did."

Aunt Edna frowned. "He's not doing well?"

Fenton shook his head.

"I've missed him," she said and she wiped her shaky palms down her face to clear the tears. "I've missed him so."

"Let me call him, Edna," Mama pleaded. "He'll want to be with you. Fenton's right. You're hurting him more by keeping him in the dark."

Aunt Edna nodded. "I guess you're right." Then she turned toward me. "I thought I told you to leave," she said. And she raised her brows.

I gave her one more kiss, hugged Mama, Zip and Mr. Bertrand, then turned to go.

At the end of the driveway, I looked back. Mama, Zip, and Fenton were all gathered around Aunt Edna. They would take care of her until I came back. I knew they would.

But I didn't want to go.

"If you change that plan, I won't go to the doctor. I swear."

My head pounded and my fingers clenched on the wheel. Yes, I had to go to school if I wanted Aunt Edna to keep her end of the deal. And she would. She wouldn't break a promise to me. I knew that. But I just couldn't leave.

Not yet.

I had to think about things, about everything that had transpired since I climbed out of bed this morning, when my future had seemed so hopeful and my aunt had seemed okay.

Turning right would send me in the direction I needed to go, Hammond. I really should get started, drive on over, get settled in. But classes didn't begin for two weeks. So a couple of hours wouldn't make that much of a difference.

I turned left.

CHAPTER TWENTY-ONE

After pulling the pink checked blanket from my trunk, I pressed the fabric to my face and inhaled my aunt. She'd saved this blanket, the same one that Big Mama had spread on the ground during those afternoons that she'd taken them to the cane fields. Aunt Edna had held onto the blanket for years, hoping to give it to me one day when I headed off for my first day at college so I could find comfort in its gentleness when I was scared or confused. Comfort in knowing that I had something precious, something that had nurtured my aunt and my mama when they were having a tough time dealing with a cruel world.

The thing was so worn and faded that you could barely tell where the pink squares ended and the white ones began. Aunt Edna had sewn new piping around the edge to make sure it held up. Consequently, it had become a beautiful collaboration of old and new, past and future, what was and what would be.

Today, thinking back to her frail body, slumped on that kitchen table, the sudden punch of the symbolism stabbed my heart. Aunt Edna and Mama, the past. And me, the future.

Right now, we were all meshed together, holding on strong. But eventually, the piping would pull away. The threads of the fabric would wear through. And right now, one of the colors in the pattern was trying to fade away.

I climbed the levee, then sat down in the bare patch of land that held my bonfire each December, the space that had been the beginning of Mama and Zip's love. The place where Aunt Edna and Mr. LeBlanc had first realized their feelings. I sat there, and I thought about all we'd shared, and all we'd yet to share. About love and life and family.

The three of us, striving to make it, striving to survive. To keep the Thibodeaux name strong. To keep our business strong. To keep the quest for our right men strong.

Mama had found hers with Zip. Aunt Edna had found hers too.

I clutched the soft fabric in my fists. She'd just realized her feelings, had finally found the thing she wanted most. A never-ending love. "God, don't take her now," I said, my teeth clenched together in fierce determination. "She deserves to be happy, if only for a little while. Please don't take her now. Don't!"

My tears caused the fabric to blur, so that I couldn't see squares at all, but merely a pale pink hue that puddled in my lap. I leaned my head forward, inhaled her sweet scent once more...and surrendered my body to sleep.

I dreamed of rose petals, red and white and pink, shifting beneath my feet. Of love. And friendship. And everything in between. Gusting breezes from the Mississippi jutted over the levee and penetrated my mind, slapped against my face, tangled my hair.

The smells of cotton candy and funnel cakes and sausage and jambalaya mingled in the breeze. A jazz band played the wedding march, faster and faster and faster. Children squealed with glee while they tossed mounds of birdseed. Horse hooves clip-clop, clip-clopped against steamy pavement and announced the bride's arrival.

I saw Mama, pulling the door open and peering inside, exclaiming in delight over the bride.

Over *me*.

I saw Aunt Edna, healthy and happy and vibrant, squealing as she rushed down the levee to meet us.

I step from the carriage, look around to see all of Grand Point attending the event. They cheer and chant and someone even starts the wave. I watch as it ripples down the levee's edge as if crossing the endzone of an LSU game.

Laughing, I turn my attention from the feisty crowd to the handsome man at the top, standing at the same spot where his wooden counterpart has climbed each year. And, like the wooden groom, waiting to capture his bride.

My heart thunders wildly in my chest and my breath catches in my throat. It is because of him that I feel this way, because of him that my life is complete, or will be, as soon as I say "I do."

"I love you," I mouth, and I wait for his response.

"Jezze," T-Roy says. I close my eyes, and amazingly, I can feel his arms encircle me, pull me close, hold me as if he'll never, ever let me go. "Jezze," he says again.

I open my eyes, lick my lips.

And kiss my right man.

Hungry to taste every bit of him, I plunge my tongue inside, moaning in contentment when his hands tighten their grip on my back. He wants me. I can feel it. And goodness knows, I want him. I don't attempt to stop, but absorb the delicious warmth of his mouth with thrusting sweeps of my tongue. His intense growl of desire gives me courage, the courage to ask for what I've never had. I pull away, panting, and open my eyes.

The wedding carriage is gone, as are the horses, the food, the crowd. Instead, the levee is cloaked in the faint blanket of darkness that composes early evening. The area that had been so crammed with people in the dream is vacant. Vacant, that is, except for two people, clutching each other like wild animals whose sole purpose in life is to procreate.

And they're ready to fulfill that goal.

"T-Roy," I whispered, shocked at what had happened, but not totally disappointed at the outcome.

"Delilah called," he said, his voice raspy. "Said you didn't make it to the school when she expected you to. She asked me to look for you."

I blinked. Didn't speak. Didn't know what to say.

"I swear, I tried to wake you, but then, well, I couldn't stop you," he said. Then he grinned, a sneaky, I-probably-shouldn't-admit-this grin. "Well, okay. I'm sure I could have, but I didn't want to."

"At least you're honest," I said, raising up and pulling away from him, then hating the cold shiver that spread over me as a result.

"I'll let them know you're okay," he said, withdrawing his cell and sending a quick text to someone, presumably my mother. Then he picked up the blanket that had slid to the ground and dusted it off before handing it back to me. "Guess you'll be heading to Hammond now."

I nodded.

"You gonna be okay? They told me about your aunt."

"I'll be fine. Thanks." I stood then I turned, looked at him, and my insides went right back to boiling chocolate in a Magnalite pot. Who in the world was I trying to fool? No one, and I mean no one, did this to me.

No one, except T-Roy Bertrand, *my* right man.

"So, how long you plan on fighting it?" he asked, interrupting my thoughts.

"Fighting what?"

"The fact that you can't live without me."

I laughed. "What?"

"Admit it, Miss Thibodeaux," he said. "I could have had just about anything I wanted a minute ago." He nodded toward the flat patch of earth that had loosened beneath our squirming.

"You always take advantage of women when they're sleeping?" I asked, "You don't even know what man I was thinking of. And if that's the only way you can get what you want, that's downright sad."

He smirked. "Bet you think you don't talk in your sleep either, huh?"

I felt the blood pool to my cheeks. "You should be ashamed," I said, and then I felt stupid, since that sounded like something Aunt Edna (or someone her age) would say.

"I should," he admitted, "But I'm not."

I whirled to leave, lost my balance, then cringed when his strong arms caught me.

"You okay, Jezze?" he asked. Dang, that voice still reminded me of cocoa butter.

I jerked away. "I'm fine, thanks. Even better if you'd leave me be."

He turned loose quick. Too quick. And I stumbled forward a couple of paces. "Tell ya what, Miss Thibodeaux," he said. "I'll make you a deal."

"What's that?"

"I'll 'leave you be,' as you asked, for the time being, but I want something from you in return."

"What?"

"I want you to think about it, about that kiss we shared outside of your Aunt Edna's, and about what we nearly shared here tonight. Think about it, every day, from now until Christmas."

I swallowed. I knew good and well that I'd be doing that anyway, but I wasn't about to admit that to the cocky butt man. "And then what?"

"Then I'll leave you alone. Until Christmas Eve."

Another swallow. And a bristle of heat on the back of my neck, but he didn't know that. "What happens Christmas Eve?" I asked.

"Then, if you can honestly say that you don't want to feel that again, I'll leave you alone forever."

I waited. I wasn't going to ask about the alternative. Surely he'd tell me.

But he waited a minute. Smiled. Well, shoot.

"And if I do want to feel it again?"

"Then you will."

"Deal," I said. Okay, so I knew I wanted to feel it again. Several times. But maybe, if I gave myself a few months, I could cool down those crazy emotions that take over whenever he comes around. Or speaks. Or touches me. Or...

Dang.

His dadgum gorgeous grin crept into his cheeks, making those dimples flat out wink at me. My stomach quivered, and so did a few other spots. Have mercy. He knew exactly what he was doing.

And it ticked me off.

"I can't marry a butt budder rep," I said. *Hah! Take that!*

He came closer. Put that one finger on my lower lip and held it there while my pride and joy tried to reach him on their own accord. Then he leaned close, slid that finger down and brushed his lips against mine.

I moaned.

And he laughed. "You realize, Miss Thibodeaux," he said, cupping my chin in his hand. "You don't have to worry about marrying a butt budder rep. If you'll recall, I haven't asked."

I whirled away and attempted Aunt Edna's kill-the-cockroach move all the way down the levee. Unfortunately, the mad punching of the balls of my feet against the soft earth caused me to lose my balance again, and I ended up barely stopping my rapid descent before I headed into the street.

I heard him laughing, but I didn't turn around. I just climbed in my car, started it, and tore off down River Road in the direction of Hammond.

While I mentally calculated how many days there were between now and Christmas Eve.

— TEA LIDS —

CHAPTER TWENTY-TWO

My first semester at Southeastern resulted in a 4.0 GPA (yay!) and an additional five pounds (not so yay). And every ounce of it in my caboose (Hey, mac and cheese happens, and those weekend trips home with Mama and Aunt Edna with all those extra beignets for the road. What's a girl to do?).

In addition, that first stint away from home produced an intense ache that throbbed through my entire body, making me wake in a hot sweat, causing my body to pulse with need.

For T-Roy.

He hadn't exactly kept his word about staying away. Well, I take that back. He stayed away, but he sent a buddy in his stead (or rather, a Boodie in his stead).

On my birthday in September, a huge box filled with sweets and gifts from Mama, Zip and Aunt Edna arrived on campus. But, in addition to the gifts from my family, a small package wrapped in shiny purple paper with a bright gold bow (LSU colors, of course) was included. The bow held a simple tag with a short inscription.

T-Roy.

Opening the box, I found a smiling, bouncy Boodie. Literally, he was bouncing. Evidently, Babineaux's had produced a new novelty item. A Boodie bobblehead. Yep, the Babineaux's mascot, complete with exposed crack in the back, was now a part of my dorm décor.

And shoot, I loved it.

I pressed his oversized head each morning then giggled when he bobbed at me the entire time I got dressed. Sure enough, the unique gift did precisely what T-Roy had planned...

Every time I looked at that silly baby's smiling face, I saw T-Roy's mouthwatering grin and deep dimples. Every time I looked at Boodie's dark eyes, I saw T-Roy's Hershey eyes staring back. And every time I saw that baby's cute little crack, well, you get the picture.

By the time the Christmas break arrived, I'd contemplated how long it would take me to find T-Roy Bertrand, tell him I'd been a fool and beg him to kiss me again.

And again.

Driving into Grand Point, I saw Fenton's black pickup at the Shell station and pulled in. (Who better than my right man's father to tell me where I could find him, huh?)

Wearing a pair of overalls on top of a faded LSU T-shirt, Fenton walked out of the station with a brown bag stuffed with boiled peanuts and a Coke. Seeing me, he grinned. "T-Roy said you'd be getting back to town today."

"I've been home every other weekend through the semester," I said. "It's not as though this is my first time back. You should've come to see me."

"The road runs both ways, cutie," Fenton said, his smile amazingly similar to his son's. "And I figured you were spending time with you aunt. But this is the first time that you'll be seeing T-Roy in a while, right?"

I nodded, shrugged. "I suppose so."

"Well, he's over in Mississippi for a spell now," he said. "Starting up some new territory that way, you know."

I attempted to disguise my disappointment. "When's he getting back?"

"Christmas Eve morn," Fenton said. "But he'll be here in time to take you to the bonfire. If'n you decide you want to go with him. Don't guess you'd feel inclined to tell me what you plan to do?"

"Don't reckon I will," I said, doing my best imitation of his thick Cajun drawl and gaining a chuckle from my future father-in-law.

Maybe.

If I can handle marrying the butt man.

"Oh yeah," Fenton said, busting open a slimy-looking shell and popping the contents in his mouth. "He told me if I saw you that I should give you a message."

My ears perked up. "What's that?"

"He said to tell you to remember that he didn't ask. He said you'd understand."

My heart sunk to my stomach, but I forced a smile. T-Roy wanted to remind me that he hadn't asked for my hand. Did he also mean he never would? Had I totally botched it by declaring that I'd never marry the butt budder man? And what if I decided I *wanted* to marry the Boodie keeper? Was I going to have to ask him? Would he make me beg? Cause I would not beg. I wouldn't. Ever.

Maybe.

Besides, I wasn't ready to get married now anyway. I just turned nineteen. I had five more years before my wooden groom would be hanging on by a thread. Might as well take advantage of the time to date.

And to give T-Roy Bertrand time to ask me.

After saying goodbye to Fenton, I started toward home. I was curious to see Aunt Edna's head. Or hair. Or hat. These days, I never knew which. According to her oncologist, the radiation treatments were taking hold, shrinking the tumor that caused those dizzy spells and nearly made her give up on life completely.

The last time I'd been home, on Thanksgiving, she'd actually gained some of her appetite back. Will LeBlanc had joined us for the holiday. He'd fried a turkey, which Zip declared a "make-you-want-to-slap-your-mama first class bird." Aunt Edna ate it with enthusiasm and hadn't been the least bit sick afterward. It was good to see her doing so well and smiling again.

Those first couple of months had been rough. She lost so much weight that she'd begun to look like the old Aunt Edna. The one who was so grumpy. And bony. And frail. But on Thanksgiving, she'd been full of life. And hope. That had been the main difference. Aunt Edna now had hope.

Mama, Zip, Will and I couldn't have been more pleased.

My pulse raced as I neared home. The Cakery was bedecked in swaths of pine garland, red bows and icicle lights, making it look like a giant gingerbread house, ready to be consumed. And from the mass of cars filling the tiny parking lot out front and spilling over to the back, there were plenty of folks from Grand Point and the surrounding towns ready to consume every bit of the treats inside.

I climbed from my Buick and slammed the door, then stood for a moment to listen to *White Christmas* piping through the speakers that Zip had mounted under the blue awnings on our shop. Several children sat on the front porch eating Christmas cookies, or chocolate cherries, or pralines, or fresh slices of doberge cake.

This was the first December that Mama and Aunt Edna had to run the Cakery without me, and astoundingly, it looked like more customers than I'd ever seen. I hoped that they'd been okay filling all of the orders on their own. Even if Zip had joined in to help, they'd still have a time trying to accommodate a crowd like this.

Knowing that this much business would require both Mama and Aunt Edna to work up front, I prayed that they'd baked enough earlier in the day to handle tonight's customers. Then, prepared to help, I stepped up my pace to get to the front door.

There were even more people than I'd thought. Folks were everywhere, sitting at the tiny wrought iron tables with their small numbered squares in their hand. They didn't look bothered by having to wait, however. On the contrary, they were all chitchatting and snacking on shortbread cookies that filled small dishes on each table.

A coffeemaker sat in one corner of the room, with a sign stating "Free Coffee While You Wait and Visit." And most folks were taking advantage of the hot, strong liquid as well as a chance to visit with friends.

Multicolored twinkle lights glittered and flashed from a live Christmas tree. A toy train circled the tree, and its individual cars each bore a letter, with all of them spelling out *T-H-I-B-O-D-E-A-U-X-S*.

My mouth gaped. Never had the Cakery been so festive. So alive. So *fun*. Evidently, Aunt Edna was celebrating life.

Anxious to tell her how wonderful everything looked and to brag on her newfound decorating skills, I turned toward the display case. Typically, she'd be standing there, talking to a customer, taking their payment or writing down an order.

But she wasn't there.

Instead, a perky little woman with fluorescent pink hair and a red and white striped strapless sequined top bounced down the aisle behind the displays, her black leather miniskirt and pink stockings visible through the glass.

Okay, I leave for a month, and an elf invades the Cakery.

"Number forty-three," she said, her tinkling voice lending credence to the elf theory. Then she picked up an open diet peach Snapple from the top of the counter, wiggled the straw around a bit then slurped it down.

"Right here, Daisey," Penny Landry said. "And I love the train around the tree, by the way."

"Did you know that brain waves can be used to run an electrc train?" Daisey asked.

"I didn't. Is that what's running that one?" Mrs. Landry asked.

Daisey giggled, with a squeal so high-pitched that I was certain if we had any dogs begging out back, they were howling.

Or running.

"Mrs. Landry?" I questioned. It'd been a while since I'd seen my fifth grade teacher, but I was more interested in how she knew the woman behind the counter.

And why I didn't.

"Why, hello, Jezze. Your mama tells me you're at Southeastern. Is everything going well?"

"Going just fine," I said. "So you know—" I was going to finish by saying "Daisey," but little miss perky beat me to the punch.

"You're Jezze?" she squealed, dropping a chocolate covered cherry, then giggling as it rolled across the glass top of the display. "Delilah's baby girl. Welcome home!" Then she scooped up the wayward cherry, tossed it toward a nearby trashcan and yelled, "Two points! Everybody cheer!"

And to my astonishment, everyone did.

When it all died down (and while I waited for the twilight zone theme music to start), Daisey went right back to boxing those cherries as though nothing had happened. At all.

"You know Daisey?" I asked Mrs. Landry. "She helps out here?"

"Oh yes, sweetie. She started a couple of weeks ago, I believe. Isn't she a doll?" She leaned close and whispered in my ear, "Your Aunt Edna really did a wonderful thing hiring her. And obviously, the whole town agrees."

"Aunt Edna hired her?" Whoa. Stop the presses. I twisted around to look at The Cakery's new (and first) employee outside of the family.

She was gone.

"Where'd she go?" I asked.

"What time is it?" Mrs. Landry snapped back, moving her attention to the large, round wall clock above the center case. "Oh, it's changing time. Changing time, everyone!" she yelled.

I blinked. Something had gone wrong in my small center of the world. Everything and everyone off-kilter.

And no one willing to clue me in.

"Green!" Daisey yelled, running from the hallway and then proceeding to finish Mrs. Landry's order.

With long, Abba-type hair, in chartreuse green.

I gasped.

Everyone else applauded.

Seeing my shock, Mrs. Landry hugged me. "Your mama and your aunt will explain, dear. And trust me, you'll love Daisey too. Such a breath of fresh air."

I watched Daisey hand the boxed cherries to Mrs. Landry. "Correct change please," she said. "Checks are fine, but no big bills. I can't count that high."

"I know dear," Mrs. Landry said. "And it's perfectly fine. Here's my check."

"Thank you," Daisey said. She didn't even glance at the rectangular paper to check the figure, just slid it in the cash register and moved to the next number. "Forty-four," she called. Then she clapped her hands together. "You've got double fours. The lucky winner for the forties. Free cookies." She picked up a handful of iced sugar cookies in the shape of Christmas trees and dropped them in a bag. "Now, what else would you like?"

"Actually," the older gentleman said, "I brought you a present, Miss Daisey."

If I thought I'd seen it all, I hadn't seen anything yet. She jumped up and down until I knew that sequined top was heading south. But it stayed up, probably due to those softball-looking boobs. They perched up high, reminding me of an upside down egg carton. (Okay, an upside down egg carton for only two eggs, but still, you get the point. Or points, I should say.)

Then she jogged around the counter with those boobs hitting north and south in record time (honestly, she'll probably have bruises on her chin) and attacked the old man. I swear I expected him to expire on the spot. Heart failure right then and there.

I could just hear the local news now.

"Eighty-year-old attacked in local bake shop. The perpetrator was last seen wearing a sequined candycane strapless top, black leather miniskirt, vinyl white go-go boots (I hadn't been able to see them earlier), hot pink stockings and chartreuse hair."

Oh yeah, that criminal should be easy to spot.

"What did you bring me? What did you bring me? What did you bring me?" she chirped, reminding me of the Minah bird that used to amaze me at the Shell station. I hadn't seen that bird when I stopped there today. Maybe the owner got tired of hearing the repetition and got rid of it. And maybe someone should tell Daisey the same thing.

"What did you bring me?" she asked again, as the crowd grew quiet, waiting to see what gift the odd woman had received.

The elderly fella crossed the room to the Christmas tree and picked up a large cylindrical package. It was wrapped in newspaper, the comics section, and topped with a red bow.

"I wrapped it in cartoons, since you like em so much," he said, grinning sheepishly.

"Oh, I do, I do," she said, then she looked around. "Can I sit here?" she asked a customer who sat at a table to her left.

The guy smiled, stood, pulled out the chair and helped her sit.

Good grief, they'd all gone mad. For one thing, the entire crowd had stopped to watch this "Daisey" creature open her package. For another, no one was manning the cash register or the display. And for another, no one seemed to care.

Eventually, Daisey achieved her goal, opening the package without tearing any of the paper. Then she folded it just so and explained that she'd read each and every cartoon later. As though the newspaper were the gift.

"There's more," the gentleman said. "Inside."

"Really?" she exclaimed, and Lord help me, I think she honestly didn't know.

Then she popped open the end of the cylinder and tilted it. A rolled poster slid out.

"Help me," she said, handing the item to the man. "I don't want to break it."

"Well, I brought you a frame for it," he explained. "It's outside in my truck and I'll fix it up for you before I leave. Then you won't have to worry about it ripping or anything."

"How thoughtful of you," she said, awe in her voice. "Can I see it?"

He nodded. Then he gently unrolled the thick paper and held it up for her approval.

"Oh. My," she whispered. "That's the one I love. It's in my book," she said, and she pointed to a booklet in the center of her table. A tourist guide of the Louisiana plantations. "It's in there," she said. "It's called..." She bit her lower lip. "It's called..." She looked to the man. "Oh dear," she whispered.

"It's Oak Alley," he said. "The one you love."

She nodded, and I noticed her eyes had filled. She blinked to keep the tears from falling. "That's right."

Everyone sat silent for a fraction of a second, then Daisey jumped up from her seat and yelled, "Time to change!"

She took the picture with her and darted to the hallway, then returned just as quickly, sporting a brunette bob.

The crowd applauded.

"Miss Daisey?" a little boy called. He sat by the tree watching the train with intense satisfaction as he chomped on a sugar cookie.

"Yes, dear?"

"Tell me something I don't know."

I held my breath. This should be interesting.

"Did you know that elephants sleep only two hours a day?" she asked.

"Really?" he asked, obviously impressed.

"Yep," she said, then she winked at the boy and he clapped.

"Good one, Miss Daisey," he said.

"Number forty-five," she called, barely skipping a beat between her distribution of knowledge (if it were actually true) and her distribution of baked goods. Then she stopped and stared at the man who'd given her the gift. "And Clyde," she said, apparently forgetting that anyone else was in the room.

"Yes, Miss Daisey?"

"I do love it."

"I'm glad," he said, his voice cracking before the second word. "I really am."

"Those cerebellum mansions have always been my favorite," she said with glee.

At that, a low snicker quivered through the crowd, but no one pointed out the obvious. Okay, twilight zone had hit in full force now, and somebody had to do something or we'd all disappear.

I was sure of it.

"Did she say—" I started, but Clyde stopped me.

"Don't tell her she's got it wrong," he urged in a panicked whisper. "She's trying, and that's what counts, right?"

I gaped at him. Then at her. What had happened to this town since Thanksgiving?

"Right?" he said, full-fledged panic in his tone now. He didn't want me to hurt her. As if me saying, "Yep, they're downright cerebral," would've done anything more than flutter right over the top of her yellow-green head (make that brunette head; I'd forgotten about "the change").

"Right," I heard myself utter, though I couldn't fathom why.

Then I performed the kill-the-cockroach, masterfully, down the hallway to the kitchen. Determined to find Mama, Aunt Edna, Zip...

And some answers.

CHAPTER TWENTY-THREE

There are some things a girl should never see. Ever. Her mother, with her back arched against a stainless steel counter, globs of purple icing on her pride and joy, and her husband doing his best to lick it off with enthusiasm...

That'd be one of them.

"Heaven help," I gasped, and I retreated. Shut the door I'd opened and tried to shut the vision from my mind.

No such luck.

Panting, I stood in the hall, trying to decide which would be worse, facing the freakfest out front or returning to my mother and Zip, possibly before they finished.

Coward that I am, I decided to wait in the hall (and no, I've never considered myself cowardly; though at this moment, I'd give the lion in Oz a good run for the money).

While I listened to Daisey charm the masses out front, and tried not to listen to Mama as Zip charmed her in the kitchen, Aunt Edna arrived.

Thank God.

She came through the front door, called out something to her new "employee," and then headed down the hall. With her arms filled with bags from the pig, she didn't even look up as she killed-the-cockroach the whole way.

"Aunt Edna," I said, sighing with relief.

"Oh, mercy, child," she said, shifting her bags to one arm and reaching the other out to grab me in a hug. "They're worse than rabbits, those two, aren't they?"

I swallowed.

She glared at the door to the kitchen. "I knew they were at it again the minute I tried the back door and it was locked. Again."

"Well, they sure didn't lock this one," I said.

"Oh, dear. You saw?"

"Purple icing."

"That does it, Delilah," she hissed. She pushed past me and headed into the kitchen while I crept along in her wake. Goodness knows I didn't want to see them if they weren't done.

Thankfully, they were.

Mama fastened the last button on her shirt just as Aunt Edna opened the door. Her cheeks were flushed and she had that "I love this man" look, you know, where her eyes are kind of glazed over and shiny, like the top of a beignet where the sugar has started to melt.

"Sorry, Edna," Mama chirped, but she sure didn't look sorry to me. She looked ecstatic. "We thought we had them both locked," she said with a shrug. Then she patted her morning glory bun, which had so many hairs sticking out of place that it looked more like a cactus than a flower.

"Don't apologize to me, you hussy," Delilah said. "I didn't walk in on you."

"You didn't?" Mama asked. "Then who—"

"Hi, Mama," I said.

I expected her to keep up the apology, but gear it toward me, or to hide her face and say something about the throes of love taking control. And the promise that next time they'd take it to the house.

But, being Delilah Thibodeaux, she stayed true to form. "Oh honey," she gushed. "You're gonna have to try that sometime. Our specialty icing sticks really good, and it makes your sweetie have to work really hard to get it off, Doesn't it Zip?"

My father, looking like he'd just taken first place in every he-man event at the Alligator Harvest Festival (or at least the kissing booth), nodded. "Yep, kiddo. It takes some work, but it's downright delicious."

"TMI, people," Aunt Edna said, whisking past both of them and placing her bags on one of the back shelves. "The girl barely clears the doors of the kitchen and you two are bombarding her with sex talk already. It's bad enough I have to live with it on a daily basis. Have some decency. Spare the child."

"Here," Mama said, walking toward Aunt Edna and handing her a plastic spoon piled high with purple icing.

Aunt Edna stared at it. "I'm almost afraid to ask," she mumbled.

Mama shrugged. "You'll never know till you try it," she said. Then she sashayed across the kitchen, pinched Zip's butt as she passed, then grabbed me up in a hug. "Welcome home, angel."

Her embrace smelled like sweet icing. Sweet purple icing. But I tried not to think about that. I simply laughed as she held me, while Aunt Edna fussed about privacy, and bedrooms, and "getting a room."

"I'm going to head out front and help Daisey," Zip said. He patted my back on his way out. "It's good to see you, Jezebel."

"Thanks," I whispered, feeling really good to be back.

Mama loosened her hold. "I've got some gumbo and potato salad at the house if you're hungry," she said.

"Phfft," Aunt Edna said, and she waltzed across the kitchen and handed me a plate filled with pralines. "You can eat good food later. Right now, let's have some sweets." She herded us to the breakfast nook. Then she sat down. "Get us some coffee, Delilah, will you?" she asked. "It's the least you can do after shocking us to death."

Mama tsked, but got the coffee. "You ain't been shocked a day in your life, Edna," she said. "And Jezebel is nineteen. She knows about stuff."

"Well, knowing it and having to see your mama doing it are two different things," Aunt Edna quipped. "Isn't that right, Jezze?"

I bit into a praline. No way was I getting in the middle of this.

Mama put a hot mug of coffee in front of each of us then got one for herself, sat down and took a sip, squinting as she swallowed. "She looks good, doesn't she?" Mama asked me. Then her eyes shifted to her sister. And shone with love.

Aunt Edna did look good, even better than at Thanksgiving. I couldn't tell if her hair had grown back or was still MIA, since a sequined red and white striped turban covered her head. But her cheeks were rosy. Her lips moist. And her eyes were happy.

Definitely happy.

"You do look good, Aunt Edna," I said. "You're feeling better, aren't you?"

As miffed as she was with my mama, Aunt Edna couldn't contain the smile that burst across her face.

"Go on, Edna," Mama said. "Tell her."

"What?" I asked, and I caught my breath when my tough aunt blushed. "What?" I repeated.

"The doctor says it's working," she said. "Tumor's about gone, and everything's looking good."

My throat tightened. Eyes burned. "That's wonderful," I whispered. "Oh, wow, it's wonderful," I repeated, and I scooted my chair closer to hers, leaned over and kissed her cheek.

"Oh good grief," Mama chided. "Now, are you going to get to the news, or am I going to have to tell her?"

What else could there be? What could be better news than that? "News?"

Aunt Edna giggled. Giggled! Then she turned to look directly in my eyes, and announced, "Will and I are tying the knot, child. Tomorrow."

The squeals in our kitchen could've been heard in Baton Rouge or New Orleans, take your pick.

"Tomorrow?" I asked, when I finally came up for air.

"I know. Short notice and all, but we figure that we haven't got any time to waste."

"Where's the wedding?"

"Oh, the levee, of course. It'll be cold, but we've built an extra bonfire this year, and we're going to light that sucker before the ceremony starts. It's another wedding cake, like yours, but not as big as Jezze's Man."

"Do you need me to do anything to help you get ready?" I asked. "Need us to work on food? Have somewhere to go for the honeymoon? Oh my, do you have a dress?"

She laughed. "Goodness child, you've always been full of questions. Okay, we don't need anything done in the food department; we've been cooking all day. And for the honeymoon, we're not going anywhere. I don't need to get too far from my doctor, just in case. Besides, we want to be here for the bonfires on Christmas Eve, and that's only a week away. And I have something to wear. Not a dress, but I didn't want a dress. Daisey designs wedding outfits, and she has one ready to go."

"Daisey," I repeated, wondering where to start.

Aunt Edna sipped her coffee, grabbed a praline. "Guess she threw you for a loop, huh?"

"That's an understatement," I admitted. "Is she really an employee? That *you* hired?"

Mama popped a warm praline in her mouth, moaned her contentment. Then she said, "Go on, sis. It's high time you fess up to Jezebel, don't you think?" Then Mama leaned forward, patted my hand and winked. "You know, when she thought she was leaving us, she started confessing all kinds of interesting little things. I reckon I've got enough on her now to last a lifetime."

"Aw, shuddup, Delilah," Aunt Edna spat, and she ate another candy.

"Well?" Mama prodded.

Shrugging her shoulders, Aunt Edna mumbled, "I made it up." She sipped more coffee and didn't look at us.

"Made what up?" I asked.

"Big Mama's request," she admitted. "She never said anything about only Thibodeaux's working in the Cakery. She just told me to watch after your mama, like I assume she told your mama to watch after me. Right, Delilah?"

Mama nodded and grinned. "Go on, Edna." I could tell Mama was really enjoying making her sister squirm.

"Oh, all right," Aunt Edna said. "I didn't want to hire anyone because—well, I guess it was because—"

"Because you didn't want to share your sister with anyone," Mama said, grinning like the cat that ate the canary. "And then your niece."

"Our family was so small," Aunt Edna said. "You were all I had. And I— I really enjoyed all the time that we had to spend together to get everything done. Just us. By ourselves."

Knowing exactly how she felt, I smiled. For the past few months, I'd lived for the weekends when I could come back home, spend time in the Cakery's kitchen and visit with them. Our time in the kitchen was special. Treasured. Filled with the sweet scents of sugar and yeast, cake and icing.

And love.

Swallowing past the lump in my throat, I said, "So what about Daisey? How did she change your mind?"

Before Aunt Edna could answer, the subject of my question shot into the kitchen like a bottle rocket, zinging past the counters and making a beeline for me. "Stand up, Jezze," Daisey demanded. "Hurry, Zip'll need me back out front soon."

I stood. What choice did I have?

She dug in the pocket of her miniskirt (yeah, I know, I was amazed the thing had room for a pocket, but it did. And to my amazement, the thing held quite a bit). She withdrew a wad of ribbon-looking stuff that I quickly realized was a tape measure.

"Arms out," she instructed.

Again, I did as told, while Mama and Aunt Edna chuckled.

Then Daisey blinked, stopped mid-motion and smiled. "I'm Daisey Leigh Mason, by the way."

"I'm Jezze," I returned.

She cocked her head to the side and stared at my mouth. "Your lipstick is too light, you know. You should try red. For the holidays."

"I'll keep that in mind."

"Did you know that the average woman consumes six pounds of lipstick in her lifetime?" she asked.

But before I could answer, she snapped back to reality and wrapped her arms around me, humming as she measured my chest. She whistled at the measurement. "Must've got em from your mama, huh? Downright blessed, I'd say."

I didn't answer. She didn't seem to require a response.

Then she moved to my waist. "Are you going to hold it in, or let it go?" she asked.

All right. This needed an answer, but since I didn't understand the question...

"Give her room to breathe," Mama said.

"Will do," Daisey said, loosening the band around my middle a bit. Then she annotated the numbers with a red marker.

On the inside of her palm.

"One more," she said, wrapping the pale green tape around my hips. "Goodness, got yourself quite a little package in the back there, don't ya?"

I grunted.

Aunt Edna giggled.

Then Miss Daisey Leigh Mason wrote the final figure, again in her palm, and left the room in a blur of red and white sequins, black leather, pink spandex and white vinyl.

"What in the world was that?" I asked.

Mama and Aunt Edna cackled with delight.

"I mean it, you two. Tell me now," I ordered.

"All right, sweetie," Mama said. "I'll start. Aunt Edna joined a cancer support group. They meet once a week at a church in Gramercy. About a month ago, Daisey showed up at the meeting."

Aunt Edna cleared her throat. "I was still waiting to find out if the treatments were working, and in all honesty, I wasn't doing so good. Cried all the dang time like some kind of wimp. Stopped wanting to make the walk over to the Cakery in the morning. Actually, stopped wanting to live."

"But you looked so good at Thanksgiving," I said. "That couldn't have been an act."

"Oh, it wasn't," Mama said. "She did such a rapid change, and that's why Zip and I were so overjoyed. We thought it was the treatment, but in fact, she'd met Daisey that week at their Tuesday night meeting."

"I swear, child. I've never met anyone like her. She came whipping in, wearing this wild scarf kind of dress thing with thousands of Mardi Gras beads and a green wig. She looked like a fortuneteller. Or a young, pretty voodoo queen. So I watched her, thinking that this girl must have her cancer licked, or she couldn't be so happy. And it made me mad. I was so jealous I couldn't see straight. I hated her for making it, for surviving." Aunt Edna frowned, shook her head.

"Then what?"

"Then she introduced herself to the group. She said, 'Hello, I'm Daisey Leigh Mason. I've just moved here from Opp, Alabama and I have lymphatic cancer. I have no family. I've had no support, until now. So, I'm declaring all of you my official relatives, at least for the next six months. That's how long they say I have. I'm supposed to enjoy life, and I've always wanted to live in Louisiana and make wedding dresses. So that's what I'm going to do.'"

"No family?" I asked.

"Raised in foster care," Mama said. "But she said her foster parents were great. She just can't remember their names."

"Her brain has been affected pretty bad by the cancer," Aunt Edna said. "We never know what she'll remember from one day to the next."

"Except for the Snapple lids," Mama reminded, causing Aunt Edna to laugh.

"Yes, she loves those trivia bits on the underside of Snapple lids. Actually, that's why I had to make another run to the pig; she was nearly out."

I looked at the white Piggly Wiggly bags on the counter (Aunt Edna had finally started requesting plastic, since the handles made them easier to carry). Sure enough, I could read the Snapple logo on the bottles inside. "Just six months?" I asked, feeling a surge of pain for the young, vibrant woman out front.

"If we're lucky," Aunt Edna said, once again frowning. "But we can't be sad, at least not in front of her. She wants to be happy."

"And the town knows, I suppose?" I thought, remembering all of the extra care that the folks in the shop had shown our new employee.

"Oh yeah," Aunt Edna said. "She talks about it, when she remembers it."

"Bless her heart," I whispered.

"She's been real anxious for you to get home, you know? Since we talk about you all the time," Mama said. "She made the wedding gown for the Jezze's Man bride this year."

"But it'll just get burned," I reminded.

"Yeah, but they always put the picture in the paper and on the news. That'll mean a lot to her," Aunt Edna said. "It really will."

"Is that why she took my measurements?"

"Oh no," Mama answered. "She's been waiting till you got home so she can start on your wedding gown. She loves T-Roy, by the way. Thinks you're getting a real catch."

"We aren't even engaged," I reminded. "Heck, we're not even dating."

"No, not yet," Aunt Edna said, reaching across the table and patting my hand. "But you will be."

"I told him I couldn't marry the butt budder man," I admitted.

"Oh Good Lord, child, when did you do that?" Aunt Edna asked.

"Before I left for school."

"You realize that I never anticipated my right man spending most of his days with a pig on his shirt either," Aunt Edna said, "But he sure enough is the one."

"Personally, I think the pig is cute," Mama said.

"Me too," Aunt Edna agreed.

I laughed. "I shouldn't have said it. In fact, I've grown kind of partial to the whole idea of having Boodie's keeper for a husband." I sighed. "Now, I'm not sure if he can ever forgive me. He sent me a message through Fenton."

"What kind of message?" Mama asked.

"He wanted to reminded me that he hasn't asked. That he hasn't asked me to marry him." I bit my lower lip. "I may have really messed things up, huh?"

"Shoot, Jezze, if that boy's got it as bad for you as you've got it for him, he'll come around. Make sure you give Daisey time enough to make that dress."

"Speaking of Daisey, I'm gonna see if she needs some help. That girl is trying to flat work herself to—well, she works too hard," Mama said. She kissed the top of my head and left the kitchen.

"Your mama ain't fooling nobody," Aunt Edna huffed. "She wants to get out there so she can rub up against Zip behind the display case."

I laughed. "You're terrible."

"Not yet," she said. "But I will be as soon as we tie the knot."

I crossed the kitchen to get the carafe of coffee from the counter, brought it back to the table and refilled our mugs. "Is there going to be anywhere for me to stay this time where I won't have to hear the action taking place in the other bedrooms?" I raised a brow.

"Oh, goodness, child. I nearly forgot. I gave your bedroom away. You'll have to stay at Zip and Delilah's place."

"You gave it away?"

"Daisey. Bless her heart, she can't drive anymore. Can't remember addresses, can't even remember how to work the accelerator on a car. I asked her if she wanted a place to live, and she said yes. I didn't think you'd mind."

"Of course not," I said. "I just hope Mama and Zip have gotten their icing fix for a while."

"Don't count on it," Aunt Edna said. "I saw her lugging two gallons of the stuff home with her yesterday. Purple and gold, of course."

"For LSU, I assume?"

"I'm sure," Aunt Edna said. "And I hope you like their fight song. You know, *Hold That Tiger*. And that's all I'm gonna say about that."

CHAPTER TWENTY-FOUR

The bride wore poinsettias. And butt budder.

No, she didn't literally wear flowers. She wore the print. But the butt budder? Well, sure. It was a necessity with her baldness, kept her scalp nice and smooth. But she'd have used it somewhere, even if she hadn't needed it for her head. The Thibodeaux women were too smart to leave home without a tube of the miracle cream (like T-Roy says, it's good stuff).

Daisey had designed Aunt Edna's wedding suit to be one-of-a-kind. And Lordy, was it ever. Probably always would be, since I couldn't imagine anyone ever duplicating its...uniqueness.

Aunt Edna was thrilled with the final product, and she sashayed her way up that levee as though her garments had been custom made by Vera Wang and her jewels loaned out by Harry Winston.

All she needed was a red carpet.

However, the folks at Harry Winston would cringe if they saw the red choker necklace Daisey had created for the occasion. Beads from the Hobby Lobby were strung together to look like poinsettias laying flat against Aunt Edna's throat. And I knew Vera Wang would never introduce a bridal suit like this, though Aunt Edna's attire did gain the same response as a Vera Wang original. Complete gasps of awe and delight, which was what Aunt Edna was going for.

The iridescent pearl sequins that covered the majority of the pantsuit (tuxedo-styled, complete with tails) caught the sunlight of the afternoon and forced the multitude of guests to shield their eyes from the glare (and yes, December in Louisiana means bright sun, even if we're freezing our hineys off).

Scattered sporadically around the suit were big, fat poinsettias formed with glittery red and green sequins.

"Do I look gorgeous, or what?" Aunt Edna had asked when she tried the outfit on for us this morning. "And don't you dare say I look like a blooming idiot."

"You look gorgeous," Mama, Zip and I had confessed. "Absolutely gorgeous."

Daisey hadn't made it to see the early morning display. She slept until noon. Evidently she'd stayed up fairly late helping Zip with the newest bonfire, the one created specifically for Aunt Edna's wedding. She had insisted on helping him complete the structure, a tall tower covered with poinsettias, while Mama, Aunt Edna and I decided to call it a night.

"I can't sleep yet," she'd claimed.

I assumed her insomnia was common. Obviously, she didn't want to miss a minute of life, particularly when those precious minutes were already numbered. However, she'd needed her rest this morning, so we all tiptoed around Aunt Edna's house to let her get much-needed sleep.

Right now though, Daisey was wide-awake, beaming at her creation. As did the rest of the town.

And who could blame them? Aunt Edna did look beautiful.

Daisey had even made a sequined hat that matched the ensemble and fit snugly on Aunt Edna's bald head (she'd decided she'd rather shave it herself instead of watching her hair come out, but she never had to do the honors. She and Daisey took turns, laughing and giggling as they helped one another maintain their slick, shiny heads).

Positively glowing with excitement (and with sequins), Aunt Edna passed through the crowd and headed to her right man. Mr. LeBlanc, believe it or not, didn't wear a pig-embroidered shirt for the occasion. Not that she'd have cared. She wanted him, period.

Pig or not.

She stood in front of the crowd and recited her vows with the back of her poinsettia-covered head facing us (Daisey had put one big flower on the hat, so that it honestly did appear that Aunt Edna had bloomed overnight, but it was pretty. Really.)

I held my breath and fought tears when the preacher, the same one who'd performed Mama and Zip's ceremony, pronounced them husband and wife.

"Beautiful," I whispered.

"Yes, it was," a deep, sexy voice said into my ear at the same time his warm palm slid across my back and settled on my waist.

I jerked around to see T-Roy, his eyes smoldering and his mouth absolutely luscious. "You weren't supposed to be home until Christmas Eve," I informed, as if he didn't know.

"I heard a couple of friends of mine were getting married. Didn't want to miss it."

"That'll mean a lot to her," I said.

"Just to her?"

I swallowed. "And to me."

The crowd cheered as Aunt Edna and Will LeBlanc passed by and headed toward the mega wedding cake that Mama had created for the occasion.

"So, Miss Thibodeaux," he said, ignoring the people shoving past us to congratulate the bride and groom. "I believe you're supposed to give me an answer."

"What was the question again?" I asked, and grinned.

"Did you think about it? About us? Over the past four months? And do you want to feel it, the way you felt when I kissed you, again?"

"Oh yeah, that was it," I said. "Now, let's see..."

He twisted me, pulled me to his chest, so my face looked directly up into his, and his lips were close enough to kiss.

"Yes," I whispered. "Every day. Every night."

I melted in his embrace, lost myself in his kiss, completely forgot that a crowd milled around us as we found each other on the bank of the levee. We'd probably have stayed there, locked in each other's arms, feeding that frenzied passion that had been steadily building for the past four months.

If Daisey hadn't intervened.

"T-Roy!" she exclaimed. "You're here!"

Hesitantly, we broke apart and turned toward Daisey. Her wedding attire consisted of a red and green striped sweater dress, I'd guess at least one size too small, but with her figure, it worked. Vinyl white go-go boots (her trademark, I'd learned). Purple fishnet stockings. And a spiked fuchsia wig.

"Where's your coat, Daisey?" T-Roy asked, sliding out of his blazer and handing it to her.

"Aw, geez, I didn't want to mess up the outfit."

"Better to have something that doesn't quite," he hesitated, "*match* than to catch cold."

"Oh all right, spoiled sport. I saw you two kissing, by the way," she said, letting him slide the jacket over her arms. "Did you know that a one minute kiss burns twenty-six calories?"

"I didn't know that," I said.

"It's true," she said, bobbing her pointy fuchsia head. "And cn average, a human being will spend two weeks kissing in his or her lifetime."

"Really?" T-Roy asked.

Another fuchsia bob. Then she shifted gears faster than Aunt Edna's transmission when she punches the pedal. "Hey, have y'all tried the strawberries yet?"

"Not yet," T-Roy said.

"Well, when you do, you can think of this. Strawberries are the only fruit whose seeds grow on the outside."

"Interesting," I said, and I smiled at her. She really was cute. And fun. And sad (No, she wasn't sad; she was happy. But it saddened my heart to know such a sweet soul would be taken from us so soon).

"But whatever you do, don't eat the bananas. We really weren't thinking when we put them out," she added.

"Why not?" T-Roy asked.

"Because mosquitoes are attracted to people who have recently eaten bananas."

"Oh," I said. Should I tell her that there aren't any mosquitoes typically swarming Louisiana in December? Nah, I didn't want to spoil her helpful tidbit. Besides, December is about the only month of the year that we aren't attacked by the monsters, so I'd just save that bit of information until the bloodsuckers returned.

"Okay, I'm going to see Edna and Will. Be back in a jiffy. By the way, did you know a jiffy is one-hundredth of a second?"

"I didn't know that," I found myself repeating.

"Sure enough," she said, then she whizzed off in the direction of my newly married aunt.

"So," T-Roy said. He ran his fingertips down my cheek, pushed a mass of long brown curls away from my face. The brush of his hand against that sensitive spot behind my ear made my eyes close. Lips part. Anticipation begin. "Jezze," he said.

"Mmmm?"

"Open your eyes."

I did. And he looked mighty serious. I blinked. "What?"

"We're going to date," he said, as though I had no say whatsoever in the matter.

"What if I—" I started, but stopped when he put that finger on my lip. *Kiss me again. Right now.*

"We're. Going. To. Date," T-Roy Bertrand, my right man, the man of my dreams, who happens to be the butt budder man, said.

I nodded, and nearly moaned at the feel of his finger rubbing up and down my mouth.

"We won't mention marriage," he informed.

My eyes widened. Did he mean, like, ever? Because I needed to provide some clarification to my former statement. I mean, sure, I said I wouldn't marry the butt budder guy. But that was before I realized that I couldn't dang sleep at night if I thought I might lose him.

"T-Roy," I mumbled beneath that intoxicating finger.

He shook his head. "Uh-uh. Not a word about it. We're going to date. For a nice, long time. And then, eventually, you'll realize that you could care less whether I sell butt budder for a living. You'll want me ro matter what, Miss Thibodeaux."

Okay. From what I heard, T-Roy Bertrand just offered to woo my heart, to make me realize that I was head over heels and couldn't live without him. Should I tell him that I'm there already? That it wouldn't take more than him asking the proverbial question for me to scream "I do?" Or should I let him try to convince me?

I smiled. "Deal."

CHAPTER TWENTY-FIVE

For our first official date, T-Roy Bertrand and I watched our alter egos burn to a crisp.

The groom wore a black tux with tails, basically the same outfit he'd garnered since that very first time, nine years ago. Except back then, he'd stood flatfooted on the ground. Now, the poor fellow was harnessed to the bride.

Literally.

Zip had wrapped a thick rope around the bride's waist and it extended over the side, where it connected to her groom. The tux-clad frame, parallel to the ground, appeared to be repelling off of the cake instead of making his way to the top. (Then again, with the way that I'd bungled things with my prospective groom, maybe he was.)

The bride wore a long gown of antique white lace and a matching twenty-foot veil that billowed across the levee toward the Mississippi.

Miss Jeansonne didn't mind giving up her position as the official dressmaker for the doomed gown. As a matter of fact, the woman was thrilled to see one of Daisey's creations on the wooden bride. "It's absolutely beautiful," the elder seamstress told her young protégé. "You're very talented, Miss Mason."

"Gee, thanks," Daisey gushed.

Evidently, the local television station and newspapers agreed with Mrs. Jeansonne's appraisement. They showcased Daisey's gown on the front page of the paper and during the opening segment of the evening news. Soon, Daisey had as many orders as she'd ever need to keep her busy for a lifetime, particularly the remainder of her lifetime.

She swapped to her purple, green and gold Mardi Gras wig (the one she'd dubbed her "celebration do") as she listened to the endless messages on the answering machine at Aunt Edna's house (Will LeBlanc's house too, since they'd decided to live at her place).

One by one, the calls came in. Some were congratulatory, celebrating Daisey's success. Some were order requests from future June brides.

Daisey cheered with each one, pumping her slender arms in the air like Rocky Balboa. Then she returned each call. She thanked each well-wisher and obtained specifics (measurements, wedding dates, etc.) from the others.

"I can't wait to get started on all these," Daisey gasped, scanning her page of notes as she sucked on a raspberry Snapple. "Oh goodness, do you think you'll be able to handle the shop without me?" she asked, turning to Aunt Edna and Mama.

"It'll be tough," Aunt Edna said, "But we'll manage."

Daisey smiled. "I hate the thought of you trying to make and sell all those cookies without me," she said. "You know the average American eats thirty-five thousand cookies during his or her lifetime. That's a lot of cookies."

"We'll make sure to keep plenty on-hand," Mama assured.

Daisey seemed satisfied with that, and she hurriedly found a pad of paper and started sketching ideas for the first of the many dresses she planned to make.

Amazed at her enthusiasm, we watched her careful strokes on the tablet. "It'll be wonderful," she whispered, gazing at the beginning of the dress.

But I knew that every person in that room was thinking the same thing as me. Not *It'll be wonderful,* but rather *It will be sad. Very. Very. Sad.*

The next morning, Christmas, I woke early, showered, dressed and headed for the Cakery. Our traditional Christmas morning involved gathering in the Thibodeaux's kitchen, drinking hot apple cider or piping cups of coffee and eating every sweet we'd decided to make for the event (with beignets, of course, topping the list).

I'd invited T-Roy to join us. Since I hadn't specified a time, other than "bright and early," it didn't surprise me in the least to see his Saturn parked beneath the oak tree behind the shop.

The wind whipped icily against my skin, forcing my eyes to tear and drip as I picked up my pace across the path. I bustled inside, surprised to see the door open and the lights on. And even more surprised to smell fresh coffee upon my entrance.

T-Roy sat at the breakfast nook, his long legs crossed at the ankles where he stretched them out across the floor. He sipped his coffee and eyed me over the top of his mug.

"And just how did you get in?" I asked, thinking that he must be talented at more than kissing. Perhaps breaking and entering was also included in his reportoire.

He grinned and lifted his key ring, which sported a shiny, new gold key. "Your mother gave it to me last night. Told me to come whenever I like. She also said to tell you that we're welcomed to take all the purple icing we need. If you know what that means."

"Thank God she didn't tell you what it means."

"Who says she didn't?" he asked, and the sneaky smirk on his face made me wonder.

And made my pride and joy burn.

"You made coffee?" I asked, trying to regain my composure. And control my body.

"I'd have made beignets too, but to be honest, I've never learned how. They're not exactly my specialty in the kitchen," he said.

"You cook?" Was there any end to his talents?

"I make a mean gumbo and a to-die-for jambalaya, but I'm at a loss in the sweet department."

"I guess that means we're perfect for each other, huh?" I blurted before thinking.

"Maybe," he said, raising his brows. "But, like I said, I haven't asked. And we're not going to discuss long-term, right? That's what you wanted. So we're dating."

That's what I wanted? Can we have a do-over on that one? I think the jury is still out. "Hmph," I mumbled, getting everything out for beignets.

"Sorry?" he asked, and it sounded mighty dang smug. "I didn't catch that."

"Didn't say a thing," I snapped. "So, do you want to learn how to make beignets, or not?"

His low, not-quite-hidden chuckle rolled over my skin like hot rum sauce on bread pudding.

"I want to learn how to do lots of things with you, Miss Thibodeaux," that husky voice affirmed.

Breathe in. Breathe out. Wax on. Wax off. Paint the fence. Sand the floor.

"Jezze?" He moved close behind me.

"W-what?"

"What are you doing?"

"Trying to hear Miyagi."

"Who?"

I blinked. Lord help me. I was losing it, right there in the Cakery kitchen, on Christmas morning, no less. "Nothing," I said. "And I want you to stop that right now."

"Stop what?" he asked, pressing his body to mine. He slid hot palms down the length of my arms, settled them on top of my hands on the counter. "What is it you want me to stop?"

"Nothing," I mumbled. "I don't want you to stop a thing. Dang it."

By the time the back door creaked open, and Mama, Zip, Aunt Edna, Will and Daisey scurried inside to get warm, the kitchen looked like it'd been in a fight with a powder puff.

And lost.

Powdered sugar was everywhere, especially all over the two of us, and the aroma of burned beignets penetrated the air, making all of them gasp. (At least I think that's why they were gasping; it could've been from the guilty looks on our faces and the way my shirt was inside-out and backwards.)

"Morning," I said, my throat raspy from panting. "Want some beignets?"

"Did any of them survive?" Aunt Edna asked.

It took less than a second for Mama's funny box to turn over. And half that long for the rest of them to join in. Shoot, I finally did something halfway wild and crazy, and my whole family knew about it. And ‾-Roy didn't help matters looking like he just took first place in the gumbo contest at the state fair.

"We didn't try the icing yet," he announced. "But the powdered sugar works just fine," he announced, which sent another bout of laughter through the crowd and turned my face six shades of red.

"You're going to regret that," I promised, raising my brows at the fellow with whom I'd just shared the most enticing cooking experience of my life.

"Oh, I doubt that," he assured, then he pulled the last batch of beignets (the only ones that actually did survive) from the fryer.

While everyone else gobbled up beignets, Daisey hurried to the front of the store.

"Go see what she's doing, Jezze," Aunt Edna said, mid-chew. "That poor thing was up most of the night designing wedding dresses, then she jumped right back up this morning. Poor thing, she's afraid time is going to get away from her, that one. And I guess it is."

Will wrapped an arm around his new bride. "Now, now, hon," he soothed. "It gets away from all of us. It's just that she can see it coming."

"I'll check on her." I started down the hallway with T-Roy following close behind. We entered the front room and watched as Daisey put Christmas presents in an industrial sized black garbage sack. Two other trash bags were propped against the wall from where she'd obviously packed them yesterday or last night.

"Whatcha doing, Daisey?" I asked.

"I asked our customers for gifts, you know?" she said, grabbing two additional small presents from the far recesses beneath the tree and sliding them in the bag. "They sure are generous, aren't they? All of these," she said, waving her hand toward the bounty of gifts contained in the bags. "New toys for the foster children in St. James and St. John Parishes."

I swallowed, looked at T-Roy, whose jaw was clenched tight.

"Do you think," Daisey started, then she smiled at us, "Well, could y'all help me take them? I've got a list of addresses, but I can't drive. And I don't know my way around either."

"We'd be glad to," T-Roy said, wrapping his arms around my waist and pulling me close. "Wouldn't we, *Cher*?"

I nodded, touched as much by his endearing term as by Daisey's huge heart. "Of course."

"Can we use your car?" Daisey asked T-Roy.

"We should use mine," I offered. "It's bigger."

T-Roy's arms tensed around me. He leaned his head around and his voice rumbled in my ear. "Are you insulting the size of my vehicle?"

Giggling, I answered, "Nope, just your trunk."

"You know what they say about men with those huge oversized trunks, don't you?" he asked.

"I don't guess I do."

"They're trying to compensate for a lack of size somewhere else."

Daisey had been squatting near the tree, but she dropped her bottom to the floor and snorted with laughter. "You two are going to make me wet myself, I swear!"

T-Roy kissed the shell of my ear then left me to pick up two of the large bags. "I'll have you know that my trunk can take on all of these gifts. No problem."

"If you say so," I teased, grabbing the other bag and then lending a hand to Daisey as she slowly stood. "You okay, Daisey?"

"Just fine," she said, though her forced smile betrayed her.

Sure enough, T-Roy fit every bag in the trunk of his Saturn. And honestly, it wasn't near as small as I'd thought.

"Well?" he said, slamming it closed.

"Yeah, yeah. I stand corrected."

Daisey had asked the customers to label each package in pencil on the bottom of the box. She sat in the backseat of the car with one of the bags beside her and worked her way through.

"Okay, this is a watch. Perfect for a teenage boy," she said. "Let's see. Okay, head over to Geismar."

T-Roy followed her directions and one-by-one, the packages were all delivered by mid-afternoon.

Feeling good about the way we'd spent our Christmas, we started driving home. We were halfway there when Daisey screamed.

"Pull over!"

T-Roy wheeled the car to the side.

"That man. I think he's hurt."

I followed her gaze. We'd passed a small community park and she seemed to be staring at a man who was bending over beside a wooden bench. To me, he appeared to be tying his shoe. Evidently, that's what T-Roy thought too.

"I think he's just tying—" T-Roy started, but Daisey had already bolted from the car.

"Hurry!" she squealed, hurdling her tiny body across the mulch-covered earth as though she was running for the gold at the Olympics. "He may need mouth to mouth insemination."

T-Roy and I were sprinting behind her, but I stopped. I couldn't help it. "Did she say...?"

I turned and saw T-Roy, big, fat tears streaming down his face as he laughed out loud. "She's something, huh, *Cher*?"

"Are you okay?" we heard her ask, and then, we heard the fellow affirm that he was, indeed, fine.

Thank God. I could only imagine folks trying to keep a straight face as Daisey informed them she'd saved someone by performing mouth-to-mouth insemination.

Amazingly enough, T-Roy and I regained our composure before she wished the guy a Merry Christmas and headed our way. "He's fine," she said, stomping past in her go-go boots. "No cause for alarm."

"That's good," T-Roy said, stifling his chuckle.

Then finally we returned to Mama and Zip's, where they'd prepared a traditional Cajun Christmas feast. Fried turkey, gumbo, potato salad, dirty rice, oyster dressing, rice pudding, you name it. Aunt Edna and Will were there, and Fenton Bertrand came too, bringing enough alcohol for the entire town of Grand Point.

By the time night fell, we were all blissfully content, sitting around the living room watching the lights twinkle on the Christmas tree while wood popped and crackled in the fireplace. Zip put his favorite CD in the player (his second favorite, if you count the LSU fight song), and soon Cajun tunes from the Coozan Band filled the house.

"Come on, *Cher*," T-Roy said, taking my hand. "Dance with me."

We danced through the living room while everyone applauded. Then he led me to the porch. Pulling me close, he whispered, "Merry Christmas," and withdrew a small box from his pocket.

Okay, I'd given him a dark green sweatshirt with a gold lion that read "Southeastern" across the top. He'd opened it earlier this afternoon, and I'd assumed he hadn't purchased a gift for me. Holding the velvet-covered box, I realized I'd assumed wrong.

Very wrong.

And to think, he said he wouldn't ask.

With confidence soaring, I cracked open the box and viewed an exquisite sapphire ring.

"That's your birthstone, right?" he asked.

I nodded. So did this mean something? Anything? Nothing? A clue. I needed a clue. But all I could think to say was, "Thank you, T-Roy. It's beautiful."

"Don't you want to know what it means?"

Yes! I took a deep, cleansing breath. Slowed my heart rate. And prepared for his proposal. "It means something?" I asked.

"It's a promise ring," he informed.

A promise ring? As in, the kind of ring a twelve-year-old gives a girl to say that when he's big enough to ask her out, he will?

When I didn't speak, he continued, "It's to promise you that I want to be with you, to date you, as long as you'll have me," he said. Which sounded pretty good, except I wanted more. "And," he added, "It's a promise that I'll never ask you to marry."

Breathe. Breathe. Which way? Oh yeah. In. Out. In. Out. Come on, Miyagi, help me out here. "Never?" I whispered.

"No," he said. "I realize that you don't want to be married to the butt budder rep."

But I do. Really.

"I also realize that you will want to. One day."

I blinked. What did he say?

"So, I promise I'll never ask you." Then the cocky thing smiled. "But I promise to say yes when you ask me."

What? I stiffened. "When *I* ask *you*?"

"Exactly."

"I'm not going to ask you," I said. And I meant it. I'm a Thibodeaux, dadgummit, and Thibodeaux women don't have to go around and beg someone to marry them. Thibodeaux women find their right man, and then they make him realize he'd rather die than spend another day without them. Make *him* beg. Which was exactly what I'd wait for T-Roy Bertrand to do. Because I would not ask him.

Ever.

"Then we can date," he said. And the weasel grinned again. Then he scooped me in his arms and kissed me. Hard.

Prepared to resist, I braced my palms against his chest. His rock-solid, firm, warm chest. And I melted, accepted that kiss as though I'd suffocate without it. But I didn't ask him to marry me. Nope. So I'd won, right?

Right. As long as I could keep it up until he realized that he just couldn't live without me in his life, in his home and in his heart.

In other words, until he asked me first.

CHAPTER TWENTY-SIX

For the next four and a half years, I worked steadfastly to complete my degree at Southeastern. Yeah, it took me a little longer than I'd planned, but that's because I took a semester off to spend time at home, to help take care of Aunt Edna during the roughest bouts of her chemo and spend more time with Daisey. But I did graduate, with honors.

In the meantime, T-Roy and I dated, and dated, and dated, with both of us dying for more.

And neither of us willing to break down and propose first.

But finally, on the twenty-sixth of October of the year I graduated college, it was time for the most talked about wedding in all of Grand Point.

Too bad it wasn't ours.

The groom wore dentures. And butt budder. Dentures in his mouth, of course. Butt budder...well, I'm assuming he wore it about near everywhere, though I didn't ask.

He also wore a green beret, a souvenir from his army days. His wife-to-be announced to the crowd that she loved the way he wore that bedet on his beautiful, round head.

No one corrected her.

The bride wore leather and vinyl and sequins and feathers in shades of pink, purple, yellow, blue, red, white, chartreuse and lavender. Oh, and she also wore butt budder.

Okay. A description of her ensemble (this may take a while). Hot pink leather micro-mini over purple fishnet stockings. Yellow off-the-shoulder top with blue, red and chartreuse sequined poke-a-dots. White go-go boots, of course. And lavender hair. Lots and lots of long spirals of sparkling pale purple hair (sparkling due to the three cans of glitter hairspray she applied prior to the ceremony).

The wedding took place on the levee, as was becoming the custom for all Thibodeaux women. And no, Daisey Leigh Mason didn't have Big Mama's wild and crazy blood pumping through her veins, but she'd been an honorary Thibodeaux lady for the past four years. Way before she'd gone and proven every doctor in the state of Louisiana wrong.

As for Clyde, well, he'd loved "Miss Daisey" from the moment she'd first served him a cup of coffee at the Cakery. And sure, she was thirty-eight years his junior, but who counts years when all your heart counts is love?

He'd used a large chunk of his retirement funds to build her a dream house fit for a queen, or at least for a Daisey. It was a smaller version of the Oak Alley Plantation. The painting he'd given her nearly four years ago was already hanging in the foyer.

Daisey had continued to shave her head, even after her hair started growing back. She really enjoyed the excitement of changing her look every fifteen minutes and, in truth, she'd become known for it. Particularly in the bridal magazines that featured her creations.

Aunt Edna, on the other hand, had officially achieved remission status after a full round of radiation and chemo, and had let her hair grow. As happens for most cancer patients, her locks came back totally different than before. In the place of her salt-and-pepper bob, she now sported a stark white pageboy that suited her spunkiness perfectly. She looked healthier and prettier than ever. And judging from the way Will stared at her now (and the way his hand cupped her left butt cheek), he thought so too.

Mama had gone all out for Daisey's wedding, with "all out" being the operative words in that statement. Pride balanced daringly over the top left side of her dress, with joy performing a similar feat on the right. Zip, of course, didn't appear to mind.

T-Roy had also decked out for the affair. I'd never seen my lover in a tux. And with the way it made my belly tingle, I was nearly ready to propose right then and there. Nearly.

But not quite.

Lately, I'd sensed his frustration, his desire to put a ring on my hand and babies in my belly. Surely he was getting ready to give in. To ask me for my hand. And of course, I'd say yes.

I just wouldn't ask him.

"Dance with me, *Cher*," he whispered the moment the ceremony had ended. His words feathered across the lobe of my ear and trickled down my neck, like they always did. And my body readily responded, growing hot and aching with fierce need.

Like it always did.

While the Coozan Band played below (Zip's gift to the bride and groom), we slow-danced on the levee. Bodies moving in harmony to the music. Sounds of the Mississippi kissing the bank of the levee penetrated the early evening. A breeze from the river misted our skin. The moment was perfect.

And I didn't want to wait any longer.

"T-Roy," I mumbled, my lips moving against his neck.

"What, *Cher*?"

"Will—"

"Jezze!" Daisey squealed, running up the levee as fast as her skinny, fishnet-embellished legs could travel.

I pulled away from the man I loved realizing that this particular perfect moment...had passed.

"Guess what?" she said, her face alive with excitement.

Clyde wheezed his way up the levee to accompany his bride, but by the time he'd arrived, she'd already told the news. The "biggest thing that ever hit Grand Point" news.

"It's Oprah, Jezze. Oprah!"

"What about Oprah?" I asked.

"She's coming here on Christmas Eve. She wants to do a showing of my gowns. Can you believe it? I wrote her and told her about my dresses, sent her pictures and all. And I asked her about having me on her network, letting me maybe auction some of my gowns and all proceeds going to help cancer in a Christmas show. According to this," she waved a white letter in the air, "she loves the idea and wants to make it a Christmas special. She wants to do it here so she can also show the bonfires! Isn't that incredible?"

I nodded, thrilled to see her so excited.

"Oh Clyde," she said, kissing her husband's cheek. "We've got to go home so I can get started on the dresses and the plans for the show. It needs to be awesome." She kissed his lips. Not a peck either. A long, wet, sloppy kiss that left him looking like a goofy kid as she ran back down the levee toward their car.

"Guess we've gotta leave our reception," he said, still grinning. "Will y'all explain to the guests?"

I nodded. "No problem."

He ran (well, as best he could) down the levee and within minutes, they were heading down River Road toward their house.

"Jezze," T-Roy said behind me.

I turned. "Yeah?"

"Were you—well, did you have something to say to me?"

I blinked. He knew I'd been nearly at the breaking point, but I knew that he was almost there too. "I don't think so, baby," I said then I kissed him. I chalked up another victory.

And another loss.

CHAPTER TWENTY-SEVEN

Two months is not a lot of time to get ready for Oprah in Grand Point. Heck, two years wouldn't be enough time to get something ready that would be worthy of the famous lady. And of course, we all think she's just super. The filé in our gumbo, so to speak.

But, amazingly enough, St. James and St. John parishes pulled together to get the site for the event, Riverside Academy's gymnasium, looking like a first-class Parisian runway. Daisey had asked every woman in the parish to model her gowns. She made sure to have a dress for each and every one, even the two elderly women from the assisted living home who'd volunteered for the job.

For me, she gave no choice in whether I'd participate. Or which dress I'd wear. I would model the exquisite creation she'd designed specifically for my wedding to T-Roy Bertrand. Of course, she'd finished the thing four years ago, so when I tried it on she had to let it out a bit for my surplus of behind. But have mercy, it still looked good. Very good. Good enough to get married in. Good enough to marry T-Roy Bertrand in, if the stubborn fool would just ask.

I'd turned twenty-four in September. It was time for Jezze's Man to reach the top of that cake. And T-Roy Bertrand knew it.

Dadgummit.

On Christmas Eve morning, Oprah arrived, and Lord help me, she's even prettier in person. We all gushed over the star and tried not to drool in our excitement. Mama and Aunt Edna took over the majority of the conversations, with both of them not the least bit shy about socializing with Oprah Winfrey. To look at them, you'd think they had just as much starpower as she.

Then again, if you asked them, they'd probably say they did.

Mama quizzed Ms. Winfrey about her thoughts on the benefits of wearing bustiers to show off an abundance of pride and joy. Aunt Edna jumped right in with questions about exactly how Oprah believed a person should breathe during power walking, and how fast the arms should be pumped. Did Oprah keep her elbows high, or low to her body? Because Aunt Edna leaned more toward high.

By the time the music had started, the runway was ready, the cameras were rolling and Daisey was beaming. And Grand Point residents were quickly growing accustomed to the brilliant smile and rich laughter of America's most famous woman, who sat front and center in the crowd (flocked by Aunt Edna and Mama, of course). Everyone was at ease, comfortable with our newfound fame.

Everyone, that is, but me.

I hadn't missed the fact that T-Roy hadn't shown all day. Did he not even want to see me wearing my wedding gown? Didn't he care? Had he decided that he'd put up with my stubborn pride long enough and was tired of waiting?

Daisey had scheduled me for last, the final dress to grace the stage. I didn't know if it was because she was more proud of this dress than any other (to me, it did outshine everything else she'd ever done, but that may have been because it reminded me of my dream. A dream that, as of yet, remained unfulfilled), or because she totally expected me to fall flat on my face when I hit that stage.

Or worse, on my ever-growing bohumpus.

"Last, but definitely not least, we have one of my very first creations. And one of my favorites. Worn by Jezebel Thibodeaux, this off-the-shoulder silk and organza floor-length gown..."

Oblivious to the remainder of Daisey's description, I walked down the runway in my wedding gown, the dress that was meant for me to wear four years ago with T-Roy, the man I loved then. The man I loved now.

And the man I should've proposed to. A long time ago.

I stopped walking. The music stopped playing. Whispers from the crowd echoed around me. Colorful lights blurred my vision of the things on my right, the things on my left. I saw nothing. Nothing at all.

Except the tall, handsome, tuxedo-clad man who stormed through the back door of the gym, taking complete control of the proceedings.

And my heart.

"T-Roy."

His eyes never wavered from mine. His pace never slowed. He strode onto the runway and scooped me in his arms while the crowd roared its approval. Then he turned his head toward Mama, Aunt Edna and Ms. Winfrey, where they sat on the front row. "Twenty minutes," he said.

"W-what?" I asked, my whole body bristling with the shock of what had just happened, with what was about to happen. Or at least, with what I sure hoped was about to happen. I held my breath. Then realized what he was waiting for.

And I was ready.

"T-Roy," I said, my voice quivering, "I've been a fool. You kncw I love you. Will you—"

He stopped my words with that blessed finger, pressing ever so slightly against my lower lip. "I told you I wouldn't ask you," he said.

I nodded. Swallowed.

"And I'm not asking now," he said.

I blinked. That's fine. He didn't want to ask. That's okay. I would.

"T-," I mumbled, my lips moving against the warmth of his finger.

He smiled. "I'm not asking," he repeated. "I'm telling."

My eyes popped wide open. And I grinned beneath that finger.

"You know where to go," he told the crowd. And sure enough, they all started gathering their things and hurrying toward the exit.

"We've got the cameras set up there, right?" I heard Oprah ask someone on her way out of the gym.

"Wh-where are we going?" I asked. "Where are they going?"

But T-Roy didn't answer. He was too busy carrying his bride-to-be out the gym.

His Saturn was parked front and center, directly outside the gym door. He walked to the passenger side, opened the door and started to put me in.

Then he stopped.

"What is it?" I asked, not at all liking the sneaky look that had crept across his face, making his chocolate eyes even darker and his smile even more delicious. I leaned up and nipped his lip. "You okay?" I asked. "Where're we going?"

"That's just it," he said. "I don't want you to know." Then he shifted me in his arms and withdrew his keys from his pocket. I heard the pop of the trunk as he hit a button on his keyless entry.

"You've gotta be kidding," I said, gawking at the opening that looked smaller by the second. "T-Roy Bertrand, don't you even think about it."

But, laughing, he put me inside (gently, yes, but still). "You told me my trunk was too small," he reminded.

"And then you proved me wrong."

"Just a little reminder that I don't have any reason to compensate," he said, reaching over me and pushing one of the backseats down, which provided a rectangular opening to the front of the car.

"I can climb through there," I said.

He raised his brows.

I thought of my shapely backside, as he called it, and knew what he was thinking. No way would my hips make it through that little hole.

"All comfy?" he asked, getting ready to shut me in.

"Wait a minute!" Mama squealed, panting as she neared the trunk.

Finally, someone to tell him to be sensible and to let me out. My mama would talk sense into this crazy man I loved.

"Here," she said, and she handed me a plastic spoon, filled with a big glob of purple icing. "I thought you might want to stop for an appetizer on the way." And she winked at T-Roy.

"Mama!" I yelled, but the trunk slammed shut. I heard the two of them mumbling about weddings and icing and something else I couldn't make out. Then I heard Mama's final shout as we drove away...

"Try not to get any icing on the dress, dear!"

Heaven help me, we're all crazy.

I tried to get comfortable, but my body twisted and turned and bashed against odd-shaped pieces of metal when my groom got a wheel in the school parking lot.

"Hey, watch it!" I yelled, but he laughed.

And dadgummit, I loved that laugh.

"Hey, are we going to a church, or the levee, or Judge St. Pierre?" I called through the tiny seat opening that separated the trunk (my current mode for transport) from the front of the car, where my husband-to-be perched behind the wheel. He tossed a small tube through the opening and muttered something, well, crude.

Without looking, I identified the pitched item. Then I took a peek. Yep, Babineaux's Butt Budder.

"You're a riot." I curled my fingers around the yellow tube so I wouldn't lose the thing in the trunk's darkened crevices. (Hey, I might need it later, you never know.)

Mama and Aunt Edna had insisted I go the full nine yards when I donned my wedding dress this morning. "Have to dress as though it's the real deal," Mama had quipped, making certain that I had all the requirements. Something old, something new, something borrowed, something blue. Now, I realized that she knew the entire time that this was, indeed, the real deal.

The mountain of crinoline layers (something borrowed) that Aunt Edna loaned me to don beneath my dress dang near scratched the hide off my legs (and my butt, for that matter, thanks to my mother's selection of something blue). I have no doubt the silky baby blue thong was meant for a woman with far less in her caboose.

But no matter. I've got a lifetime supply of butt budder.

Howling with laughter, T-Roy took a curve on two wheels. I whacked my head on a piece of metal and jabbed my cheek with the end of my spoon. Then I glared at the purple heap. Yeah, I knew what she'd intended for it, and what the driver of this car intended for it.

And he could forget that now.

"I'm eating the icing!" I screamed through the rectangular hole. "Hah!"

I watched him shake his head, and dang it if those dark waves didn't make my insides flutter.

"What do ya think she gave me for a wedding present?" he asked. Then, to my utter astonishment, he reached across to the passenger's seat and held up a whole gallon of Thibodeaux's Specialty Icing. "Hope pride and joy are ready for some fun."

My chest started to tingle at the thought. Shoot, not only had my mother and her sister sold me out, my own body was in on the act. "Traitors," I said to my boobs, spilling out of my dress, as though they wanted to help him get there quicker.

Then I poked the spoon in my mouth and rolled my eyes to the top of my head. "Mmmmmmm, butter cream."

Letting the sugar coat my tongue, I attempted to relax and remembered the one thing I'm sure my groom forgot.

"T-Roy?" I call, in my sweetest voice.

He lifted his hand to shift the rearview mirror then he eyed me in its reflection. And raised a brow.

"We don't have a marriage license."

Te-dah. Now he'd have to have some cooperation on my part, wouldn't he?

Nope.

He opened the console and withdrew a sheet of paper, waving it in the air triumphantly.

"We didn't take a blood test," I spouted.

"Don't need one in Louisiana."

"We didn't apply for it!"

"I did. It just takes one of the parties to apply here, *Cher*. Guess you've never had a reason to check out Louisiana marriage requirements, huh? Good thing I did. Of course, Delilah and Edna helped. I had to have your birth certificate."

Well, shoot. It wasn't as though I didn't want to marry him, but they'd done all the planning and I hadn't even been involved. Wasn't there some kind of rule against that? And where the heck was he taking me?

"T-Roy Bertrand," I started, but then the car stopped.

My groom climbed out.

I stuck my head as far as possible through the opening and tried to look around. I saw sky. And heard cheers. Then the trunk opened, and T-Roy slid his arms beneath me and cradled me, then lifted me out.

Cameras flashed, making me blink. The entire crowd from the gym had reinvented itself around the levee, with all of them circling the largest bonfire, Jezze's Man, where the groom stood proudly, finally, beside his bride.

I looked at the two wooden structures on the top of the cake. "I nearly didn't make it, did I?" I whispered.

T-Roy laughed then carried his bride up the levee, where the same preacher who'd performed the ceremonies for Mama and Zip, Aunt Edna and Will, and Daisey and Clyde awaited our arrival.

We were nearly to the top when I spotted the one person who could make this day complete. My eyes watered, throat closed in, heart clenched in my chest.

"Fenton," I whispered.

T-Roy stopped walking when we were even with his father.

Fenton Bertrand withdrew a pale blue handkerchief from his pocket, dabbed his eyes. "T-Roy said this is where all Thibodeaux women get married. And it's where he first found his love for you," he said.

I swallowed. The man hadn't ventured down River Road since his wife had lost her life on one of its curves, hadn't attended a wedding since her passing either. Yet, he'd confronted both obstacles today to be here for me.

And for his son.

"Thank you," I whispered, and I graciously accepted his tender kiss on my cheek.

The ceremony was perfect, though I barely heard the preacher's words. I only remember the one thing that mattered most. My right man. And the fact that I'd finally have him. To love and to cherish. Forever.

Our reception was covered on all of the local and national news media, particularly since it involved the wooden groom who'd been climbing that mountain for fourteen years finally reaching his goal.

The newspapers loved it. The television stations loved it. And Ms. Winfrey loved it, particularly when Zip pulled out the additions for the structure, just before they set the flame.

Twelve, small wooden fixtures to surround the cake. All of them peering up at the bride and groom. Apparently wondering how long it would be...before they'd meet their parents. I'd always said I wanted a dozen.

CHAPTER TWENTY-EIGHT

Clyde Roussell never expected to survive his young bride, but approximately two years after they'd pledged their vows, that's exactly what happened.

The doctors, when they'd professed to know the future, had given Daisey six months. But she'd proven to be stronger than even she would have dreamed, living six years after their original proclamation. And in those six years, Daisey Leigh Mason Roussell accomplished more than most people do in a lifetime.

Her wedding gowns were world-renowned, and with the abundance of patterns and styles that she'd left on the surplus of writing tablets in her home, Clyde, Edna, Delilah and I could make sure that they continued to be produced for many years to come.

As Daisey had instructed, Clyde vowed to continue donating the profits from her business in equal portions to support both foster children and cancer research.

News of the sweet lady's passing touched all of America, with flowers coming from all over and cards of condolences pouring into the small post office at Grand Point. Oprah made another trip to the tiny town, just to pay her respects to the woman who'd touched her heart.

And Daisey's wake? Well, it could be described in two words...

Completely Daisey.

She'd planned it to the smallest detail. She wore traditional Daisey attire. A sequined, red, yellow and purple poke-a-dotted top with a green feather boa draped around her neck.

The shirt caught your attention, but it was the hair that kept people circling the funeral home every fifteen minutes. And Daisey had planned it that way. Aunt Edna, following Daisey's specific instructions, shooed everyone out of the mourning room every fifteen minutes. When they'd all been herded outside, she'd say, with true Daisey panache, "It's changing time." Then, a few minutes later, she'd reopen the doors and the crowd would once again make their way to view Miss Daisey.

And see what color of hair she'd selected next.

Before the night ended, Daisey had sported pink, green, yellow, purple, red, chartreuse and white. And, as she'd directed, her final wig was the celebratory purple, green and gold that she'd loved so much.

Clyde bid her farewell and promised to see her soon, which he did, a mere three months later.

I had no doubt that we'd been blessed by Daisey's presence in our lives. She'd taught us how to live, how to love, and how to be loved. She'd shown us how to enjoy the butter cream in our cakes, while also embracing the coconut that found its way in every now and again.

I was glad she lived long enough to find her right man and to share a few years with her adoring Clyde. And I was glad that she had witnessed my wedding and had been an active part in its success.

But I regretted that she couldn't be here now, to see the product of our love, vibrant with life. And feisty with Thibodeaux blood.

My mama peered over the top of the clear bassinet and ogled the squirming, rolling butterball that composed the newest, and much needed, addition to the Thibodeaux/Bertrand families, while T-Roy and I watched.

And beamed with pride.

Aunt Edna cooed at the chubby faced little girl, writhing and stretching and acting as though she were chomping at the bit to start living.

I figured if she took after her namesake, she probably was.

"Why look, Edna, she has your double chin," Mama said, smirking at her sister, who promptly stuck her tongue out and pointed a warning finger at the child's proud grandmother.

"Will you give her to me, Mama? I want to hold her again," I said, and I watched my mama swaddle my baby and deliver her to my arms.

"She's beautiful, Jezze," T-Roy said, leaning over the bed to view his firstborn, his beautiful, perfect baby girl.

Fenton stepped forward, smiled at the new arrival. "Tell me her name again, Jezze. All of it."

I put a finger in the cleft of my baby's chin and whispered, "Delilah Ann Isabelle Sylvie Edna Yasmin Bertrand," I said. "But we'll just call her..."

"Daisey," they said in unison.

I nodded. "Just like your name, Mama. Taken from members of the family, and Sylvie for T-Roy's Mama."

Fenton dabbed his eyes.

"Um, Jezebel?" Mama asked.

"Yes, Mama?"

"Sweetie, we've never had anyone in our family named Yasmin. I'm fairly certain of it."

I grinned, shrugged and winked at Aunt Edna. "No biggee."

ABOUT THE AUTHOR

Renee Andrews spends a lot of time in the gym. No, she isn't working out. Her husband, a former All-American gymnast, co-owns ACE Cheer Company, an all-star cheerleading company. She is thankful the talented kids at the gym don't have a problem when she brings her laptop and writes while they sweat. When she isn't writing, she's typically traveling with her husband, bragging about their two sons or spoiling their bulldog.

Renee is a kidney donor and actively supports organ donation. She welcomes prayer requests and loves to hear from readers! Write to her at Renee@ReneeAndrews.com or visit her Web site at www.reneeandrews.com.

Renee Andrews on Twitter:

www.twitter.com/reneeandrews

And if you're a fan of edge-of-your-seat suspense, check out Renee's other pseudonym, K.A. ZAiNE, at www.KAZAiNE.com.

www.ingramcontent.com/pod-product-compliance
Lightning Source LLC
Chambersburg PA
CBHW071254170626
46809CB00001B/208